MONDAY, SUNDAY

FENTON GRACE

HANOVER
PRESS

DEDICATION

À John Rechy,
pour tout ce que vous m'avez appris.

1

At 3 PM on a crisp Monday, the first Monday in May, Laney Secord was in the kitchen making orange spice cookies when she heard the doorbell over the churning of her KitchenAid mixer. She turned the machine off, the bell emitting its final chimes. Who was it? She rarely had visitors—one of the perks, or drawbacks, of living in a postage stamp-sized town. The mailman had already come and gone, and she wasn't expecting any packages. Brian knew to go around back.

The doorbell rang again.

"Coming," she said, though she doubted whoever was at the door would hear her. Brushing her hands on her drawstring pants, she looked to see whether her camisole had any flour on it—no—and whisked to the front door.

She moved gracefully, and although she was very attractive—a still-blonde thirty-two, with blue-green eyes (she was never sure which)—she had virtually cloistered herself in her sprawling home. Out of necessity, she had morphed into the perfect homemaker, a dutiful mother, a meticulous organizer. To alleviate the monotony, she resorted to gardening, pondering a move away from Plainview, searching the self-help aisle of the closest bookstore for something to ease, to expunge, her grief. But for her efforts all she had to show was that dread, that platitude: Experience.

She opened the door to a boy, sixteen, maybe seventeen, wearing spruce green pants and full Eagle Scout regalia. A clipboard in his hands, he launched into what sounded like a rehearsed speech—

"Mrs. Secord, the Boy Scouts are planning an expedition to Mount Rushmore this Fourth of July to learn about our greatest presidents and to study the environment. We're going around the neighborhood door to door to raise money so that the boys in my troop will have an opportunity to attend. I have an information sheet here which explains my fundraising activity. Would it be possible for you to make a donation to help..."—he quickly peeked at a note clutched in his palm— "a needy boy out?"

She knew how difficult it was to go door to door and ask for money from strangers. She was impressed he had used her name, even though he had addressed her as Mrs. and not Ms. He was so well spoken, and his voice, though it had changed, was innocent, as if his whole world were Plainview, the Boy Scouts, and dreams of Mount Rushmore.

"That's quite a ways from Colorado. Of course," she said. "My son just happened to join the Cub Scouts."

"Brian?" he said.

"You know him?"

"Only a bit, since he's new. I'm a troop leader and I hope to show him what scouting's all about."

She smiled, his unabashed eagerness setting her at ease. As she looked at him—a score of colored badges on his sleeves and pockets, badges with insignia, a depiction of a tent, a cross— she thought of Brian, who was so proud of his uniform with its single patch, that of the Tiger Cub. "My handbag is in the kitchen. Come in."

He glanced over her head, at the chrome chandelier hanging from the vaulted ceiling of the foyer. He brushed his feet against the jute doormat. He was a well built boy, as large as a man, though he had the gangliness and awkwardness of an adolescent.

He closed the door with a soft click. Manners, she thought.

Her innate shyness, the shyness she thought she had discarded while in college, came back to her: Why? she wondered.

"What part of town do you live in?" she asked, trying to overcome that pesky timidity.

"Grove Street. Near Center Pond, ma'am." He sounded nervous, but as he strode through the foyer his gait suggested a bolder, more imposing presence.

"Please, call me Laney."

"Laney," he repeated softly. "That's a nice name."

"Thank you." She could not help but notice the smooth, supple youthfulness of his skin. She wiped her hands on the side of her pants to clean bits of dough off her fingers.

He took a step to the left, as if to adjust his stride. "I'm Christopher. Christopher Hendrickson." His voice cleaved onto every syllable of his name, hammering the consonants as if banging nails into wood studs. A small pimple graced the center of his forehead, where his bangs parted. The pimple probably bothered him, but she found it endearing: a touch of purity, of innocence.

"Do you go to Plainview High?" she asked.

"Yes, I'm a junior."

"How do you like it?"

"It would be even better if I was a senior." His eyes danced. She could tell he was joking. She gave him a quick grin.

His footsteps followed quietly behind her down the hall. He reminded her of Jay, though not physically. Even at his young age he was taller and more muscular. Yet they had the same

3

easygoing, reassuring manner.

She turned, noticing that his eyes seemed to be searching over her, but was he actually looking at her or at the small, still-life watercolor on the wall behind her?

They reached the kitchen. "Are your son and husband home?" he asked.

Why did he want to know? "As a matter of fact, Brian's at a Cub Scouts meeting."

"Of course," he answered instantly.

Because the topic of death made people uncomfortable, she debated whether to tell him about Jay. He was just a boy. She decided to be frank: "My husband passed away a few years ago."

"Oh, I'm sorry. I didn't mean to..." His lips twitched as if he was about to say something more, but he put a finger to the corner of his mouth.

"It's quite all right." She sauntered to the sink to rinse her hands. "Would you like a soft drink?"

"A glass of water would be great."

"Give me a moment," she said.

"No *problema*." His voice became deeper.

As the water ran over her hands, Christopher placed his clipboard on the counter near the breakfast area. He was fidgeting toward the kitchen island, closer to her, as if he were listening to music in his head. When he noticed her watching, he stopped.

"You can have a seat if you'd like," she said.

He smirked, angling around the stool and spinning the seat before spreading his legs and sitting down.

"You must be getting ready to go off to college soon?" she ventured.

"If my SAT's are good, I hope to get into Boulder."

"Boulder's my alma mater."

His eyes lit up. "For real?"

'For real': She was struck by the enthusiastic way he used the expression. "What do you want to study?" she asked.

"Business."

The confidence of his answer impressed her. He would probably be quite successful in corporate America.

"For me, it was psychology."

"Nice." He let his voice trail off in such a way that suggested he was referring not to psychology but to something else.

She turned off the faucet and watched the water flow down the drain, drying her hands on a towel propped against the granite backsplash.

His eyes darted about the room. She put the towel on the counter, where a picture of Jay was set in a silver frame. In it, he waved hello—or goodbye—while trekking up a trail. It was the last photo she had taken of him.

Christopher's feet tapped on the footrest of the stool, unsettling her. She noticed him scratching or reaching for something in his pocket. She cautiously filled a glass of water using the automatic dispenser on the refrigerator door. Her twitching fingers cooled. As she handed him the glass, he stood and pulled a stool from the island and offered it to her.

She tried to dispel the flush of her cheeks. "Such a gentleman," she said, half sarcastically, half flirtatiously.

"I try," he said, picking up on her sarcasm, his eyes narrowing, suggesting that he enjoyed her tone. "At sixteen, you have to keep up your image." He gave a quick wink.

The wink struck her as odd. Perhaps he was trying to imitate what he saw older men do. At the same time, she found the gesture charming.

Sixteen, she thought.

She sat on the stool and took her bag. She smiled awkwardly. Christopher, with his youthful manliness, an innocence blurred by impending adulthood, was beguiling her.

"I'll take whatever you can give," he said. "We almost have enough for our whole troop. The Cubs won't be joining us, though. They're too young." His feet shuffled against the stool: Tap, tap. He grabbed the glass of water and drank half of it in a single gulp.

"You must be thirsty."

"I've been pounding the pavement all afternoon."

The edges of her lips curled upward. She unzipped the side compartment where her change was. Reflexively, her eyes returned to him, from his face to his body. His tight uniform caused her to daydream. She told herself he played baseball. He had a baseball player's thighs and hips. He liked things like archery, fishing, and swimming, but he wasn't the best swimmer. He was a sinker. Like Jay.

The pimple on his forehead seemed to grow larger. His fresh, pearl-white skin marred by that single flaw. She cast the thought out of her mind. She rifled through the change, searching for quarters. Why was she looking for change? She was not going to give him her parking money.

She turned to him and felt his eyes linger, then rise, from her breasts. As she glanced at his thick blond hair, his soothing blue eyes, his jaw that was becoming more square, she suddenly stopped: Why was she checking him out?

She rummaged through her wallet. Bills and bills, ones and

twenties and fives indistinguishable. She began to arrange them, heads up, the way she liked them. Although she didn't make eye contact with him, the black granite countertop on the island gave a distorted reflection of his spruce uniform, his badges of honor. She set the bills on the table between them.

He leaned forward on the stool. He was so close she could feel his breath on her face.

"That's more than generous," he said, his voice almost dissolving into a whisper.

"You're welcome."

Faint blond whiskers sprouted from the lower part of his chin. One day he might have a cleft, like Jay.

As she fastened her bag, he put a hand on her arm. "The boys and I can't thank you enough." His fingers spread lightly across her skin, causing the fine hairs on her arm to tingle. "You're really helping a boy in need."

She smiled, taking her hand and closing her bag.

"You have such a beautiful smile," he said.

His compliment was genuine and heartfelt but unnecessary. She smiled uncomfortably. Why did he continue to flirt?

"Thank you. That's very kind." Standing, she set her bag aside, and he stood next to her. How tall he was! Suddenly he seemed less of a boy and more of a man. She gazed at the money on the table.

"I really mean it, Laney." He leaned forward, gently taking her elbow in a hand, and kissed her on the lips.

She tipped on her toes, enjoying the touch of his warm, soft lips. How could he be kissing her? She shouldn't have flirted with him. He was impressionable. She had misled him. She stepped back. She watched him slowly open his eyes. His lips, full and bright, would not close. Yes, he was beautiful. She found herself becoming lost in the sensation of his breath that smelled of mint, his eyes, his long lashes, his uniform.

"Nice," he said.

He leaned forward, but she put her other hand on his shoulder, halting him.

"You're beautiful," he said. He tilted his head at an angle as a prelude to kissing her.

"It's my fault. I'm sorry." She lifted the bills off the countertop and placed them in his hand.

He looked stone-faced, as if he didn't hear her. His fingers gently held her hand. He would not let go. She put her other hand on his fingers and took his hand away. "It was nice meeting you," she said.

"You didn't mind, did you?"

She felt her mind changing.

"Yes?"

She tried to remain implacable, but her hands trembled.

"Could I kiss you again, Laney?"

"No, that's okay. Best of luck with your trip."

He stared at her for a few moments. She remained as still as her limbs would allow. He began to walk toward the door. He scratched his chest above the patch with the cross. What was he thinking?

His hand lingered to the middle of his chest. Then he withdrew it. He shook his head, placed the money on the table by the telephone, and left.

***

She stood in the kitchen, listening to his feet tap over the hardwood floor. His footsteps stopped. She stared at the bills on the table. Was he going to come back?

She looked around the room, as if to see whether anyone had witnessed what had happened.

The house was empty, still. The front door closed. Why did she let him kiss her? Why had she flirted with him?

A part of her felt invigorated. A young boy had found her attractive. He had said she was beautiful. Indeed, she did have as good a figure as when she was twenty. Still, she was uneasy. A boy half her age should not interest her. She should have maternal feelings for him, not feelings of... arousal.

In the three years since Jay's death, she frequently received admiring looks from strangers. Men at the shopping plaza blatantly stared at her, many a whistle from a passing car at the gas station. However, she had never felt the desire to respond. She could see they only wanted her body, sex. But now the rigid strictures she had imposed on herself—the commands not to look at or touch another man—were disassembling. How could this boy have kissed her?

She fidgeted with the picture of Jay on the counter, placing it behind another photo of them, their parents, their best friends Dan and Erin, and their children, taken one Christmas. Why had she betrayed Jay a couple of months later? That snowy day in February when he was back in Boulder visiting family, Dan had persuaded her to go out for dinner and drinks. Erin had stayed at home. In their drunkenness Laney and Dan ended up on the living room sofa, later vowing never to speak of what had happened—actual intercourse. Months later, Laney, in her guilt, confessed to Jay. He was incensed. She made him promise not to say anything to Dan. He said he forgave her, but in the ensuing days and weeks things changed between them. He did not appear to trust her. They went through a period where they didn't have sex. A few months later, he died.

She looked at the dough in the KitchenAid mixer. She turned the machine to the lowest setting and watched the dough churn round. What did Christopher want? To tell his friends that he had seduced an older woman?

She turned the mixer off, taking the bowl and placing it on the granite counter. The dough was too smoothly beaten, like a paste for hanging wallpaper. It had the texture of glue. She dumped it down the garbage disposal.

Gazing out the window, she noticed, near the breakfast nook on the counter, that he had left his clipboard. She gravitated to it.

His name, "Christopher Hendrickson," was handwritten in capital letters atop the information sheet in red ink. The writing was that of a man, sloppy and large, disrespectfully disproportionate to the page.

What if he came back? She felt frightened and at the same time expectant. She wanted to get the clipboard back to him. She could call Brian's troop leader and find out whom to give it to. She waited, staring at the clipboard, at his name. She flipped through the pages.

On the last page there was a handwritten note:

"Henry Miller said growth is an unbridled leap, without the need for experience."

On the bottom corner of the page, a doodle was drawn in red pen. The sketch was of a skier hunched over, going down a mountainous slope. He had goggles on and a scarf that blew back from his face.

She traced a finger over the drawing, imagining there was a

connection between her, the ink, and the boy who had probably just been passing his time—by kissing her! How adventurous, impulsive, and free-spirited she once was herself. In moving to Plainview, she had become a facsimile of herself, suburban and reserved. She had never wanted to be a stay-at-home mom—as much as Jay had made her appear to be. She wanted to wait to have children; he didn't. She wanted to live in the city; he fell in love with rural Plainview. There was a significant part of her—a part she couldn't share with anybody—that was thankful their path to gleeful domesticity was destroyed. She was now free to do as she chose, but the wants she once had—to have a fulfilling career as a psychologist, with clients and an office of her own, to mingle with friends at art galleries, cafes—had vanished along the way, not to be replaced by other wants, and so she was like a prisoner counting down the days of a sentence, never sure what day it really was.

She returned the clipboard to the counter, as if it belonged there. He was not going to come back.

Maybe he would after dinner.

Needing to cease her mind's wandering, she went upstairs to the master bath to freshen up before Brian came home. Taking the bath mat from the side of the tub and placing it outside the shower door on the grayish white marble floor, she turned the water on to a massaging flow. She hesitated before stepping in: Did she really need to shower?

She looked at her reflection in the ceiling-high mirror behind her. Is this what the boy saw: a kind, though overly pale face? The shapely curves of a mature woman, one who was—she was certain, despite what Madison Avenue led people to believe—in her physical prime? A slender neck, a pert mouth? An overall tenderness about her that made strangers feel they knew her, like a sister or a wife?

Or did he see something in her that she couldn't see herself? She twisted to catch every angle of her face, her shoulders, her hair.

As she undressed, she wondered what he might do if he saw her like this, completely naked. Would he pin her against the vanity, wrap his arms around her? She felt her throat tighten. She visualized him beside her, his shirt neatly tucked in. She saw his badges, his tight, spruce-colored pants, his soft pink full lips. His mouth and his skin.

No. What was she thinking? What would she want with a boy?

Her eyes drifted to the vanity, where a can of Barbasol shaving cream sat in the corner. Jay had always insisted on using this foamy, alcohol-saturated brand, even though she had told him it would dry out his skin and age him prematurely. She could not get him to switch, and in time, she started using it.

Behind the canister, she glimpsed a prom picture of her and Jay, taken in her parents' back yard. He seemed to be watching and, with his lopsided smile, censoring her. She could not escape his memory. What was she doing, fantasizing in the nude? He was a minor.

She gathered her clothes from the floor, not wanting to put them on, but not wanting to linger naked either. She lay her drawstring pants across her chest to cover herself, clinging to them. The marble floor was cold on her feet. She needed to go finish dinner. Brian would be home soon.

***

She and Brian always ate in the dining room, even though there was a sizeable table in the breakfast nook of the kitchen. Eating in this room, with its sliding glass doors to the deck facing the back yard, made their meals sacrosanct. The house felt lived in, used.

The pork was dry and the broccoli overcooked.

She watched Brian pick over his food. He had his father's eyes: brown and deep-set and beautiful. She tried to engage him in conversation, but he was not talkative. Since he had started second grade and joined the Cubs Scouts, he had grown distant from her. He began to spend more time alone, retreating to a private world she knew less and less of and becoming silent whenever she entered his room. Yet his teachers said he was animated at school and showed no signs of maladjustment.

During dinner, she waited for the doorbell to ring. She expected Christopher to come back for his clipboard, but he never did.

By 8 PM Brian was tucked snugly in bed. He insisted on wearing his Spiderman pajamas, even though the webbed collar pinched his neck so tightly he needed a bigger size.

Each night, she read to him from a book of myths that she had purchased at a flea market at Plainview Elementary. It was a children's book, a hardcover, the dustboard edges slightly frayed. Tonight she read him the myth of Ariadne, who left the thread for Theseus to find his way out of the labyrinth after he slayed the minotaur.

As she read, Brian lay stone-faced, staring at the ceiling as if he were waiting for her to leave his room and let him go to sleep. She, in turn, was unable to follow the storyline. Her mind drifted back to Christopher, his fidgeting, the gulping of water.

While she read, she felt as if she were nodding and saying "Uh-huh" during a conversation she wasn't paying attention to.

When she finished the story, Brian's head poked from the covers. He opened his mouth to say something, then closed it. He looked at the wall beside the bed, where a 49'ers football poster hung.

"Is something the matter?" She brushed a hand through his bangs, but he took a hand from under the blanket and put it on hers to stop her.

"What's wrong?" Her voice rose in concern.

"All the other boys' fathers are going to the Cub Scouts meeting on Saturday," he said.

"I'll go with you."

"No, you can't. We're making Mother's Day gifts."

Yes, she remembered, this Sunday was Mother's Day.

"Who's going to help me?" he asked.

"Maybe Mr. Wexler can?"

He stared at the ceiling. Finally, he spoke: "How do they make thread?"

His precociousness always startled her. He was referring to the myth she had just finished reading. "Thread? I think machines make it. Why?"

"But they didn't have machines then, did they?"

"How did Areead—" he struggled with the name—

"Ariadne," she corrected him.

"How did she make the thread?"

She didn't know how she had made the thread. Maybe she spun it. "I'll find out," she said.

He was not satisfied. "If Daddy had thread, couldn't he find his way out of heaven?"

"I've told you. Once you go to heaven, you don't come back."

"Because of the brainerism?"

"The aneurysm. The brain aneurysm."

She had counseled him time and again, but he too seemed to feel guilt over Jay's death. An aneurysm meant nothing to a seven-year-old. At times she had considered whether her telling Jay about the tryst with Dan might have triggered it, but the doctors said shock could not have been a contributing factor. Although the rational part of her mind told her that there was no connection, she had not completely convinced herself.

She took the book of myths from the bed stand. A picture of Jay holding Brian as a toddler was set in a clear frame. She did not have all the answers. A father was something she could never be. She thought it best to change the subject. "Maybe one of the other boys' fathers can help you with your project."

He turned to the wall and pulled the sheet over his head.

She was about to put a hand to his forehead, but stopped. "Don't worry. Everything will be all right." She did not sound as convincing as she had hoped.

He pulled the blanket and sheet to his chin. She tucked the edges under the mattress. He was so snug he could barely move, but that was how he liked to fall asleep. He looked like a corpse.

She stood from the bed and turned the light on the bed stand to a soft glow. She waited for some sign that he was going to re-open his eyes—to ask for the light to be turned up—to say that he loved her—but he pretended to be fast asleep.

She walked toward the door. His Cub Scout uniform was neatly folded on the chair beside the bureau. He insisted on folding it himself, so that the Tiger Cub patch always faced up. He didn't like her to touch it except for washing. Would he have let his father fold it if he were alive today?

She took the uniform and went downstairs to launder it. As she held the tiny pants and shirt, seeing the small Tiger's head on the pocket, she thought of the badges over Christopher's uniform. She could see the colors of each of them—red, green, brown. The symbols and acronyms were a blur of half-formed images and letters. None except the cross registered.

She tried to form a clue as to what she was feeling. Her mind grappled with the words: longing, infatuation. Surely, she should have relegated him to some unimportant part of her brain by now, five hours after he had come—and kissed her.

She went into the kitchen and sipped a cup of chocolate milk while the wash ran. The money, the bills now carefully arranged, were still on the table. She looked at the clipboard. The name in red—Christopher Hendrickson—in large block letters—stared back at her. She couldn't take her eyes off his penmanship. In his handwriting, she tried to decipher some meaning, some connection to his hands—they were thick, steady, like a man's.

She flipped to Christopher's note: "*Henry Miller said growth is an unbridled leap, without the need for experience.*"

2

On Tuesday, after Brian left for school, Laney attempted to follow her usual routine, but was unable to concentrate. She had a hard time finishing her Rice Krispies but forced herself to because she knew she would not be able to tolerate the handful of vitamins she had taken otherwise. Her eyes kept darting to the table beside the folded laundry where Christopher's clipboard rested. She doubted he would come back today.

The sun shone brightly through the window. The yard outside was lush; the garden too lush. She had planned on gardening this morning, but her thoughts circled around Christopher. Should she mention anything about him to Erin? Erin was a good listener, a trained social worker like Laney, but she was puritanical and judgmental. She would tell Dan, her husband, and they would sit her down and tell her she should see a therapist. Laney knew that therapy would fail her. She would feel obliged to make up some story so the therapist could see the roots of her feelings. Some fabulous tale of her being molested as a child. Some childhood so traumatic that the therapist could not help but feel sorry for her.

As she looked about the house—well kept, sturdy and impressive—arcs and angles and expansive panes of glass, she found it hard to believe that she owned the property outright. Jay's death had triggered the mortgage insurance. Life insurance— both work and personal policies—plus Jay's inheritance from his father—ensured she would never have to work again. But in some ways, the house, regal and serenely austere, was less of a safety net than a burden. Although three years had passed since his death, she couldn't give up his home. She would lose her final connection to him. Selling it would be tantamount to admitting failure, failure to adjusting to life as a single mother, to remarrying perhaps, to reentering the working world, to making new friends, to developing hobbies, to do *something*.

She was hesitant about moving to Plainview when Jay was offered a lucrative job here. She did not believe she would find suitable work, but Jay persuaded her, saying she could always commute to Denver or even study for a master's degree in psychology, to become a therapist.

She drifted to the spare bedroom she used as an office, to the computer. She would find out, for Brian, how Ariadne had made the thread. She began a search and scanned through several sites. She read that Ariadne was the daughter of King Minos. Ariadne's mother had slept with a beautiful white bull and had given birth to a creature who was half-man, half-bull, the minotaur. Minos was so disgusted by the minotaur that he banished the creature to a labyrinth from which it was impossible to escape.

Athens, a foreign land, sent Theseus and several other young men as tributes to Minos. Although Ariadne was in love with Theseus, Minos ordered him, as he did with all the tributes, into the labyrinth to fight the minotaur. Confident that Theseus could kill the minotaur, Ariadne gave him a ball of thread so he could find his way back out of the maze. However, after he killed the minotaur and escaped, he abandoned her and left her broken-hearted.

Had she read all this to Brian, or did the children's book offer a sanitized version of events? She empathized with Ariadne's being abandoned: How could Theseus have left her?

Laney printed several pages, forming a faint parallel in her own life with Jay's death. The past, she told herself, *move on.*

She could find nothing about how Ariadne had made the thread.

In the corner of the screen, there was a blinking ad for low-priced Caribbean cruises. She hadn't taken a vacation since Brian was born. Where might he like to go: Hawaii, Disneyland?

She went to Google and typed "vacation spots." A half hour later, she was still combing through site after site, none of which interested her except for one, a link for Mount Rushmore, where Christopher's troop was planning their excursion. On screen, the faces of Washington, Lincoln, Jefferson, and Roosevelt stared back at her. At the bottom of the page, "organized tours" flashed. She clicked on the link. Pictures of schoolchildren appeared. Further down on the page, there was a photo of a Boy Scout troop standing at an observation point. One of the boys was holding a small American flag. He was eleven, maybe twelve. He looked so innocent, so patriotic. She was reminded of Christopher's eager eyes, and a wave of regret passed through her.

The statement on Christopher's clipboard about growth and experience came to mind. She went back to the search engine and typed "Henry Miller." A color picture of Miller appeared on screen. She learned he was a writer, notorious in his private and professional lives. Banned books, dalliances with all sorts of interesting women—including Anais Nin. Laney had heard of her, but she found nothing about an unbridled leap.

She sat still, staring blankly at the screen. She went to the history menu then clicked on the page about Mount Rushmore. She found the Boy Scouts of America home page. A section on age restrictions was featured on the index. She clicked on that section. She read a paragraph about legal responsibilities of parents, reaching the words "age of consent." Age of consent: that meant when a child was legally considered to be an adult.

She clicked her way back to Google and typed "age of consent." In an instant, thousands of matches were found. She scanned the listings: conspiracy theories, United Kingdom.

She re-typed: "age of consent by state." There were only two results. The first one seemed perfect: Alaska, Alabama, Arizona, Arkansas. She clicked the link. As the page loaded, a sense of dread overcame her. What would she do if the legal age for a consensual relationship was eighteen? Sixteen? What difference would it make? What did the laws of society matter when she knew, within herself, that he was too young?

She closed her internet browser. She lingered for a few minutes with her eyes closed, turned off the computer, then went to the kitchen.

She pretended to clean, but when she reached the cabinet by the telephone, the Plainview phone directory caught her eye. An image of the local church spire graced the cover. White, pointed, wooden. A grove of trees in the background. This was the same church where Jay was put to rest.

She slid the directory from the shelf. It was a slim volume, with the Yellow and White Pages combined, the smallest phone book she'd ever seen. She and Jay had had a laugh when it landed on their doorstep. They had moved to a town, population 3023, where everybody would know everybody else's business.

Her mind tossing and turning, she took the directory to the breakfast table. Christopher represented an impossible bargain, a made-to-measure catastrophe.

She really should give him his clipboard back.

She flipped through the White Pages section, to H. Skimming down the list, she found one 'Hendrickson, William'. Not an old-fashioned "Mr. and Mrs." as other couples were listed. Did Christopher have a mother? The question unsettled her.

The street address, 16 Grove Street, she committed to memory.

There was no harm in going to see where he lived. In Plainview, it was called being neighborly.

She chose a baby pink Lycra tank top. Tight-fitting. Form fitting, but the built-in push-up bra was a necessity because otherwise the straps would show. Cut-off denim shorts. She had not worn them since her honeymoon in Fiji. Wooden slides, with a strap against the big toe, a steal for $8.99 at the new supermarket. She painted her toe nails a pale blue to match the shorts, put on mascara, eyeliner, lipstick, rouge, probably too much because she was not accustomed to using so much makeup.

I am only trying to look my best, she told herself, as I would for any stranger.

At 3 PM—the time she figured Christopher would be home from school —she arrived at 16 Grove Street. The sun was still shining. All the trees and lawns were in their deepest, fullest green. Beads of sweat formed on her arms.

She parked her Volvo station wagon along the embankment. She and Jay had bought the car when she was pregnant. It was slightly beat up from the Colorado winters, had some electrical problems, but she did not want to trade it in. Like the house, it was supposed to have been the start of a big family. They were going to have another child when Brian became a few years older.

Her hands grasped the leather steering wheel. She looked

through the windshield. Her eyes were drawn to all the spots. The wipers would only make it worse, she thought. It was better to leave the smudges there. *Don't make things perfect. Stop looking at them and they will go away.*

She looked at the passenger's seat, at the clipboard, at the note about Henry Miller. *Go, she told herself. Be as bold as Christopher was in the kitchen.*

The house down the drive was a bastardized ranch with a small column on each side of the portico. The foundation looked off kilter. In today's market, with Plainview becoming a choice spot for young professionals, the house was a tear down, with unkempt overhanging trees, dirt patches on the lawn. A teal blue clunker was parked outside the detached garage, facing the street.

In contrast, the mailbox at the end of the driveway looked pristine. A hand-painted robin was perched atop the wooden cage, with its flag, tilted half up, half down, and painted red to match the robin's breast. The box looked as if it could have been the handiwork of Christopher.

She took her checkbook from her handbag and laid it atop the clipboard. She slid her black and gold Cross pen out of the sleeve of her checkbook and placed it in the glove compartment.

She put the car in gear and drove around the mailbox into the dirt drive, parking directly behind the teal blue car.

She took the clipboard and checkbook and stepped out. The car before her was no clunker. It was a mint condition Ford Galaxy, with a flawless paint job and gleaming chrome trim. What she had initially thought to be a jalopy was a collector's dream.

As she made her way to the portico, she wiped the perspiration from her arms. Her palms felt clammy. The sidewalk had recently been patched with cement. On the edge of a square, the initials "CH" and "4EVA" were etched. They were the markings of a boy—a youth who thought he would live forever—and she felt a twinge of regret for coming here.

She exhaled a final breath, searched for the doorbell—there was none—then knocked, once, twice, then a pair of louder knocks because she felt the first two were inaudible.

She waited, tapping her toes in her sliders. She looked back at the driveway, at the Galaxy. Perhaps no one was home.

The door opened. A middle-aged man, forty-five or so, with thick hair—various shades of light browns mixed with grays—hunched under the door frame. He was about six feet four and wore a white T-shirt, blue jeans, and black cowboy boots. He had pale blue eyes almost the color of the Galaxy. His face was handsomely rugged, as if he spent a great deal of time working outdoors.

He had to have been Christopher's father—the eyes, the hair, the height.

"Mr. Hendrickson?" she said.

"Yes." He had a paternal, benevolent expression as he craned his neck forward.

"I'm Laney Secord. Your son—I believe I have the right house—Christopher?"

"Yes," he said.

"He came by my house yesterday to ask for a donation for his trip to Mount Rushmore."

His brow scrunched in puzzlement.

"A Boy Scout trip?" she said.

"I don't know anything about a trip to Mount Rushmore."

23

She was perplexed. Had Christopher made up the story about his trip? Was his fundraising effort a ruse? At the same time, she felt titillated, flattered that he might have come to see her merely to kiss her.

"Your son left his clipboard at my house, on Heather Lane. I didn't have my checkbook handy, so I thought I'd drop by."

He scratched his neck, lifting his hand to his mouth, just as Christopher had done in the kitchen, not taking his eyes off her.

She sensed that he was scrutinizing her, possibly mistrusting her. "I'd like to write him a check." She offered him the clipboard.

He looked at it. She moved it closer, and finally he took it.

She peered over his shoulders, hoping to see Christopher.

"I'll be happy to give this to Chris. I'm not sure why he didn't mention anything about the trip to me."

"He's not home?"

"He should be, but I don't know where he is."

A stout German shepherd rushed between them, barking. She put her hands near the dog's muzzle so he could smell her.

The dog jumped up, putting his nose against her thighs and resting his chin against her shorts. Drool drizzled over her hands. "Good doggie," she said. Her checkbook she allowed to fall to the ground while the dog slabbered her hands.

"Butch, easy!"

"It's okay," she said.

Mr. Hendrickson grabbed hold of Butch's collar.

"Such a nice dog." She continued to pet Butch, who kept slobbering. Drool slid down her thighs.

"Butch!" he scolded.

"That's okay, really."

Mr. Hendrickson bent down to pick up her checkbook.

With saliva-coated hands she took the checkbook from him and proceeded to open it. She leafed through the register. "I seem to have forgotten my pen," she said with an absentminded touch.

The dog started to lick her knees.

"Butch, easy!"

"I guess he likes me."

"I'll get something to write with inside."

She kept petting the dog.

"Here, why don't you come in?" He looked behind her.

She turned, expecting to see Christopher, but no one was there. Was he looking to see whether someone was watching them? "Why thank you," she said.

How exhilarated she felt upon entering the house, relieved and yet also, a tad guilty.

No entry hall separated the living room from the front door. The air was stale, like that on an overcast, humid day. A stuffed plaid armchair was positioned next to a mismatched striped sofa, each facing a large-screen TV that dominated the room. A pair of sneakers, laces still tied, were propped against the base of a brass torchiere, the shade of which was tilted, perhaps to allow easy access to the switch. It was apparent from the decor that the house had not known a Mrs. Hendrickson.

"My name is Bill, by the way."

She reached out a hand, flickering her fingers. "It's nice to meet you. I'd shake, but I think your dog might get jealous."

He laughed. "The bathroom's down the hall."

"Thank you." She gave a gallant smile. *Neighborly*.

She walked down the narrow center hallway off the living

room. A floorboard creaked under her feet. The bathroom was small, with just enough space for a tub, a vanity, and a toilet. A pair of shag rugs—one blue, the other yellow, both ratty—covered the linoleum floor, but it was still obvious that the linoleum was lifting in various places.

She rinsed her hands. The medicine cabinet had no door. An array of razors and combs, Bayer aspirin for children, a rusty pair of tweezers, an uncapped bottle of Flintstones chewable multi-vitamins were crammed on dusty shelves. On the vanity, only two toothbrushes stood in a ceramic holder attached to the wall. The lid of the toilet seat was up.

No, no woman could have possibly *ever* lived here.

A bath-sized towel was lying atop a waist-high basket fixed between the tub and the door. She dried her hands on it and noticed hanging half-way out of the padded beige lid a pair of spruce-colored pants. She recognized them as Christopher's Scout uniform. On the floor, by the bottom of the hamper, there was a pair of briefs. Inside the waistband, she could make out the blue and yellow bands. The Fruit of the Loom brand. The tag was facing up. Waist size 30. A blanket of shame rushed through her.

She left the underwear on the floor, then returned to the living room. Mr. Hendrickson had stepped away. She heard sounds emanating from the other end of the hall and walked toward them. Had Christopher come home?

The door to the kitchen was open. A plastic trash can stood beside it. Behind the door Mr. Hendrickson was taking a pitcher of iced tea from the refrigerator. No, Christopher was not there.

He stepped beside her, placing the pitcher on the counter. "I know I have a pen in here somewhere," he said, flummoxed, rifling through a drawer. Nails clanged against one another, pieces of paper ruffled, a chrome corkscrew flashed, a coupon fell to the floor. She was going to bend down to pick it up, but the feeling she had in the bathroom—that blank wave of shame—came back and discouraged her.

"Ah-hah," he said, "so this is where it ended up. Chris will be happy I found it."

So he calls him 'Chris.'

He took out a palm-sized aluminum cartouche and opened it. A colorful array of hand-tied fishing flies attracted the sparkle of his blue eyes.

He placed the cartouche on the table. "Please, have a seat."

His eyes seemed to roam over her briefly, and she felt uncomfortable. He watched her seat herself at the laminate table, on a chair with a torn seat.

He untangled a fly, his large fingers quivering around the barely visible fishing line. "Wouldn't you know, absentminded me forgot your pen."

As he returned to the counter, she found herself looking at his shoulders and back, the backs of his legs, to his feet. He was in good shape, with only a hint of softening. She could see where Christopher got his physique.

He returned with a ball-point pen and she smiled, awkwardly. While he fetched ice from a crank-type metal tray in the freezer, she set about writing the check, signing her name and writing the date first. How much time would she have to wait before Christopher would arrive? She looked at the cheap plastic wall clock. It was 3:15. He must be due soon. She didn't have much time. Brian would be home at 4:00.

He set a pair of tall glasses, each emblazoned with the head of a horse shaped like a gun going through a "D"—the Denver Broncos emblem—on the table next to her. Football glasses: such a bachelor.

"Have you lived in Plainview long?" she asked.

"Going on two years. Two and a half maybe." He scratched his head. "I think I've seen you in town. At the Pioneer Market?"

She was embarrassed: She didn't recall ever seeing him, and the thought that he had seen her, admiring her perhaps, made her uneasy. "I do shop there from time to time. The supermarket gets so crowded."

"Where did you move from?"

"Beckle's Ridge, a spit of a town up north. Pretty, but it makes Plainview look like a metropolis."

She chuckled, thinking how unusual it was to hear the word 'metropolis' juxtaposed with 'spit' in casual conversation. She wrote the name Christopher Hendrickson slowly on the check.

"And you?" he asked.

"I've been in Plainview for eight years, right after I graduated from college. My husband moved here for work."

A look of surprise came over his eyes. "Oh? What does he do?"

"He was in computers." Should she explain? Yes, she needed to be truthful— "He passed away a few years ago."

"I'm sorry." But was that?...—Yes, it was!—The edges of his lips curled into a smile.

She smiled back nervously. She told herself she should not have mentioned her late husband. She had to fill in an amount on the check. How much was appropriate? Twenty-five, forty: the numbers seemed arbitrary, but fifty seemed just enough. She wrote the numbers slowly, daintily, then spelled out "Fifty" on the line below. She took a final look at the check, examining her signature—yes, it was legible enough—then tore the check from the register. She recorded the check number, amount, and payee in the log. She did a quick accounting and balanced her account, then placed the check on the table, sipping her iced tea. The tea needed more sugar.

He glanced at the check.

"Have I spelled your son's name correctly?" she asked.

"Yes." As he breathed, she thought she detected the faint smell of liquor. The check shook in his hand. She casually looked around the room, at the waste basket and the counter, for signs of bottles, but saw none.

"That's an awful lot of money for a kid," he said.

A jolt of panic shot through her. She had not wanted to attract his suspicion. "Your son seems like a nice young man. My son's a scout too." She smiled.

His eyes became more vibrant. "You have a son, too? How old?"

"Seven."

"That's the best age. After that, reality sets in and boys can't stand being kids anymore."

She chuckled, the word 'boys' reverberating as if he were repeating it: Boys, Boys, Boys. Christopher was not a young man, but a *boy*.

"Any other children?" he asked.

She wished for a moment she could retract the mention of her son. He was taking an interest in her. It was the outfit, she thought. She was all tarted up, and there was no way to stop him from responding. "No, just the one."

"Me too. One's enough to keep your hands full." His

shoulders danced slightly, and she was reminded of the eagerness Christopher had displayed in the kitchen. She looked at his eyes—they did not seem bloodshot. Had he actually been drinking or was she being paranoid? He was so steady and assured, his gaze imperturbable as a rock.

She glanced overhead. Slightly over five minutes had passed. The longer she stayed, the more she was sure to send the wrong message. It was better to go now, she concluded.

She finished her iced tea. "I didn't realize how late it was. I do appreciate your hospitality, Mr. Hendrickson."

He paused, half squinting. The awkwardness of the moment increased. "Please, call me Bill. It's Laney, right?"

"Yes," she said.

His lips twitched a bit, and he stared, blinking, at the table. Maybe he had been drinking.

"I'm not sure about this donation. It's so... magnanimous."

His use of that word surprised her. First metropolis, now magnanimous. Was he a Word of the Day freak? He certainly was not a country bumpkin. But drunk?

His eyebrows arched as if he detected that she was curious about him. She tried to conceal any interest by forcing her eyes to wander, but he pushed his body closer to the table. It seemed as if he could twist it in his arms and crumple it between his legs. She could feel herself pulling back, although her body moved only centimeters at most. She scolded herself again for choosing such a large amount.

"My son should be home soon. Are you sure you don't want to give this to him yourself?" His head tilted, staring at her eyes.

She felt guilty and wanted to escape. She should not have come in the first place. "That's very nice of you, but I really need to be getting home."

"It was nice of you to stop by. I hope we have the chance to see each other again." He paused, as if expecting her to say something, but all she offered was a small smile which she quickly retracted.

His eyes roamed over her shoulders down her bare arms. "This is very nice of you to help my son. I would like to repay you. There's a great new seafood place by the interstate. Maybe we could go to dinner this Thursday, if that would work?"

Of course, she told herself. The tight pink tank top. The short shorts. The daintily painted toe nails. Of course he would ask her out. "I...," she stuttered... "have to check my calendar."

"Sure." He gave her a torn piece of a menu from "3P," the Plainview Pizza Parlor, and wrote his phone number on it.

Why couldn't she have said, 'I'm seeing someone' or 'I already have plans'? Or 'No?' Grow up, she told herself. *Laney Secord, you are thirty-two. You can say, 'No!'* But she felt guilty for having come to see his son.

"I really need to be going," she said, taking the number and placing it in her pocket.

"I didn't mean to make you feel uncomfortable."

At once, she felt honored that he had respected her enough to realize that he had crossed a line with her. "No, I'm fine," she said.

He nodded, remaining a few feet from her.

They shook hands, and she drove away down Grove Street. She shouldn't blame him for responding to the visual clues she had provided: her bare legs, her bare shoulders, her wholesome face. A week ago, she would not have fathomed going to a stranger's house to talk to a boy. Now, a man she knew nothing about asked her on a date. She had entered a world she knew of only through case files, conjecture, and theory. Christopher's seemingly humble origins, the father who might have a drinking problem, the mother who was absent from the picture: all classic ingredients for dysfunction. But she was not sitting behind a desk contemplating the fates of strangers. She was driving her run-down Volvo, asking herself why had she gone to see Christopher. She should have confined herself to the safety of her imagination, where the antidote to loneliness was a pint of Ben and Jerrys and a tearjerker. Then she would not have been forced to lead on a man who was too *old* for her, too rough around the edges.

She had travelled the wrong way down Grove Street and ended up in the small town center. Damn this town!

Plainview was in full suburban swing—housewives fussing with errands, day crews whittling away shifts, a policeman directing traffic around yet another public works project. What was she doing here? Why didn't she move? How did she let her life stop?

She looked into the rearview mirror. She had no one to blame but herself. She had waltzed down a blind alley, unsuspecting, a walking target. Who did she think she was? Swabs of mascara and eyeliner, blotches of rouge on her cheeks: a veritable clown. Ready for the Big Top, starring in her very own freak show, the one, the only, Laney Secord.

When she was midway through an intersection, a Cadillac moving in a perpendicular direction pulled before her. The driver of the Cadillac, an elderly woman, blared her horn. Laney jammed on the brakes. Her Volvo skidded to a stop before the driver's side door. Laney's light beamed red. The woman gave her a look that said, "Damn you!"

Laney's fingertips palpitated. She could not take her eyes off the frail woman: a hive of bluish white hair, chin barely poking above the steering wheel. Terrified. Laney could have killed her, but she was more frightened by the prospect that one day, she would *be* her, alone, scared, almost invisible.

The driveway to 6 Heather Lane was empty as usual. She took her checkbook and the black and gold pen from the glove compartment. Deceitfully and damnably she had behaved.

With head and shoulders slumped, she made her way to the front door. When she reached the unweathered, spotless welcome mat, she couldn't conceive that it was only yesterday that Christopher had come by. Time was spinning. She thought of herself standing at the Hendricksons' door, looking for the doorbell. That there was none should have been a warning.

She stepped inside and immediately scurried to the master bath, fetching a bottle of make up remover and proceeding to spread the lotion around her eyes, her mouth, her forehead. Her blond hair she brushed aside. She rubbed the cream into a lather and let it set. As she stood over the vanity, prom picture by her side, she felt tears rush forth through the suds and the dissolving make up. She quickly took handfuls of water and pushed the water into her eyes, watching as the lather flowed down the basin. She looked into the mirror. No, she reminded herself, nothing was wrong.

3

After being at the Hendricksons' house, which was a third the size of her own, Laney felt less claustrophobic, less restricted, but still, she did not feel at ease. The walls of the hallway looked overdecorated. The kitchen, the room she came to live in day after day, seemed strange. It, unlike the outdated kitchen at Bill's, was equipped with all the finest appliances, but she didn't know what to make of them. She knew she should be preparing dinner, but she didn't know what.

It was 4 PM and Brian was due home from his Cub Scouts meeting.

She had changed into a pair of flared capri pants and a conservative V-neck knit shirt that hung loosely about her. She gazed at the refrigerator. She could start with a salad. She always started with a soup or a salad, to help keep her figure and to develop good eating habits in Brian. Yet it was too hot for soup, and salad seemed so bland.

The phone rang, but she let the answering machine pick up. It was her mother: "Where are you? You know I hate these machines. Dad wants to know if you're coming to Santa Maria this summer. For the Fourth. Call us. Someday. Please." The machine beeped as her mother hung up.

Laney immediately hit 'erase' on the machine. She did not want to go to Santa Maria. Her father loved the California coastal resort because he could play golf and smoke cigars with his Knights of Columbus buddies, but she would be stuck with her doting, prying, loving mother. Mother who still tried to tell her how to dress, how much make-up to wear, how to raise Brian, how she should remarry. In her subtle ways, she would suggest that Laney would never find anyone like Jay, the implication being that she did not deserve him.

She wanted to skip dinner altogether.

She heard the front door open, then close. Brian's feet slid across the hall. He would not pick up his feet, no matter how much she scolded him.

He walked in, looking adorable in the blue polo shirt she had bought for him in Boulder over Easter. His wind-breaker was tied around his waist. It was so warm out he didn't need a jacket, but she had insisted he take one in case it cooled off. He put his Spiderman lunch box on the butcher block table, keeping on his little Tiger Cub backpack, which he had begged her to buy.

She closed the refrigerator door and noticed that he looked disappointed, as if he too were a stranger in his own home.

"Can't you say hi?" she said.

"Hi." His voice was weak and unconvincing. He had something on his mind, but as with his father, she would have to draw it out of him.

"How was your day?"

"Fine."

"What did you do?"

"We made elephants and giraffes and lions out of cardboard colored paper then we played kickball but we didn't get to finish because Mrs. Peeler made us come back in."

"That sounds like fun." She smiled at him, hoping for a smile in return, but none came. Nothing she could do could wipe away his look of concern. "Is something the matter?"

"Who's Christopher Hendrickson?"

How did he know Christopher Hendrickson's name? Did they know each other? Or had he seen him yesterday and not said anything? "He's a boy who lives not too far from us, on the other side of Plainview. Why do you ask?"

"I saw him on the way home from school and he asked me about you."

"Today?"

He nodded.

"Where?"

"At the bus stop. When I got off the bus."

The bus stop: Just down the street in front of Mrs. Flaherty?

"Mom, maybe he can come in for dinner? He's an Eagle Scout." His eyes lit up. "He said he can help me with my Mother's Day project. I'll never finish it without someone to help me. Please, can he come over?"

Was Christopher waiting outside? She could feel herself becoming more tense. "I thought the troop leader was helping you."

"He doesn't have enough time for me. He's always helping the other boys. And sometimes he gives me funny looks. I don't think he understands. Christopher said he could make it nice for me. He hasn't eaten dinner yet. Can't he come over?"

He sounded so pleading and desperate. Did she have any choice? Christopher had come all this way, again. Even if dinner was not such a good idea, perhaps at least she could go talk to him about helping Brian. "Is he still outside?"

"Yes, outside. Hurry before he leaves."

"Will you be okay upstairs?" she asked.

He nudged her toward the door, as she wondered: Could she

really have Christopher over for dinner?

She told Brian to go upstairs and to stay in his room while she went outside.

Christopher was not in her yard or on the street. She continued down Heather Lane toward the bus stop.

All the trees—the maples and the pines—were verdant green. The street itself was pristine, newly paved, with new yellow and white lines freshly painted. She did not cross the street because the other side of Heather Lane was still undeveloped, with nothing but weeds, wild blackberries, grapes flourishing by the stream.

There was no sign of Christopher at the bus stop. A dirt path next to the stop led to the woods, and she saw a maze of lines and curlicues that resembled footprints.

She stepped off the road down the path, dirt creeping into her sandals, scratching, biting her feet. Down the path, old broken bottles, rusty pieces of cans, a corroded newspaper, lined the embankment separating the road from the woods.

Christopher was nowhere in sight.

She mounted the embankment and proceeded into the woods, where the sun could not filter through the trees. Fallen dead leaves, wet underneath her feet, formed a mat over the ground. She hadn't been in these woods in years. The feeling of the leaves prickling her feet brought back the memory of when she and Jay had first traipsed through these woods after their offer on the house was accepted and they were in escrow. They had walked hand in hand, feeling they had found something special, something momentous. Their world away from the world.

A leaf slipped into the strap of her slide. She slinked down on a hollow stump and fished it out. She looked at the leaf.

Green and robust. A waxy finish. Strong, tender veins. The tree from which it fell towered overhead. She could see Jay pinning her against a tree, saying, "I love you with all my life, Laney. Nothing will ever destroy that."

Not even infidelity with his closest friend? Her foot skated back and forth against the wood sole. She took a breath. She did not see Christopher anywhere. She couldn't expect him to be hiding in the woods.

She stepped around the tree stump and cleared a few leaves with her hands, making a small hole in the earth with the tip of her sandal. She knew she should be returning home, to make sure Brian was okay, but the woods offered a respite from her routine, with no burdens or responsibilities, no pestering calls about visiting Santa Maria pressing down upon her. She could see the roof of Mrs. Flaherty's house next door peeking through the trees. She took off her shoes and placed them atop each other in the hole, becoming lost in a daydream, thinking of how as a child she used to play alone in the woods of the backyard of her home in Boulder. She would dance and sing and pretend that the trees were her audience, and the hours would rush by and soon dinner would be served.

As she abandoned herself to these memories, she heard leaves crunching behind her. Christopher, twenty yards away, was pulling himself up a small hill by the low-lying branch of a tree. She hastily put her sandals back on.

Had he been watching her? She had not been doing anything odd, except daydream, but she felt uncomfortable.

He walked toward her. His blond hair was scattered over his forehead. He was wearing blue jeans and a white polo shirt, similar to the one Brian was wearing but Christopher's lacked the horse emblem on the chest. Out of his Eagle Scout uniform, he looked more boyish, gawky, even younger. She would have thought he was fourteen or fifteen if she had not known his exact age.

"Christopher, hi." Her voice was hesitant and unsure.

He did not offer a greeting in response, as if he too were nervous and ashamed.

"My son said you came by the house a few minutes ago," she said.

He walked closer, slowly.

She was struck by his resemblance to his father. He had his father's build, similar bone structure to his face, an equally thick mesh of hair. She envisioned how he would look as a man: His stomach becoming softer and fuller; the skin under his eyes sagging, the skin on his hands becoming coarser and thicker. She imagined his father as a boy: Slim and smooth and tight and hormones oiling his face and deepening his voice and broadening his chest.

"I went to your house today and met your father," she said, her voice nervous, too nervous. "You left your clipboard and I brought it back. I left a donation."

He crinkled his lip between his thumb and forefinger. He seemed so unlike the young man she had met yesterday, so shy, unsure of himself, awkward and nervous. The skin on his face and neck was soft and supple, with a small fold under his chin, which she wanted to caress.

"I haven't gone home yet," he said.

She had forgotten what his voice sounded like. She was surprised how deep it was—deeper than his father's, but not as certain.

"Brian said you offered to help him with his Cub Scouts project."

"The Mother's Day gift? Sure," he said. He nervously rubbed his nose, wiping his hand over his forehand and through his bangs. "Whatever he wants. If it's okay with you." His other hand flew into his pocket, and he appeared to be fumbling with something, or merely scratching, something.

Jarred, she tried to ignore his nervous tics. "He would appreciate that a lot," she said. "I'm a little confused. Your father didn't seem to know anything about a trip to Mount Rushmore have been."

His eyes narrowed. "I must have forgot to tell him."

Was there really an excursion to Mount Rushmore, she wondered. "I talked to your father for a little while," she said. "He seems nice. I'm sure he's very good to you."

He shrugged, pushing a foot against the trunk of the tree and stepping forward. He moved with brusque movements, and suddenly he seemed more like the young man she had met yesterday. She was startled by the abrupt change in his demeanor, but cast it off to adolescence. She forgot how teenage boys could be all tough and uncaring on the outside but inside so vulnerable, afraid, and sensitive.

"When I kissed you yesterday, were you surprised?" he asked.

She wanted him to keep his voice down, even though nobody else was around. "Yes, I was, very much," she said.

"Why did you stop me?"

"I didn't think it was right."

He smirked, kicking a dead branch with the tip of his sneaker. "I kissed the girl I brought to junior prom last year. She would have done more, but I didn't want her to." His eyes had a knowing look, then it vanished, as if he caught himself. He raised his shoulders meekly. "Did you tell my dad I kissed you?"

"Of course not."

"He wouldn't have cared."

"I don't think that's the case at all."

"All he cares about is fishing," he said.

"That can't be true."

He scattered a mass of broken leaves and pine needles by his feet. "We used to fish all the time but not anymore." There was a note of anger in his voice. "It's boring," he said.

Despite his air of indifference, she could tell he was scared and hurt. Perhaps his father had not shown him how to express his feelings. Her own father did not know himself: He would find a way to deal with something else, like fixing the lawnmower or tinkering in the garage.

Christopher stepped closer. "I knew you were different from other people in this town. When I saw you at the first Cub Scouts meeting, when you dropped your son off—do you remember?"

The truth was, she remembered dropping Brian off but she hadn't spotted Christopher. She would have remembered if she had. "Last fall?" she said.

His eyes danced. "You do remember."

The edges of her lips tensed. Had he plotted to see her when he came to her door yesterday?

"I wanted to see you again, for a long time." He looked relieved. "You're not from Plainview, are you?"

"No, Boulder."

"Right—where you went to college, I remember. I'm not from here either."

"No, Beckle's Ridge."

He looked surprised. "You know it?"

"Your father told me."

He seemed disappointed. He stood next to her, breathing slowly and heavily. He scratched his stomach, lifting his shirt to reveal a flash of his belly button, a flash of hair above his belt, then he let the shirt fall, his pinkie pointing at, beckoning to, her.

"Yesterday, in the kitchen," he said, "you wanted to kiss me, didn't you? You were looking at me."

"I'm terribly flattered."

His arm slipped around her waist. Her body tightened. He gently pressed against the small of her back.

"We can keep it a secret," he said. "You can trust me. I'm an Eagle Scout."

She stifled a temptation to laugh. "I have a son."

She could see in his eyes that he would not listen to reason. He was sure he knew everything.

"You're so beautiful," he said.

She could feel herself blush. She knew he meant it. She wanted to tell him that he was very handsome himself, even more than his father.

His head tilted and he closed his eyes and he tried to kiss her. She put a hand to his lips. "Christopher."

He moved his head aside. "Just one kiss, please?"

She stepped back toward the stump, freeing herself from his hands.

"I could get in trouble for something like this. Serious trouble."

"I won't tell. Don't worry," he said.

"It's not as easy as that."

"No one has to know." He looked at the ground by her feet, then stepped forward, his eyes alight with desire. He held onto her arm, his head trembling. Despite his bravado, she could tell he was afraid, and she wanted to hold him.

The trees behind them rustled loudly, and he turned suddenly, letting go of her.

She was going to explain how a relationship between them would not work, but no sooner than her lips parted, the trees behind them rustled again in a loud whoosh, and there was a screeching noise. Frightened, he scampered off, through the woods.

4

The rustling of leaves turned out to be nothing more than a gust of wind, and the screeching just a pair of large crows loudly calling to each other.

Laney searched the area. No one was near. Christopher had vanished. She was confused: He had come across town to see her and though outwardly he seemed headstrong and impulsive, he was so skittish on the slightest noise he ran away.

She walked away, feeling as though his hand were still on the small of her back, pushing her down Heather Lane, invigorating her with the surety of being desired. Still, as she looked back, at the woods, she was unsettled. She could see his eager eyes—soft and entreating—and his skin, so pure, smooth, and fresh—all of which spoke volumes more than anything he had said. Yet why couldn't he have talked to her? What did he want? To kiss her? Could a simple kiss be so important, so all consuming? Or was it some sort of a juvenile game for him? Could his feelings for her really be genuine?

What feelings did—*could*—she have for him? How could she allow herself to pursue a relationship with someone half her age, someone underage? To do so would be a compromise of her morals.

She immediately headed upstairs, where Brian was busy working on his surprise for Mother's Day.

He quickly turned his back to her and huddled around his project. "Mom!"

She caught a glimpse of wood, then looked away toward the

door. "I'm sorry, honey. I should have knocked."

He fumbled with a paper bag and some cloth.

"You can turn around now," he said. The blanket from the foot of his bed covered the project, rising in several places, at odd angles. What was he making? He couldn't be crafting this all by himself: He was too young. He was probably just staring at it, day-dreaming.

"Christopher couldn't come to help. He had to go home for dinner."

"With his mother and father?"

She knew Brian, consciously or not, was making a point about Christopher having both parents. "He just lives with his father," she said.

"He doesn't have a mother?"

"I'm sure he does, but they don't live together anymore. Sometimes mothers and fathers don't get along, and one of them moves away."

"Don't they come back?"

"Sometimes they just come to visit and they go off to their own house."

He gazed at picture of Jay on the bed stand. "If Christopher lives in Plainview, can't you call him and ask him to come over sometime?"

"What did Christopher say to you outside, at the bus stop?"

"He asked why you weren't married."

"What did you tell him?"

"Daddy died."

"Anything else?"

"He said he thought you were very nice."

'Nice': What would Christopher have meant by that? Or was

Brian remembering correctly?

His eyes were twinkling—why, why? But she was afraid to press him too much. She had better not raise his suspicions. "If Christopher comes back again, if you see him somewhere, will you let me know?"

He nodded, almost smiling, and she started to leave.

Had she said something she should not have? Was she involving her son unnecessarily?

Feeling slightly worn, Laney went to the master bedroom, ruminating on his need for company. He only had her and her mother and father—Jay's parents lived far away, in Oregon. He had only seen them once in the past two years. She was an only child herself, and she knew how lonesome it could be. At least she had had the neighbors' children to play with.

Lying on top of the satin comforter on her bed, she closed her eyes and quickly fell asleep. However, a couple minutes later, she awoke, surprised at how tired she was.

She closed her eyes again, telling herself she would dream of something fantastic.

She moved her hand around the pillow, repositioning the clumps of down under her head. She could see the woods behind the bus stop, the branches of saplings swaying, the pine needles being brushed aside.

She opened her eyes. She stood and walked to the white wicker dressing table. She picked up the phone and dialed the Hendricksons to call Christopher. She was surprised she had remembered the number.

"Hello?"

She recognized Christopher's voice by the way it deepened and then let up.

She wanted to hang up.

"Who is this?" he said. "Laney, is that you?"

How did he know it was her?

Her lips parted, but she hesitated, staring at the wall. She didn't know what to say. Then instantly, she spoke: "Christopher." She did not say his name as a question or a statement, but rather as an admission.

It sounded as if he was moving the phone around.

"Christopher, why did you run away?"

His voice became harsh. "You're wasting your time if you think you're going to get my father to love you as much as I do."

"Christopher."

"I'll kill him," he said. "I'll kill the son of a bitch."

Then the phone rang and Laney woke up. She had been dreaming. Still lying on her bed, she felt her heart racing. Sweat exuding from her forehead, she sat up and stared at the phone, listening to her voice on the machine. "Hi, this is Laney. We're not here at the moment, but please leave a message."

"Laney, it's Dad. We're making plans for Santa Maria. Can we count you in? We're thinking of flying in on the second..."

Her father continued speaking as Brian entered the room. "Mom, aren't you going to answer the phone? It's Grandpa."

She stood and walked to the dressing table. Regret stirred through her for not returning her mother's call. Her head throbbed as she tried to push aside the dream she had just had. Still, the images and sounds were all a jumble: Christopher, Santa Maria, I'll kill him, Mom.

Her father was still talking to the machine: "We'd really like to wrap up our plans by the weekend before all the best fares are sold out."

She picked up the handset. "Hi, Dad."

"Laney, hi. Mom said you didn't call her back."

"It's been a busy day."

Brian was tugging the sides of her pants. "Please, can I talk to him?"

"Dad, Brian wants to talk to you."

She handed Brian the phone.

"Hi Grandpa." A wave of excitement rushed through Brian's voice as he held the phone with both hands.

While Brian and her father spoke, she continued to hear Christopher's perplexing voice: I'll kill him. Jarred, she could visualize herself at the Hendricksons' front door, Bill guarding it, she was petting the dog. Christopher was walking up the sidewalk, a gun in his hand. What was she thinking? Why was her head pulsating, the sides of her skull clenching?

Brian lifted the phone over his head to hand it to her. She was lost in her reverie, her headache, but she took the phone nonetheless. "Dad, I'm not sure about Santa Maria."

"Mom!" Brian said.

His cry was shrill, and her forehead tensed.

"We'd love to see him," her father said. "Are you okay, Lane?"

"Yeah, it's just that..."

Brian was tugging at her pants again. "Can we go, Mom? Please? Please."

She tried to ignore Brian. "Dad, I have an interview this Friday, the one that my friends set up. I might be starting work soon. I don't know if I can get the time off."

"Can't you ask them for vacation time in the interview?"

"I don't know. They're really busy now. That's why they need me."

"Why do you want to go back to work anyway? If you need money, all you need to do is pick up the phone."

"It's not the money."

"Then what?"

Brian tugged at her pants. "Please?"

She looked at Brian, holding the phone a few inches from her ear. "Just a moment." She put the phone back to her ear. "I just need to think about it. What *I* want, for a change."

"What do you mean?" her father said.

What do you think I mean? she wanted to scream, but out of deference to Brian, she held back: "I'll call you later, okay." She hung up the phone.

"Can't we go?" Brian said.

She gently pushed his back. "Come on. Let's get washed up for dinner."

"But Mom."

She was going to explode. "No, but Mom nothing."

***

After she loaded the dishes and utensils into the dishwasher, she dried her hands and walked to the cabinet by the refrigerator. She pulled out the telephone directory. She felt no hesitation. There was no dilemma, no agonizing, no internal debate that left her perplexed.

She dialed the number, and the line on the other end rang.

The line kept ringing.

Her mouth tightened. This was not so easy.

As she was about to hang up, a man's voice answered. "Hello."

It was Bill. She hesitated, thinking of what to say.

"Hi, Bill. It's Laney Secord."

"Laney, it's nice to hear from you." He sounded surprised.

"Bill, I'm sorry, but I checked my calendar and discovered I already have plans for Thursday. Dinner with friends."

"Maybe we can make it another time."

Was that a question or an invitation?

"Well, sure. Let me give you a call."

She heard a sigh, or a groan, then he spoke: "You have my number." He sounded disappointed.

She listened for a beat. He hung up. She heard a click, then a barely audible hiss, and silence. A droning, disappointing silence. She had managed to extricate herself from the date, but his response—curt, though not without a hint of caring in his tone—puzzled her.

She hung up, and as she looked at the phone, she recalled her dream of calling Christopher. In it, he had threatened to kill his father—Where would that anger have come from? Did she imagine it, or had he said something to give her pause: "All he cares about is fishing," he had lamented in the woods, suggesting he felt unloved. Is that why he wanted her love?

She had to think of something other than the Hendricksons— but as she looked at the kitchen cabinets—antiqued, brushed steel handles and knobs, with substantial back plates behind every pull, fine maple grain—none of it seemed as important as the fact that yesterday, Christopher had been in this room, and despite physical evidence to the contrary—all reason, all rationality—he hadn't seemed to leave.

***

Although she normally fell asleep by 11:00 or 11:30, tonight Laney sat on the side of the bed with the lamp on, staring at the crystal Waterford clock that her aunt had given her and Jay as a wedding present. It was 12:30 AM, Wednesday.

The house seemed empty, though Brian was just down the hall. A notice from his Cub Scouts troop sat on the end table, advising of a troop gathering this Saturday at 8:30 AM at Plainview Elementary. She tried to recall the first time she had brought him there to join the Scouts. It was a weekday evening in October. There were several excited boys along with their fathers, a few mothers beside herself. Several older men—troop leaders—were present, as well as a dozen or so Boy Scouts who were talking among themselves. She could see the teenaged boys huddling, but nowhere amid them could she see Christopher. A leg, a torso, could have been his. She transposed his features onto another boy. He was so striking. Why hadn't she noticed him last fall? Maybe she had changed over the past several months. She no longer had a steady companion, a presence, in the house at all times, and she had begun to feel her isolation more than ever. Brian was at school more often than last year, enjoying his time away from her.

She watched the minute hand move from the six to the left of the six. There was no second hand on the clock but still the minute hand moved. Then it stopped moving. She watched and waited for it to move again. Another minute passed. On and on she watched the face of the clock until the minute hand approached eight. She thought of nothing. She liked being lost in the absolute nothingness of the slowly moving clock, the ticking clock that offered a consistent hum as the seconds passed. Fast, regular, sharp clicks for each second, sounds that blurred one into the other. She could see herself slowly dissolving into the face of the clock. Her blond hair and green-blue eyes reflected in the chrome face around the dial. She moved a hand and caught a distorted glimpse of herself. She could not see her mouth or her nose nor even her eyes. She was becoming a faceless nonentity. This realization did not frighten her, but rather comforted her, because as she felt herself drift into nonexistence, she would have no need to sleep.

5

Laney knew it was Wednesday only when she looked at her packet of birth control pills, which had a pill marked for each day. The pills eased her period and her chronic headaches, but now the palm-sized packet was nearly empty. She'd have to refill it soon, though she didn't want to go back to the doctor and be examined, questioned, and condescended to in order to get another prescription.

She hadn't slept all night, except for the hour beginning at 5 AM. The hour of sleep made her all the more tired. Images of Christopher's face, his body, would not let up.

As Brian was leaving for school, he asked whether something was wrong. She wanted to tell him that she had a lot on her mind, that she felt pressured, overworked, unmistakably hollow. But he would not understand, and she did not want to burden him. Her role was to be the protector, the person he could always come to. So she told him that she had a slight headache, that she was sure it would pass, that he should not worry but enjoy his day at school. As she kissed him goodbye, he said, "How do you know it's not an aneurysm?"

She knelt before him. "When Daddy died, he didn't have any pain. Something went wrong in his brain."

He looked at her, mistrusting. "Was he happy when he died?"

Had somebody suggested that his father was unhappy? Perhaps he had seen something on television. She cast aside her doubts. "Yes, he was very happy because he had a son he loved very much."

What she said did not seem to register. Brian offered no reaction, no awareness that he had heard her. After he walked out the door to the bus stop, she could feel his presence beside her, as if he were still in the doorway asking questions, and she was kneeling before him, offering rationalizations. He was like Jay in that respect—he would bring up a subject only to drop it moments later, seemingly satisfied. Later, he'd bring up the subject again and ask a bit more. More and more he'd pry, and then finally he'd be fully satisfied. He'd have no want of questioning, no consciousness that he was ever concerned. Because Brian was so much like his father, she felt Jay was with her. His death once seemed her own, but over the years, she relegated his absence to its proper place, to memory. Ironically, this process of accepting his death reaffirmed that she was still alive, if only to face the neverending cycle of want and mollification that masqueraded as minutes and hours.

By 9:20 AM she felt in desperate need of sleep. She tried to yawn, contorting her facial muscles and opening her mouth, but her throat, vacant of air, refused to cooperate. She was about to go back to bed when the phone rang. The ringing, hard and fast, jarred her. Her head pulsated with the harsh, grinding, successive trills. Blood rushed to the periphery of her skull. She watched the black cordless phone on the white wicker dressing table with the beige carpet underneath, debating whether to answer it, listening to the piercing, spasmodic sound that seemed to press against her, swallow her almost, even push her aside.

She thought it might be her parents pestering her for an answer about Santa Maria. Or Bill—to ask her out again.

The machine started to pick up, playing the outgoing

message. Would it be Christopher, to thank her for the check, to apologize, as only an adolescent can or would, for running off in the woods?

She lifted the phone from the cradle and said hello.

"Laney, it's Erin."

The sound of her best friend's voice seemed anticlimactic. It was devoid of the harshness, the rudeness, the slap in the face that the ringing seemed to augur.

"Hi," Laney said.

"You're still coming over, right?" Erin had a careful, coldly mellifluous voice that reminded her of her mother's.

She had completely forgotten that they had a shopping trip planned, to help Erin prepare for a dinner party on Saturday. "Erin, I'm sorry. I barely slept last night."

"What's the matter?"

"A migraine," she said, half hoping that Erin would detect her lie because she had told Erin that the birth control medication had helped her manage her headaches.

"Oh, honey, you get some rest."

Erin let her off so easily, with so little struggle. "I'm a liar!" Laney wanted to scream. "Don't believe a word I say. Can't you see I am falling apart all over again? Just like I did when Jay died. I am the woman who slept with your husband. How can you trust me? How can you talk to me? Are you that blind? Don't you want to know what's on my mind?" but her sleep-deprived state left her vanquished. Her voice betrayed all that was inside and took on a martyred, motherly tone that sounded devoid of guilt. "That's okay. I think it's passed. I can meet you in an hour."

***

She drove to Erin's house and dutifully took her to the sparkling clean—almost antiseptically clean—new supermarket in the shopping center by the interstate. It felt great to be outside. Laney usually shopped at the smaller market, the Pioneer Market, where Bill had said he had first seen her, but Erin had a lot of shopping to do.

The center was appointed with dueling fast food outlets, one Mexican, the other old fashioned burgers, a multiplex, a discount book store, a chic clothing store with a sign that said "Mother's Day Sale." Laney couldn't keep her mind off how everything and everybody in Plainview was changing. This was not the town she had moved to eight years ago. Her fellow shoppers seemed more tanned, better dressed, more diverse even. No longer were they all housewives and elderly folks but a smattering of young women and men too, a man that looked Indian, a black man by the checkout counter.

Had the town truly changed, or was her perception of it changing, as if she was more readily aware of things outside herself? Or maybe the lack of sleep was now catching up with her, and winning.

While everybody shopped, she was struck by the air-conditioned quiet, the inaudible hum of freezers and laser eye scanners and sliding glass doors, hidden cameras watching and recording and preserving for today and all of eternity every nod, every turn, every glance that she made. The shopping foray seemed a mirage, even Erin before her, in her gray fleece sweats, her neatly bobbed hair dyed nutmeg, her lithe frame which twisted as she pushed her cart down the aisle. Erin's hair glistened shades of red and brown in the glow of the omnipresent fluorescent lights. She filled her cart with enough sundries and comestibles to furnish a time capsule. The heaping cart made Laney think that she was just taking with her what she could before a bell rang for her to stop.

"Are you all right, Laney? You're awfully quiet."

They were in yet another canned goods section.

"You look pale," she added.

"I'm fine."

It saddened her to think how close she and Erin once were. They used to be so similar. But Erin had transformed herself into Mrs. Suburbia, the perfect wife and mother of two—a darling boy and girl—the doyenne of a rambling home in one of the more exclusive developments in Plainview. She had a part-time nanny, she did not work, and she had no outside interests to speak of except for throwing dinner parties and trying to fix up her single friends. Marriage and family life had become everything to her. Gone was the tennis playing, wisecracking, spunky redhead that Laney had met in college, where Erin's talent for putting down a few too many earned her a certain reputation. After she met Dan, she changed. She spent her junior and senior years studying, boosting her GPA to a solid B, even joined a Christian Bible group. Dan didn't ask any of this from her, but he did not complain either.

Laney moved her virtually empty cart out of the way for a teenage mom to pass.

"Didn't you bring your purse?" Erin said.

Laney knew that she was referring to the beaded purse that Erin had given her, not for her birthday or any other occasion, but just because she said she had found one that she thought suited her. Laney didn't like to carry purses—she could only think of putting keys, lipstick, and a wallet in them, and she could do without the lipstick.

"It's at home," Laney said.

Erin's tongue clucked. "Women who don't carry purses intimidate men."

"I'll take my chances," she said.

Erin's brow arched. Then, in practically the same instant, she put the back of a hand to Laney's forehead. "I shouldn't have dragged you out."

"I'm fine. Really."

But there was a hint of question in her voice that she herself detected and could not suppress. She tried to think of a way to ask her whether she knew anything about Christopher Hendrickson. Erin knew all the town gossip. She could mention Bill, but she would have to explain how she had met him. She decided to be direct—

"Erin, did a Boy Scout come to your door the other day?"

"On Monday? The Hendrickson boy. The one with the pimple?"

"Yes," Laney said, chuckling. "Do you know him?"

"I've heard a thing or two about the father. Supposedly he's divorced and has a little drinking problem. But what's worse is... No, I shouldn't repeat it."

"What?"

"It's nothing." She dropped another can in her cart.

"You can't just lead me on and then just say it's nothing. Come on."

"I'm sorry. I shouldn't have said anything in the first place. I'm trying to turn a new leaf. I've been reading this self-help book. It says people who gossip aren't happy with themselves. I know it's simplistic, but I think there's a germ of truth in there, somewhere."

Laney felt uneasy. She knew that Erin's home life wasn't perfect. Dan wouldn't have cheated on her otherwise. But because Dan had cheated with *her*, she felt all the more guilty: How good a friend was she? She did not have the strength to tell her what had happened that cold, silly night when she and Dan had fucked. Christ, how much they had wanted to be with each other! She wished she could forget. Fortunately, their feelings for each other were purely carnal, and temporal.

Did she know Dan had cheated on her? Could she ever forgive either of them? Laney was torn: she could not be truthful to her. There was too great a risk in speaking the truth. Look what had happened after she had told Jay.

Erin placed a couple of jars of olives in her cart. "Why do you ask about the Hendrickson boy?"

"I'd never seen him before. That's all." *Why did she have to say: 'That's all?' She was being defensive.* "Did you give him any money?"

"Ten bucks or so. Dan took a liking to him. He brought him out to the garage and gave him some fishing tackle."

Laney recalled that she still had Jay's fishing tackle in the basement. She could probably give that away as she did with his clothes: Would Christopher want any of it?

"I met the boy's father the other day, too," Laney said.

"Where?"

"At the Pioneer Market," she said, lying. "He asked me out on a date."

"You didn't say yes, I hope."

"He's pretty good-looking, in that rugged, cowboy sort of way."

"Look, I have the perfect guy for you. You'll meet him on Saturday. He's an accountant. Never married, no kids, not gay.

Thirty-four. Sweet as molasses."

"You know I don't like molasses."

"I really think you're going to like this guy. He's so sweet. And he might make partner soon."

"You really don't need to set me up."

"I'm just trying to be a friend."

"I appreciate it, but it's really not necessary." *Was that what she was saying: That it wasn't necessary to be a friend?*

"Fine." She tried to mask her disappointment, but the edge in her voice gave her away.

"Besides, I'm not sure if I can make it Saturday. Brian has a Scouts gathering."

"My sister will watch Brian. You need some activity in your life. That's why I pushed Dan to get you that interview. All you have to do is show up. He'll do the rest." They reached the checkout line. The black man she had seen earlier by the manager's office door was talking to a female customer. He wore an assistant store manager badge. He was more attractive than she had thought. She had never seen such an exotic-looking man in Plainview before. His thighs seemed to lift him upwards rather than ground him. His hair was closely cropped. He put an arm on the counter. The tendons in his forearm rippled. After the woman he was talking to departed, he turned and looked back at Laney. He seemed to be aware that she was staring at him. He smiled at her. *Why was she checking this man out? She had never dated a black man before.* Embarrassed and confused, she looked away.

Erin was unloading her purchases onto the conveyor belt. Laney looked at her pixieish features. She always felt a little too fleshy beside her elfin frame, even though Jay had told her she was beautiful, perfect. Still, she had not completely believed him.

On the way out, the assistant manager asked if they needed help with their bags. "No, thank you," Erin said with a forced, curt smile as she proceeded to head toward the door. Laney followed, careful not to look at him.

Once outside the store, Erin turned to her and said, "I don't know why they hire people like that."

"Erin! How could you say something like that?"

"Well, at least they haven't moved into my neighborhood yet."

"Erin!"

She shrugged her shoulders. "That's the way I am. And nothing's going to change me."

Laney looked back at the man as she stepped through the sliding glass doors. Once again, her eyes caught the man's powerful legs. As her eyes roamed up to his face, he gave her a broad smile. She again looked away.

***

Laney had been sitting on the patio overlooking the backyard at Erin's house for only five minutes but already she was restless. Erin's kids, Luke and Samantha, were splashing each other in a shallow, above-ground pool set up near the swing set. They screeched and laughed. Everything seemed so simple for them—their only concern, to enjoy themselves. Samantha, five, yelled for her brother to stop, but Laney could tell she really didn't want him to. How had pleasure had become so complicated for her?

Luke, Erin's four year-old, came waddling over, his wet swim trunks dripping. He was carrying a plastic, inflated ball. "Mrs.

Secord, would you throw this to us?"

"Sure," she said.

He handed her the ball and ran back, saying, "Wait, wait." Then he scampered into the pool, where his sister stood ready.

Laney rose, holding the ball. Erin opened the sliding glass doors from the family room, carrying a tray with a pitcher of lemonade and several small sandwiches.

"Do you need a hand?" Laney asked her.

"No, that's okay. I can manage."

Laney turned back to the children. Where should she throw it?

"To me," Luke called eagerly. "No, me!" Samantha shouted. They jockeyed in front of each other to better position themselves.

Laney threw the ball. They reached up, pushing each other out of the way. The ball hit the bar of the swing set. The children moaned.

"Sorry," Laney said.

Luke crawled out to get the ball. She thought how Brian might enjoy playing with them. The three of them used to play together until Brian started school.

Erin placed the tray on the glass-topped iron table. "Those kids will wear you out. Sit down. Relax."

I'm just getting warmed up, Laney thought. *I can't relax*, but she obeyed. She always did as she was told: That's why everyone liked her.

She looked back at the kids, who were now trying to drown the ball in the water. She tried to think of a clever way to ask what gossip Erin had heard about Bill Hendrickson, but the sliding glass doors opened and Erin's husband, Dan, walked onto the patio. The door he left open.

He seemed to have gained ten pounds since she last saw him about a month ago. All the weight gravitated around his middle and below, giving him a pear-shaped appearance. His eyes too were puffy.

"What are you doing home?" Erin asked him.

"Can't a man want to see his wife and kids?" He did a double-take as he saw Laney and said, "Laney!" He gave her a quick peck on the cheek. Then he turned to his wife, leaned down and kissed Erin on top of her head, his eyes peeking up at Laney.

Samantha and Luke stopped playing in the pool. "Daddy!" they shouted, scrambling out of the pool and running toward the patio.

Samantha clung to her father's leg, Luke proceeding to take the other. Dan took the beach towel that was draped over the empty chair. As he held it up, a larger than life size depiction of Mickey Mouse unfurled. Dan wrapped the towel about his legs, covering Samantha and Luke. They giggled and twisted underneath.

"Are you hungry, hon?" Erin asked.

"Starving."

"Samantha, why don't you help me go make Daddy another sandwich." Erin led Samantha through the sliding glass doors, closing them behind her.

Luke stuck to his father's leg, but Dan rubbed the towel on his wet head, mussing his hair, then grabbed a rubber ball at the edge of the patio and motioned with the back of a hand for him to run. Luke ran toward the fence at the edge of the property. Dan threw the ball, but Luke missed.

Laney was amazed they did not even need to speak. She and Brian could never relate in such a natural, almost preprogrammed fashion.

As Luke chased after the ball, Dan turned to Laney, his forehead gleaming in the sun. He had lost so much hair over the past year.

"How are you?" she said.

He walked toward the table. "I'm really overworked."

"Daddy!" Luke had the ball and was ready to throw.

"Just a minute, son. I'm talking to Laney, okay?" He pulled a chair beside her and sat down. "I never get to talk to you anymore."

"You're never here when I drop in." She could feel her eyes betraying her.

"Is that just a coincidence?"

"You think I'm avoiding you?"

"Erin and I have been going to marriage counseling," he blurted nervously, as if the whole point of his conversing with her was to tell her this.

She wasn't going to give him the benefit of her reaction.

"We're trying to be honest with each other," he continued. "We're at the point where I think I should tell her about what happened between us."

A stab of anger rose through her. "That was a long time ago," she said coldly.

"And you regret it?"

The sliding doors opened. Laney slinked downward, her spine pressing against the back of the iron chair. Samantha walked out with a plate. Her mother followed, carrying a glass and a larger plate.

Dan took on a serious look. "Honey, I was just telling Laney I got promoted. I was made a Senior Vice President today."

"That's wonderful."

"Wonderful nothing. That's another twenty-five G's."

"Dan!" Erin said scoldingly.

"Please. Laney has more money than all of us. She's the day trader."

"No, I gave up on the stock market."

"But weren't you up like 150 percent?"

"I just got tired of all the ups and downs."

"You're not nervous about Friday, are you?" he asked.

"I haven't had a job in five years. They might laugh at me."

"It's just an accounts payable job, entry-level. The whole thing will be really informal. I'll stop by to make sure it goes okay."

Accounts payable, she thought. Well, it was a start.

Erin poured each of them a glass of lemonade. "I'm trying to make sure she'll be here for dinner this Saturday. I've invited Alex."

"Alex? The Mormon?"

A Mormon C.P.A., Laney said to herself. Thrilling.

Erin put the pitcher down. "Leave the matchmaking to me, Mr. Senior Vice President." She stood over Dan and kneaded her fingers into his shoulders. "I'm so proud of you."

"Not so hard," he said.

Erin took her hands away. He didn't seem to notice how she looked hurt. "Why don't you just let Laney bring whoever she wants this Saturday," he said. She doesn't need our help getting a date. Look at her. She's a knockout."

Erin's eyes grew circumspect. "Alex is a good catch."

"Maybe she's not interested."

"Dan, please."

They seemed to have forgotten she was there.

"When she's ready, she'll be ready," Dan said.

"Don't pressure her."

"Me pressure her? You're the one who keeps saying, it's been three years, three years." They both stopped, looking at each other. Laney repositioned herself on her chair and took a sip of lemonade. *I'm not here, she told herself. I didn't sleep with Dan and I didn't tell Jay before he died. This is all a mirage. My life is a mirage.*

"We didn't mean to...," Erin started to say, but Laney interrupted:

"No, no. Some things are better left unspoken." She shot a cool look at Dan.

Laney left the Malloys at 1 PM. Seeing Dan sent her thoughts reeling. There was a time when Dan would call her, to apologize, to say he had made a mistake. He and Laney had been drinking and it wasn't right of him to take advantage of a friend. There was a time when he would never have broached the subject. They agreed that their fuck had no impact, that they needn't tell anyone because it was meaningless. Why had "therapy" changed him? Did he realize he was unhappy with Erin? Did he want a divorce now that he was doing well financially? Was it just a process of growing older, of facing the truth, of taking responsibility? Or was he hoping to kindle a romance with her?

Now, after she thought she had slipped all knowledge of the tryst squarely away, under the furthest recesses of her mind, it had resurfaced. She could still see Dan kissing her on the living room sofa. Dan knew Jay was away in Boulder visiting family. Had he planned on seducing her when he invited her? Why hadn't Erin gone to dinner with them? Laney had once believed that Erin knew that she had screwed Dan, but convinced herself she couldn't know: There was no way she would have remained friends with her.

Laney could not forget the look on Jay's face when he returned home that Sunday: He was not the least bit suspicious. He told her how much he had missed her, that he would love her forever, words she did not want to hear.

She had begged Jay not to say anything to Dan. He didn't. Yet she had imposed an impossible burden on him—she insisted he keep quiet while she had told all.

When she was alone with his body, at the funeral home, she said, "I made a mistake. I'm not perfect. I'm sorry." But there was no response, no reaction. Couldn't the dead even whisper? No, touching his cold lips, his hard forehead, his lifeless face did not provoke response, a forgiveness, merely stillness, and departure.

As she drove—lunch at Erin's house, the splashing of water, the cucumber sandwiches, the sweet lemonade became a collage. Erin and Dan—their heads only—were cut and pasted before her on the windshield, and she felt as if her insides were twisting. Just below her solar plexus, she could feel a pounding, and nauseousness.

She needed aspirin. She drove to the supermarket where she and Erin had shopped. She pulled into the parking lot and squeezed by a line of cars near the burger joint and slowly passed the first entrance of the supermarket. The large windows had a multitude of signs covering them—she looked inside and could make out the cashier lines under the lights. She kept driving, going even more slowly past the second entrance.

She continued through the parking lot, traveling the outside perimeter of stores. She went around the entire mall and became bottlenecked in a row of cars trying to enter the drive-through lane of the Taco Bell. Through the first entrance she glimpsed several supermarket employees talking to one another. She was looking for the assistant manager—she could see his white teeth, his exotic skin, the triangular corners of his eyes. She wanted to see him. Only to see him, nothing more, to verify whether he truly existed or whether she had imagined him.

No, she didn't need aspirin. She extricated herself from the row of cars and exited the shopping center, proceeding down Taunton Street through town. The image of the manager smiling at her passed through her mind, but instantly the image was crossed with Christopher standing in the woods, leaning against the tree, pulling himself up by a branch. She passed the gray clapboard post office and saw the School Zone sign. She turned right onto a side street which led to the school.

The high school, the hub of Plainview's and three neighboring towns' public school systems, stood behind an expansive campus with a baseball diamond and tennis courts to one side and a football field to the other. Behind the mid-century brick, glass, and concrete main structure, spanned more fields. Laney had been here before, to bring Brian to a play, also to an outdoor fair.

She did not pull into the parking lot. She drove down the street which led around the front of the school. Green, hardy trees with full branches wove one into the other. She could see nothing but tree trunks and leaves and branches and soil. She looked down the street. Nothing. No cars. Just the winding pavement until a small hill blocked the view ahead.

She pulled to the side of the road and parked in the dirt embankment. She held her head against the steering wheel, keeping her eyes closed, exhaling, but the deep breath she wanted to release only came in a small spurt. She felt anxious and also angry with herself. She had come to see Christopher, but told herself she should not have.

She put the car in gear and made a U-turn toward the front of the school. She turned left onto another side street which led to the fields in back. Wide open space—crisply shorn fields of green grass with scattered brown patches from too much sun—stretched from one end of the grounds to the other. Groups of students—girls on one side of the field, boys on the other—were playing soccer. She pulled onto a short street which formed the edge of the field and parked.

The field was set perpendicular to her car. There was a total of four matches being played at once—two boys' and two girls'. She scanned through the teams playing. Most of the students were wearing the green and gold uniforms of the Plainview Chieftains. Half of the boys were shirtless.

The darker-haired boys caught her eye first—they were easier to spot in the sunlight. She looked past them, searching for boys with lighter-colored hair like Christopher's. One was short, another a redhead, another pudgy. A shirtless boy with tufts of dark hair spurting from underneath his arms whizzed by the pudgy one and kicked the ball to a teammate who attempted to score a goal, but the goalie leapt up and caught the ball against his chest. He kicked it to his teammates. The goalie's hands, his back sweating, lifted in triumph when a teammate scored.

She looked away toward the brick school building. She could not fathom what she was doing. *He's not here, she told herself.*

She continued to stare blankly through the windshield, oblivious to the hurrahs and cheers from the field.

I am here, she told herself. I am actually at the school. I wish that I could dissolve into the brick or the concrete or the soil like the light posts and girters and pipes. I do not belong here. In an instant she could see Christopher kissing her in the kitchen, looking at her, his lips twitching, inquiring almost, semi-closed, saying nothing. She had come to relive that moment. Yet she realized that would be impossible. Still, she needed to know whether Christopher was here. She wanted to see him at play, in his natural environment. Then she could go.

She stepped out of the car, unwrinkling her blouse and jeans. She first had to pass the girls' field, where cloisters of girls had congregated around the goal line because their game had stopped. No one seemed to notice her. Keeping her head down, she approached the group of boys at play. She continued to look down, as if not looking at them would make them less likely to notice her. *I've seen enough, she told herself. I can go now.*

She continued down the field, slowly making her way toward the first goal post. The goalie was hunched down, his hands on his knees, intently staring at the field before him. No one even notices me, she thought.

She heard a car pull up behind her. She turned around and saw that it was a police cruiser. She turned back to the field, pretending not to have noticed it. Why has a cruiser come to Plainview High? The heckles of the boys and the screeches of the girls became louder. *I need to walk along, disappear around the other side of the school. I should have never come. He is going to see my car...* She turned her head slightly, putting a hand on her hair as if to rearrange it. Out of her peripheral vision, she saw a police officer stepping out of the cruiser. She caught a glimpse of his short, round body before she turned away. She tried, unsuccessfully, not to look back. He was walking by her, stopped beside it, placing his hands on his gun and baton. She breathed, trying to relax. She turned her head back to the field. *I am going to be arrested. He will take me to jail. I am a trespasser. What I am doing is illegal.* He stopped walking. *Let him handcuff me and drag me away. I was wrong. I am guilty.* She could see herself in jail, waiting for the jailer to unlock the cell, but the jailer had already come and talked to her: *'Why did you do it? You had everything. A beautiful home, a beautiful son, people who loved you.'*

She pretended to watch the game: She couldn't see any of the boys—they were a blur, a mass of motion before her, tipping in unison from side to side like a ship on heavy seas.

The officer was coming closer. He was a few yards away. Her eyes gravitated to the instruments attached to his belt: the gun, holstered; the baton; a walkie-talkie; a pepper spray bottle; handcuffs. She forced a smile.

"Good day, ma'am."

"Good day, officer." Her eyes kept hitting upon the handcuffs, and unconsciously, she grasped her wrist.

"Is there something I could help you with?"

"I just came to take a little breather," she said.

He looked at her circumspectly, turning to her car, which was down at the other side of the field. "That's quite a walk."

"I need the exercise," she said, unable to read what he was thinking.

His posture loosened, and he took his hands off the gun and baton. "I thought I was the only fan of the Chieftains."

Fan, she said to herself. He thinks I'm a fan.

"Real talent out there," he said, nodding toward the field. He had a lilting drawl to his voice, almost a Southern accent, not clipped like the locals.

"Absolutely," she said.

"Those girls are the best though, aren't they?"

Just go along with him, she told herself. "Yes, they are."

"They just might take the state championship after all." His eyes were focused on the other field where a large-boned girl was passing the ball. "I come out here myself from time to time. The boys, they just don't got their act together. You'd think they'd learn a thing or two from the girls."

Say something. Make it up. "They're getting better, though."

"Indeed they should." His eyes roamed back from the field. "Do you know the girls' coach?"

"No."

"I'll introduce you." He pointed to the girls' area of the field. "Chris Wilkins, by the way," he said.

Another Chris, she couldn't believe it.

"Pleased to meet you, Officer. I'm Laney Secord." She said her name in a way that gave the effect of a shrug.

"Secord, on Heather Lane?"

"Yes."

"I've seen the house on patrol. Very, pretty house," he said with an awkward pause. He kept walking, intently, and she followed. He blew his whistle and waved a hand to the physical education teacher near the middle of the field. The teacher, who was repositioning a cone, lifted her head and saw Officer Wilkins. She waved back and smiled enthusiastically. A ball from the boys' game at the edge of the field rolled out of bounds in her direction. She bounded down the field while the girls continued to chat with one another. Officer Wilkins stepped forward to meet the girls' coach, but Laney stayed where she was. *Go forward, an inner voice said. I don't want to.*

She watched as Wilkins met the girls' coach. A couple of

boys ran towards the girls' field. One was shirtless and dark-haired. The other was Christopher. Christopher tapped a hand on the other boy's shoulder to pass. As the other boy stopped, Christopher ran around him and entered the girls' field. Laney's eyes widened and her heart began to race. She had come to see him, but she did not want him to see her. The ball continued to roll toward her. *I can go now, she thought. It's not too late. He doesn't see me. This is wrong.*

She watched as his white T-shirt undulated in the gentle breeze. His hair looked dark in the sunlight. He wore the green and gold shorts of the Chieftains. The shorts looked too small for him, too tight.

Although her eyes were on Christopher, she tried to concentrate on the ball that was rolling closer. As the ball neared her, a lithe blond girl who reminded her a bit of herself at that age stepped between her and the ball, and with some fancy footwork, danced it back into the field toward Christopher. He came closer to Laney but still did not notice her. The blond girl zigzagged with the ball, tauntingly tapped it toward Christopher, then raced forward to steal it from him. The group of girls, watching, laughed. The blond girl kicked the ball between her feet. At one point, she lunged forward as if she were the ball, pulling her head and torso back to confuse him. The girls hooted.

Officer Wilkins and the girls' coach walked over to Laney, obstructing her view. "This is Stephanie Breen."

"Pleased to meet you," Laney said. *He won't see me, she thought.*

Miss Breen was a heavy-set, compact woman with square shoulders and muscular legs. She was Laney's age or a few years older, but her hair, dark and cropped short, had turned prematurely gray.

The women shook hands. "I haven't seen you at any of the games," Miss Breen said.

"I never seem to get the chance. My son keeps me too busy."

Miss Breen winced, as if the sun were in her eyes, though it wasn't. "We're always looking for volunteers."

Laney feigned a look of interest. A group of boys started cheering. Wilkins and Miss Breen turned, and Laney stepped aside to see Christopher kicking the ball back and forth while the blond girl darted in front of him trying to steal it away. He trotted it aside, she lunged toward him, but he took the ball with the side of his heel, tossing it to his other leg, lifting his leg, twisting his body so that the ball ran up to his chest and then down his arm. He let the ball fall off his hand to his other foot and performed the same maneuver, but this time, he leaned his body sideways so that the ball went under his arm, to his back, crossing his shoulders and travelling to his other hand. He bopped it off his head a few times, then he stopped, letting it roll slowly down his forehead, down his nose, to his lips. Then he chipped the ball with his chin to his pelvis, which he jutted outward, buffeting the ball to a teammate.

Miss Breen blew her whistle. "Such a show off, that boy."

Christopher looked toward the source of the sound. He saw Laney standing at the edge of the field. She looked away.

A group of girls ran toward the boy with the ball while Miss Breen sprinted into the field, continuing to blow her whistle. Laney had to turn back. Christopher stood where he was, in the girls' field, alone and still, his eyes on Laney. The distance between them was no more than twenty yards, but she felt as if they were orbiting one another, slowly turning, the field was rotating. He continued to gaze at her. She stared back. Officer Wilkins did not seem to be standing next to her, the boys and girls were not rowdily competing for the ball, Miss Breen was not blowing her whistle.

The cheering suddenly stopped, the boys and girls moaned, and Miss Breen took possession of the ball. Wilkins' walkie-talkie buzzed with the static of a dispatcher's voice. He took the call, indicating he would be leaving. *Aren't you going to take me, she thought. No. They don't want people like me. This is my punishment. This field, this boy.* The tension that had connected her and Christopher slowly dissipated. As she watched him, his eyes tightly held her gaze, as if trying to maintain the tension, to regain what had been lost. The sun briefly hid behind a cloud, the slight overcast seeming a heavy pall. He continued to look at her. The sun reappeared from behind the cloud, but he seemed like a far-off vision across the ocean, unsure and out of focus. She turned away.

6

When Laney returned home from the school, she felt downcast and ashamed. Why did she have to go to see Christopher? Couldn't she have foreseen that someone at the school—a teacher, security—might have stopped her to question her? Compounding her gloom was the way she had held Christopher's gaze. She had looked away only when it was too late, only when she had wanted to break the bond of interest between them. Yet her looking away—because she felt she had to, because Christopher had to have known she did not want to—only furthered their bond, giving it life, credence, possibility.

The uncertainty of this possibility frightened her. As she went upstairs to her bedroom, through this house that should have been so familiar but looked stranger by the minute, she felt as though something within her were attempting to break out, struggling to become free. Could it have been her dormant sexual yearnings, awakened by Christopher? No. They didn't exist. And if they did—if she had been looking at Christopher, at the supermarket manager, they certainly held no importance.

Her limbs were unsteady, her gait tentative. She had not felt so nauseated since she was pregnant with Brian, when in the early months of her pregnancy unremitting morning sickness had caused her to wish she could will him to be born rather than wait until her body was ready. Now, she was sure that in a matter of time—hours, minutes, at most a day—she would be free of her desire for Christopher just as... No, she was contradicting herself—She had no desire for Christopher. None whatsoever. These damn headaches were the culprit.

She took an aspirin and washed her hands and face at the vanity mirror. Fine lines had formed around her eyes, on her forehead. Her hair, like Dan's, was thinning and receding. There was no way Christopher could have any desire for her either.

Her hair was a mess. She took a pair of scissors and started to trim it, stopping just at the moment she thought she was going to make herself look worse. But as she held the scissors in her hand, pressed the cold steel blade against the side of her neck, she had the concrete, unsettling feeling of being victimized. Held by the throat and with force. She could not make out her assailant's physical characteristics, only blacks and grays and fleece and a mask, but she could feel him, and she could almost sense her struggle.

The blackness—perhaps it wasn't the assailant's mask, but his face—could it have been the supermarket manager?

How foolish she was, to succumb to fantasy. The rape was not real and should not be real. Could Christopher have incited *deviant* sexual desires? No. Did she feel guilt, a need to punish herself, for having gone to the school? No, these strange thoughts could only be explained by boredom, inactivity. They had nothing to do with her true feelings, real desires. She had to go back to work.

Just as she was set to prepare her résumé for her job interview on Friday, she heard a car pull into the driveway. She poked open the curtains and saw Bill's blue Galaxy being parked. Why was he coming to see her? She readjusted the drapes back in place and stepped away from the window, toward the hall. She did not want to face him, not after she had just gone out of her way to see his son.

She slowly went downstairs, and as the doorbell rang, she listened to the chimes echo until the last chord softly dissolved. She waited for a few moments. He had surely seen her car in the driveway. She had to answer the door.

Do not be afraid, she told herself. This can't be anything serious. Finally, she opened the door, as if she had just rushed to it.

Bill was looking at the side of the house—something there had caught his eye, but she could not tell what.

He wore a white, short sleeve white Bermuda shirt, blue jeans, and black cowboy boots—virtually the same outfit as yesterday except for the shirt, but she could tell he had made an effort by the way his hair was styled, with a dollop of gel. A face that looked more radiant, because it was freshly washed and shaven.

"Hi," she said in an overly friendly, an overcompensating tone.

"Hello," he said exuberantly. "Sorry I didn't call. I found your address on your check." He brandished the check she had given him. "I couldn't give it to Chris because it's too much. It was very generous of you, but I don't want him to get the wrong idea, that having money is too easy, you know. I'm trying to teach him the value of a dollar. He's just a kid."

Jolting her, the image of Christopher standing in the field, staring at her, sweating, muscles pumped, came to mind.

"Yes, I understand," she said. "I could write another check—something smaller, say twenty, twenty-five dollars."

"Great," he said.

Next to the door, there was a pot of wilting gardenias. He leaned down and looked at the planter. Water had pooled around the base. "Would you mind?" he asked.

She wasn't sure what he was asking, but she said, "Sure."

"These are getting too much water and not enough sun." He moved the planter a foot away from the house, toward the edge of the sidewalk, so that the awning did not cast shade on it. "This should do it. They'll come back in no time."

"That's so nice of you," she said, impressed by how neighborly he was acting. The door seemed an awkward barrier. "Why don't you come in?"

"Thanks." He brushed his feet on the welcome mat—the same gesture Christopher had made before entering her house. As he stepped in, she noticed he was looking up at the chrome chandelier, as Christopher also did. Was it that impressive? Was the house that nice? Or did father and son have such similar outlooks, such similar thoughts and perspectives?

"This is a very nice place you have," he said. He was taller than she had first thought, over six feet two perhaps, but not quite so tall as Christopher.

"Thank you. Could I get you something cool to drink?"

"Sure."

When they reached the kitchen, he found a stool at the island where Christopher had sat and twirled about. Bill's eyes roamed the granite countertop while she went to the refrigerator. As the moments passed, he became less stiff and more relaxed. Christopher himself changed from one moment to the next, something she had attributed to his youth, but now she began to wonder whether the change in comportment was a family trait.

"This is really a fabulous kitchen you have," he said. "Do you like to cook?"

"When I'm inspired. But it's a lot of effort for just the two of us."

"I can empathize."

Empathize: another word that disrupted the picture she had of his being just a country bumpkin.

"Since Chris's mom and I divorced," he said, "my workload around the house has doubled."

He was divorced: surely, that couldn't have been the secret Erin had alluded to. There had to be something more. Could he have been married several times, perhaps, each marriage ending badly? She looked back from the refrigerator door. "Do you work in town?"

"No. I've been wanting to open another business since I sold my heating and air conditioning shop up in Beckle's Ridge. I toyed with a few things—restoring cars, motor bikes, even, believe it or not, a gift shop. I'm sort of a jack of all trades. But I'm just waiting for the right opportunity."

A gift shop?—She couldn't picture him in one at all. And a jack of all trades?—His house needed so much work. She held up a pitcher. "Is lemonade good?"

"Wonderful." The inflection of his voice rose a beat.

He's *too* nervous, she thought.

"At least I've been able to spend more time with my boy."

She set a glass of lemonade on the counter. "Your son is such a sweet kid."

"Boys aren't what they used to be. Pretty soon he'll be running me out of the house."

She thought of Christopher dashing down the field, bouncing the soccer ball on his knees, his tight shorts gripping his thighs. She immediately tried to cast off the image. "That's what our parents probably said about us," she said.

He stood, taking his glass to the window. She watched the back of his shoulders, his neck, the backs of his arms, his head.

His hair was still thick, though it had turned ashen and was no longer blond like his son's. He was an attractive man. He had a fatherly aspect that made her feel comfortable. But she caught herself: She didn't want to be at ease with him, not because she found his character distasteful, but because even though he was unaware of it, he held, by virtue of his relationship with Christopher, a relationship with her which was more complex than he realized.

"Gardening is one of my hobbies," he said, turning from the window back to her. "You mind if I have a look?"

"You'll embarass me," she said.

"Don't be silly. I'll be glad to help."

He walked to the French doors off the breakfast nook that led to the patio.

"I believe they're locked," she said.

"You're not afraid of that murderer running loose in town, are you?"

"Murderer?"

"You haven't heard?

"No," she said rather quickly.

"They found some woman's body by the interstate. I forget her name. I'm not that good with names. She was young, early twenties."

A prickly sensation tingled her arms. A stranger was in her house. She knew his name, where he lived, but she did not know him. *Could... this man be a murderer?*

"You look like you've seen a ghost."

She should not have let him in. Her nerves were getting the better of her.

"Don't worry, it's not me."

"No, I didn't think so." Instantly, she felt relief: He could read her, just like his son had known she had found him attractive. "It's just a habit of mine," she said, "I always lock the doors."

It was true: though there was little crime in Plainview, she kept all the doors and windows locked. She was fastidious about turning on the house alarm too, though few came to her door except the occasional deliveryman, the Jehovah's Witnesses, and now, the Hendricksons.

Because Bill was having trouble with the lock, she went over to help him. As she stood beside him, he stepped aside to give her room. That he was giving her space—physical and by extension emotional space—set her at greater ease. He was not a murderer, no. He stood near the table, watching her unlatch the lock, entirely relaxed and giving himself over to her as a husband or family member might in admiring her skill.

When she opened the door, he casually passed by her, his eyes on the garden by the deck. A feeling overcame her that he was not merely attracted to her but that he genuinely liked her. He seemed to belong in this house, the way he flowed in, then out.

Despite her misgivings, she could find no reason not to like him. He had asked her out on a date, she had said no. He was acting graciously and gentlemanly. The fact that he was so well behaved, combined with the suspicions that Erin raised, cast an air of mystery over him. There were no signs that he had been drinking now, and he probably hadn't been the other day at his house. Perhaps there was a serious reason that he had moved from Beckle's Ridge. Could it have had anything to do with Christopher?

She watched as Bill knelt before the tomato plants. It had

been too hot and dry this season, and she knew she should have spent more time watering and pruning her plants. She returned to the center island of the kitchen and took a sip of her lemonade. The thought of Christopher gulping down his water the other day returned to her. She tried to cast the image aside, but it stuck with her as she went to her handbag. She took her checkbook and had a sensation of deja vu: Christopher was still sitting on the stool, waiting for his money, waiting to kiss her. She could see the check sitting on the table by the door. How much had she written it for? Probably twenty-five dollars. Why she hadn't just given Bill a check for the same amount? No, she had felt guilty. She had been trying to compensate for the impropriety of Christopher's kiss. How had she arrived at a point where she believed she could simply write a check for her problems to disappear? Or did the check merely make her problems, and desires, seem more palatable, more acceptable?

The French doors Bill had left open. She now could hear birds chirping in the trees in the back yard, calling to one another in a round of measured, precise notes. No, none of this—her life, this house, this yard, what she was doing, thinking or feeling, had anything to do with Christopher. She hastily took the black and gold Cross pen that she had concealed at Bill's house in order to be invited in and wrote a check for twenty-five dollars, making it payable to Christopher Hendrickson but writing his name as impersonally as if she were paying a utility bill.

She walked to the French doors with the check and saw Bill coming out of the garden with several tomatoes in his arms.

"You really do have a green thumb," he said, grinning as he walked toward the deck, holding the tomatoes against his chest. "I could have picked a few more, but they could probably go another day or two."

"I'll be sure to gather them."

"If you need a hand," he said, ascending the stairs of the deck, "I'll be glad to help."

"Thanks," she said with a small smile. She held out her hands, one still holding the check, to take a couple of the tomatoes. He leaned forward so that the two that were against the top of his stomach rolled into her hands. As she touched his body, she could feel her shoulders tensing and pulling back slightly. She watched his tan arms press against his sides, contrasting with his white shirt. She pulled back farther, so as to reposition her grip on both the tomatoes and the check, but one of the tomatoes fell—splat—between them. They both bent down to pick it up, but they knocked into each other. They laughed. Catching herself, she stopped. She was looking at his large hands, one of which could have easily held two or three tomatoes—or her. He became silent. Was he aware that she was looking at him?

He proceeded to pick up the broken tomato, scooping the seeds and juice into his palm. He glanced at her and smiled. Then he looked down her chest to her legs.

She stood. "I'll get a paper towel." She slowly went to fetch one, and returned to the deck and handed it to him. He already had most of the seeds and pulp in his hands and plopped them in the towel which he placed before her, as if an offering. He smiled at her again—a longer, more deliberate smile.

"I have your check inside," she said.

He followed her back into the kitchen where he laid the tomatoes on the table in the breakfast nook while she tossed the other tomato away.

"I was taken by surprise when you called yesterday afternoon."

He paused, expecting her to say something in response, but she remained quiet.

"You know—well, of course, no, you wouldn't know—" the water in his eyes reflected the lights overhead, "I haven't dated anyone since my wife and I split. It's kind of awkward for me, the dating stuff. So I wasn't sure when you said you'd call if you would. Or were you saying that to be polite?" He walked around the breakfast table, still holding a tomato in his hand.

"No, not at all," she said, hoping he couldn't tell she was lying.

His appearance—his soft eyes, the skin of his face which hung loose around his jaw line and was probably firm and taut in his youth, as Christopher's was, gave him a genial aspect. As he moved to the counter where she stood, she expected the conflicts within to stir, to gather momentum, to propel her from the island away from him. But because of his benevolent smile, his warm-hearted voice, she felt drawn to him, physically and emotionally.

"I hope I'm not being too personal, but I like you better dressed like this," he said. "You don't need make-up."

She felt flattered, but instantly, she tried to quell the feeling. He was being too personal. "Thank you."

"How long has your husband been gone?"

"Three years now."

"Do you think you're ready for a relationship?"

A relationship?—He was moving fast. "When I look back," she said, "I suppose I've been ready for some time. But my son is my focus and the right person hasn't come along."

"Have you given anyone a chance?"

The feeling that he was pushing her, pressing her for a

commitment, an admission of interest, returned, and her fingers twitched with discomfort. He stood next to her. She had the sense Christopher was beside her, preparing to lean in to kiss her. But she knew her allowing him to kiss her, her going to the school this afternoon, had been wrong. She looked down, at the granite countertop, picking up the check, inching back at most, repositioning her body, gathering her strength—Then she looked up. "I can't promise anything, but yes, if you'd like to go out, we could. My friend Erin is having a dinner party this Saturday. I'll have to check with her to make sure she has space."

He smiled boyishly. She wished for a moment that he would defer his decision, that she hadn't invited him to the dinner party, and that whatever had prompted her to ask—Was it guilt, a latent yearning to grow?—had not surfaced.

"I look forward to it," he said. "This really makes my day."

Her regret temporarily intensified. She cast her feelings aside and gave him a small smile. "Why don't you take the tomatoes with you. There's no way I can use them all."

"You know, Laney, you really are a very nice person."

'Nice,' what did that mean? Christopher had used the same word, flirtatiously.

In her mind, she had nearly accused Bill of being the town murderer, but still he thought she was 'nice'. But because he had said her name—even though he said it casually and without affectation or purpose—she felt they had entered a pact: an unsigned, unwritten but binding agreement. And she was powerless to object to it.

7

After dinner that evening, a few minutes past 8 PM, while Brian was asleep, Laney sat down for some much-needed rest in the family room. She reclined in an overstuffed armchair that Jay had purchased. The TV was tuned to Anderson Cooper on CNN, but she left the volume muted.

Wearing the gray loose-fitting sweat pants that she liked to lounge around the house in and a University of Colorado T-shirt that was getting rattier though more comfortable by the year, she perused the Plainview *Gazette*, a small tabloid-sized paper full of such hard news like raccoons causing a ruckus at the Chapertons' house, the 4-H club stealing first prize—yet again—in the regional horticultural meet, and Mrs. Clapp taking orders, already, for her famous Thanksgiving pumpkin pies. On the front page, which she glimpsed last, she noticed a lengthy article with the headline "Murder Baffles Authorities." Was this the murder that Bill had referred to?

According to the article, the body of a 28-year-old woman who worked as a waitress at a local saloon was found badly decomposed by the interstate. Yes, Bill had mentioned that the body was found by the highway.

Forensic evidence showed she had been raped. The circumstances were similar to another murder in Plainview that occurred near Christmastime: Both victims still had their glasses on when their corpses were found. Glasses—what a strange way to pick, if not mark, his victims.

Laney was unaware that there had been an earlier murder.

She had become so isolated that she had not heard two of the biggest news stories in Plainview in years. She turned to the back pages of the paper, where the story was continued. The Employment classified section briefly caught her eye. Yes, the job that Dan had set up for her would be a good step toward meeting other people, to find out what was happening in town.

As she read more about the murdered woman—no children, had moved to Plainview five years ago when she started at Dorsey's Bar and Grill, Laney heard a noise outside the window and she put the paper down. The noise sounded like footsteps going down the sidewalk. There was a rustling of leaves, then the noise stopped.

No, it was nothing. Perhaps a stray cat, a raccoon, the wind. Imagine if this house were old, she told herself, the noises would be magnified tenfold.

Moments later, the noise started again: the sounds of bushes being disturbed, a branch crackling against the side of the house. Nerves, she told herself. The account of the unsolved murders was unsettling her.

Soon, as she held the paper before her, the absence of noise began to disturb her. She went to the window beside the fireplace and pulled aside the curtain. She cupped her hand to the glass. She couldn't make out much because it was dark outside and light in the room. In an instant, a face stared in at her. She startled back. Then the face vanished. She turned off the lamp, stood still for a moment, heard nothing. How vulnerable she was, living with just Brian in this cavernous house, with acres of woods surrounding it. Her body could be dumped in the bog across Heather Lane and no one would find her for weeks, months even. Her mouth dry, her breathing accelerating, she walked to the window on the other side of the mantle and peeked out the curtain.

She could barely discern the shadowy outlines of bushes in the darkness. A brusque clanging came from the front step. Someone had tipped over the watering can by the foundation plantings! She rushed to the hall to check the deadbolt on the front door. It was locked.

Through the window beside the door, she saw a bright flash. Looking through the peephole, she saw a beam of light snake across the lawn, thrusting down the sidewalk toward the side of the house.

"Hey you!" a man's voice called.

He can't be talking to me, she thought. She drifted toward the stairs. She should call the police. No, she was overreacting. The noises stopped. The house alarm was set. If someone tried to break in, the police would respond. After an instant, she heard footsteps on the sidewalk, and the doorbell rang.

She waited for a moment, regulating her breath. "Who is it?" she called from the stairs.

"Officer Wilkins of the Plainview Police Department."

The police? The officer from the school? What was he doing at her house? She had not done anything wrong. No, she had just gone to the school... and watched.

She walked to the door, to make sure it really was Wilkins outside. Through the peephole she saw the heavy-set officer, still in uniform, his badge gleaming back at her. Her fear of the unknown murderer gave way to trepidation. She could not ignore him; she would only invite suspicion. "One moment," she said, going back to the hall and disabling the alarm. Then she returned and slowly opened the front door.

Beside the officer, Christopher was panting. His hair was disheveled, a grass stain discolored his jeans, a streak of dirt stretched down his forearm. What had he been doing outside? The officer was pressing against Christopher's back, virtually holding him, cornering him like a wild animal, so that he could not flee. He too had several leaves stuck to his uniform.

Christopher turned slightly, out of discomfort. One of his wrists was locked in handcuffs. She was aghast. They had scuffled. Did Christopher say something to the cop? Was Wilkins going to arrest him, her?

Wilkins spoke in an officious, ominous tone: "Miss Secord, I found this boy snooping around your backyard. Do you know him?"

She tried to smile, but her lips tensed. "His name is Chris Hendrickson. I know him and his father. He's a student at Plainview High."

The officer's eyes rose in surprise.

Did he believe her? "An Eagle Scout," she added, hoping that Wilkins would see that Christopher was a respectable boy.

He seemed to wince.

She scolded herself—it was such a stupid thing to say. *Stop being so nervous.*

"Your next door neighbor called because she heard some noise around her house. The boy says he's not robbing you."

She had to think quickly. "No, no, officer. Chris asked if he could look around my yard for signs of animals or other things his troop would be interested in. For a Boy Scout project. There are a lot of unusual creatures around here, because of the swampland across the street."

She was unable to read the officer's expression. He pulled

Christopher toward him, as if ready to take him away.

A surge of panic raced through her. Her body, her limbs, lurched forward through the doorway, toward Chris. "My son, Brian, is a Boy Scout, too," she added. "A Cub Scout. And Chris has been extremely helpful with him this year."

Wilkins fidgeted for a moment, nervously tugging the unattached handcuff while looking at Christopher. "Son, why did you try to run?"

"I was scared. I'm sorry," he mumbled.

Yes, apologize, she thought. She watched the officer's handcuffs, hoping he would unlock them and set Christopher free, but he didn't move.

"Do your folks know about this?" Wilkins said.

"No." Christopher cast his eyes cast down at the marble floor of the entry.

Why didn't he lie? Now his father would have to know. "His parents are divorced," she said.

Christopher looked at her, his eyes scrutinizing hers, as if questioning how she knew his family situation.

She opened the door some more. She had to deflect suspicion from Christopher. "Officer, it's really a strange coincidence, seeing you twice in one day."

"Yes, it sure is." He maintained a poker face.

"I was really impressed with the girls' team today. I think you're right—they just might make the state finals." 'Finals,' she wondered? Should she have said 'playoffs,' 'championship'? Could he tell she wasn't a fan?

"We shall see," he said, uncomfortably shifting a step away from Christopher, his demeanor hardening as he looked at him: "You really scared the hell out of Mrs. Flaherty."

"I'm sorry," he said, his voice now, suddenly, somehow, deeper, as deep as a grown man's.

Officer Wilkins seemed to be looking behind Laney, over her shoulder—for something, somebody, in her house.

Was he distrustful or merely being nosy? "Officer, it's my fault. I didn't think of the neighbors. I'll be sure to call Mrs. Flaherty first thing tomorrow morning to apologize."

Christopher turned down to look at Wilkins, who was several inches shorter than he was. "Sir, I do apologize for this. I didn't mean to cause a problem. I didn't realize how late it was. I'm trying to finish my project by Saturday."

Wilkins was not completely swayed: "Son, when a police officer tells you to freeze, make sure you do that or you risk getting shot." He pushed him against the door frame. Christopher's body tensed. His eyes grew white.

She stepped forward, ready to plead with the officer, but she noticed that he was reaching into his belt, fishing out the key to the handcuffs. He unlocked the cuff on Christopher's wrist, setting him free.

Christopher took a step away from the officer and pressed his feet into the ground, as if he were about to run. Her heart pounded. But he didn't move. He was just stretching. She nervously, as casually as she could, brushed a leaf off Officer Wilkins' uniform, eliciting a look of surprise, followed by a boyish smile.

"Son, you should give Mrs. Flaherty a call yourself and apologize for disturbing her."

"Yessir."

"I'll take you back to your father."

She couldn't allow him to take Christopher home. She would

have to explain to Bill why he'd been at her house—and Bill would ask why she hadn't mentioned anything about giving him permission to enter her yard.

"Officer, I wouldn't want his father to become alarmed, seeing his son in a cruiser. I could easily give him a ride home. It's not too far."

"But you have a young son, don't you? He's not at home?"

"Yes,"—her voice was becoming unsteady— "but my mother is in town, visiting, and she will be able to watch him. I'll just wake her." Did he believe her? What if she were asked to produce her mother? What if he checked the garage and noticed only one car, her car, in it? She should not have lied. Now, she was trapped.

"I suppose I could," he said slowly, his drawl returning, "leave him in your care. Son, you're not hurt, are you?"

"No sir, I'm fine."

"How old are you?"

"Sixteen, sir."

"And you're really an Eagle Scout?"

"Yessir."

"Then you should know how to stay out of trouble. I hope we don't have a problem again."

Christopher's face became indignant. His mouth opened, slack-jawed.

He seemed about to say something, in protest perhaps, that the officer was being unfair, that it wasn't his fault—but she boldly interrupted before he had any opportunity to speak—
"No, you won't. I assure you."

"It's Laney, correct?" Wilkins asked.

"Yes." She gave a small smile and gently laid a hand on

Wilkins' shoulder, feeling as though she had succeeded in manipulating him and warding off his suspicions.

"The problem around here, Laney, is we have a lot of nosy neighbors." He smiled—a curious smile, his eyes scanning. "You never know who's watching." He paused for a moment, grasping his baton, his gaze bearing down upon her. "Take care now." He walked down the sidewalk, looking back only once.

What did he mean— 'You never know who's watching'? She felt—even though Wilkins' back faced her—that he continued to stare at her, circumspectly, watching for signs that she had lied to him about Christopher's reasons for being at her house, about her mother being upstairs. She tried to look away, so that the weight of her stare would not cause him to feel that he was being watched, but she couldn't avert her eyes. His blue uniform was like a magnet, the polar opposite, to her field of vision.

When Wilkins returned to his patrol car, Christopher entered the foyer and she closed the door behind him. Peering through the curtains, she watched Wilkins drive away. After his cruiser had disappeared, she continued to stare at the empty street, half-fearing that he would return. But the still, dark night showed no signs of being disturbed, and after a few moments, she became satisfied that he was not going to come back.

Christopher tapped his feet anxiously on the marble floor, jittering, as if he were about to step closer to her. Her eyes gravitated from his new athletic shoes, to his jeans, to the shirt that hung over his waist. He twirled the corner of his shirt nervously in his hands. His clothes were dirty, but still, he was a picture of perfection. They were alone. Brian was asleep upstairs. Although they were out of public view, her tension increased: Anything she would do—touch him, hold him—she had to blame on herself.

He stepped toward her, apparently interpreting her silence as an invitation. Was he going to touch her, to kiss her again?

She moved toward the hall, and he stopped, the eagerness in his face slowly giving way to melancholy.

"Why did you come here tonight?" she said, her voice scolding.

He avoided eye contact with her. He looked at the chandelier, at the mirrored sconces on the wall. Then, in the reflection on one of the mirrored panes of a sconce, she noticed him looking at her. "I wanted to see how you lived. I wasn't going to disturb you. I had it all figured out. I was going to say I was taking a shortcut back home and I lost my way. Why did you have to tell him I was working on a Boy Scout project? That's something a two year-old would do."

"Why didn't you come to the front door?" she said indignantly. "The police patrol this area. Didn't you think someone might find you snooping? What if I was asleep? Or I got scared and called the police? Weren't you afraid he was going to arrest you?"

"Don't worry, I didn't tell him anything. He wasn't going to arrest me. I'm an Eagle Scout." A smile took over his lips, a grinning, boyish smile, one that suggested he relished being a naughty teenager.

How could he be so naive? Didn't he understand the trouble he could have caused her? "Christopher, you can't just go into people's yards in the middle of the night."

"It wasn't that dark when I came." His foot tapped on the floor, once, then twice.

He was so nonchalant. How could she break through to him? She wanted to shake him, to wake him to their predicament, but she was afraid to have any physical interaction with him. "I didn't think that officer would ever leave."

"I'm sorry," he said. "I just wanted to see you."

She watched the angles in his face—his jaw, his cheekbones, his mouth, which protruded outward, almost too much. Every time she saw him, she became rapt by something new, something strangely beautiful that she hadn't noticed about him before. A feeling of tenderness began to fill her. "Does your father know you're here?" she asked.

"No. I told him I was going to the movies with a buddy."

"Christopher..."

He interrupted: "My friends call me Chris. We're friends, aren't we?"

His comment caught her off guard. They were friends, of sorts, but it was a friendship by default. "You can't just keep coming by like this."

"I don't have your number," he said sweetly, his voice cooing as if he were speaking to a schoolgirl that he was trying to woo.

Don't play into his charms, she told herself. "You know what I mean. People will talk."

"But you came to see me, today, at the school."

"I was just passing through."

His eyes narrowed, pressing down upon her, to quietly acknowledge her lie. She could not deny, as much as she wanted to, that they had a connection. Every moment she was in his presence, she could feel nothing but a strong pull, a gravitational tug, a yanking that made her want to be closer to him. The solution, obviously, was not to be with him, to avoid him, but a greater part of her—almost the whole of her—yearned to be with him. "I'll get my son," she said.

"You don't have to give me a ride home," he said. "I can walk." He took a half step toward the door.

"No. I don't want to risk the police coming back and asking questions, like why I let you walk home alone at 8:30 at night."

He gave her the same look of receptive passivity as at the school field. His lips were quivering. She glimpsed his brow, his thick neck, the Adam's apple that protruded sharply. Faster than he realized, he was becoming a man.

She ascended the stairs, sensing with every step that his eyes were moving with her, holding her. She did not look back.

She went to Brian's room and woke him. Although he thought that something was wrong, she reassured him, telling him to go back to sleep. She carried him against her shoulder to the stairway, remembering how she used to carry him as a baby, thinking how it was never easy to carry him—the weight always surprised her.

At the stairs, she did not see Christopher. She thought he might have left, as he had vanished in the woods on Tuesday afternoon. A part of her was relieved. She looked at the base of the stairs, into the foyer—he was gone. When she turned to bring Brian back to his room, she saw Christopher staring blankly at a painting on the wall. It was one of her favorites, an impressionistic view of the California coast, a painting which Jay had purchased during a family outing to Santa Maria.

She descended the stairs, Brian was awakening, but she put a hand atop his head so he would fall back asleep. When she reached the hall, Brian lifted his head and looked at him. Christopher waved, smiling. He seemed to take on a brotherly, almost fatherly aspect. She looked at the painting behind him. As she examined the jagged, rocky cliff over the ocean, she realized the memory of the trip had been lost and could now only be revived in broad details: joy, being with Jay. Nothing specific came to mind. She scavenged the recesses of her memory. All she could come up with was the artist's studio where the painting was purchased—a wooden ramshackle built beside a restaurant. The artist himself was lost—just a fragmented depiction of a middle-aged man. She could not recall any other painting in the studio. How all the years since had been lost. With them the touchstones she and Jay had taken for granted.

Brian was awake now, and Christopher was clowning with him, making faces—closing one eye, sticking his tongue against the inside of his cheek, curling his lip backward, arching his eyebrows—causing Brian to become more agitated atop her.

He stuck his tongue against his upper lip and bugged his eyes out. As Brian covered his eyes, squirming against her, she saw Christopher less as a big brother or a father but as a child himself: a youngster, someone who needed scolding, reminders, constant attention.

"I'll get my keys," she said.

As she began to turn toward the kitchen, Christopher raised his arms and lifted Brian off her. Brian nestled against his shoulder and neck, holding his hands to his chest. She gave a small smile, departing down the hall, perplexed. How instantly and interchangeably Christopher and Brian were friends, brothers, father and son. She walked, zombie-like, into the kitchen, back into the hall, to the front door. Brian was fast asleep again, his Spider-Man pajamas stretching across his back, legs, and arms, the fabric seeming an extension of Christopher's own clothes. Confusion and uncertainty coursed through her, but as she stepped forward to take Brian, she realized what she felt more than anything else was fear.

8

Laney drove down the darkened street, Brian asleep on the back seat, Christopher sitting quietly beside her in front. In this area of Plainview, which was mostly uninhabited except for a smattering of houses hidden far back from the road, street lights were few and sharp twists in the road were common.

She drove slowly, with the high beams on. At every pothole or break in the pavement, she checked to insure that Brian was still sleeping. She repeatedly glanced in the rearview mirror, thinking that the police might be following them. She felt guilty: If she had not gone to the school, would Christopher have come to see her? Moreover, since leaving her house, had Officer Wilkins called Bill to verify her story? If so, would he be waiting for them at the Hendricksons' house, to ask more questions?

Christopher evinced only a touch of jitteriness. His head was turned toward the passenger window. His hair, thick and unruly, had its layers protruding in odd angles, and could use some restyling. He could not have been looking at anything but his own reflection because it was so dark out all he would be able to see were rows upon rows of tree trunks passing by.

She continued to concentrate on the tortuous country road. What was he thinking? Why couldn't he say anything more to quell her concerns? Surely, he was a boy, used to making mistakes and not attaching much importance to them. But this was no mere mistake, nor even a simple error in judgment. It was a complete, utter miscalculation, one that didn't involve just him but had potential repercussions on her and her family.

The stretch of road ahead was secluded and shrouded by groves of fir trees. They hadn't passed a car since they had left her house. She had to make sure he would not behave so foolishly again.

She slowed down and navigated onto the embankment. Christopher looked to see where they were, his eyes widening in surprise as he scooted against his seat. She switched off the ignition and headlights, causing the interior of the car to become nearly pitch black. She paused a moment for her eyes to adjust. Brian was barely visible in the back, still sound asleep.

"Why have you kept coming to see me?" she asked.

"I like you."

Didn't he understand—she was old enough to be his mother. "I'm twice your age. If the authorities thought something was going on between us, it could cause me a lot of trouble."

"All we did was kiss. And I kissed you."

She shook her head. "It doesn't matter. I'm the adult. It's *my* responsibility. What if Officer Wilkins called your father?"

"I suppose he would have picked me up." He shrugged his shoulders defiantly. "Why did you ask my father to dinner this Saturday?"

"I think he's a nice man."

"Do you like him as much as you like me?"

She could not answer him. If she would be truthful, he would only be encouraged.

"I'm sixteen," he said. "You think I don't know anything?"

What did he mean by 'anything'? Images of him strutting across the soccer field, sweat soaking his T-shirt, his shorts zealously clinging against his muscular thighs, his slender hips, assaulted her. She could hear Brian's breathing, labored and rhythmic, ticking away the moments like a clock. She became more aware of how close Christopher was sitting to her, how small she was in comparison to him, how his knees jutted against the glove compartment because the seat was pushed too far up.

He repositioned himself in the seat, to face her, trying to make his large frame comfortable in the passenger compartment. Instantly, her body became rigid, pulling back. "We've only known each other three days," she said.

"I know I like someone the moment I meet them," he shot back confidently.

There was not the slightest doubt in his voice, and as he sat there, so close to her, his body pushing against the console between them, his head nearly touching the roofline—she thought how easy it would be to touch him. His skin was so taut. The sinewy muscles on his face and arms pulsed even as he tried to sit still. Christ, why couldn't she stop looking at him? Did he notice that she was staring at him?

He was gazing at the dashboard. He started to flicker the louvers of the air conditioning vent, retreating into himself. "Have you mentioned me to my father?" he asked quietly.

"No, why would I?" Her eyes lingered over his chest, up to his neck, to his chin and cheekbones. She noticed that his earlobes were attached to the sides of his face, as hers were.

His eyes caught hers: "You tell me," he said with a self-satisfied grin.

So he did detect her interest. His grin, the way his eyes eagerly tried to dance with hers, so as to prolong the moment of her observing him, so as to create a full-fledged seduction— was proof. Perhaps he knew her better than she had thought.

Perhaps he had been waiting for some sure sign from her that she wanted him. What sign was that?—But to look at him, to not turn away!

Now that he had the confirmation he needed, he was calm, as if cautiously planning the next move of a rook or a knight, thoroughly plodding his mode of attack. She had yielded to her feelings. He had won a small victory in catching her offguard. The rest of the play was now predetermined: He understood she was attracted to him.

He exhaled slowly, deeply, his body and limbs filling the passenger seat more amply, as if he intended to inch closer and closer to her. The prospect that she was attracted to him did not frighten him—No, it had encouraged him, imbuing him with confidence, with certainty, with increased desire.

He was looking at her arm, bare except for a short sleeve. His fingers twitched. In his face, in his blue eyes that were unmoved, she could see that all her explanations and rationalizations were transparent. He could have touched her at any moment, and if he did, she did not know whether she would have resisted. "I *do* like you," she relented.

"Then why do you have to go out with my father?" His voice cracked, then steadied itself into a low murmur. "We could go somewhere."

"You mean to get a cup of coffee?"

"No," he scoffed.

Then what, she wondered?

"*You* know," he said, raising his brow, provocatively.

She edged farther back on the seat. Her spine pressed against the driver's door panel. What was he proposing? Something here, something now? No, he had to have meant a casual meeting. Panic raced through her. Did he mean a clandestine rendez-vous or an actual date? The image of the motel by the interstate flashed as though it were before her. No, she told herself, she did not desire to go to the motel, she had merely seen it in passing, last week, last month sometime. *He is not serious. He means he would like to get to know me better. Christ, he is a boy.* He is not proposing sex or dating but friendship, companionship.

His chest heaved. There were pieces of grass stuck to the sides of the shirt, and she wanted to pick them off, blade by blade, and wipe the dirt off the fabric, off his arms, off his ruddy cheek, his small, pert nose.

"My father won't know," he said. "No one has to know."

A secret relationship. Furtive meetings. Not being able to tell anybody. No!—She couldn't have any future with him! She had to maintain control.

She started the car, steadying it onto the roadway, turning on the headlights, telling herself to be careful, to drive slowly, to breathe. She turned back to Brian, curled in a ball. *No one has seen us. The police officer did not suspect anything. There is no crime.*

Her car started to veer into the oncoming lane, and she corrected her steering. She had to make him understand. *Stop shaking. Remember, he is just a boy.*

"What happened to your mother?" she asked.

"What do you mean?"

She wasn't going to allow him to be evasive. "Where does she live?"

"I don't know." He turned to the window and wiped the condensation from the glass. He started to hum, making a hollow, popping sound with his tongue against his cheek.

Rather than let the matter go, as she might with a peer whom she would not want to annoy, she persisted: "Do you see her?"

"What's the point?" His eyes couldn't conceal his hurt. Nervously, he turned to the back seat and glanced at Brian. "Tomorrow, he won't even remember he saw me tonight."

She couldn't get him to focus. His sitting beside her, being himself—distracted yet caring—began to unnerve her.

She turned the corner, onto Grove Street. She had done all she could. They approached the Hendricksons' house. There was no police car in sight. "I'm going to ride down a little farther so your father doesn't see my car," she said.

"Listen to me," he said, his voice shaking. "Don't go out with him."

"I have to. I invited him."

"Laney, please. I'm asking, I'm telling you. I don't want you to go out with him. *Ever.*" His voice became fierce and angry. She began to feel afraid. What might he do—strike her, make her cry? His hand stretched toward her arm, and she watched it, and her arm, near his fingers which were not quite still. She turned the steering wheel. He took away his hand, snapping the air conditioning vent closed with a sharp flick.

When she stopped the car, he opened the passenger door with a brusque push. He hesitated before stepping out. Despite his aggressive stance, she could see in his eyes an inherent warmth. Had he resigned himself to their not being able to see each other? Was he surrendering?

"Don't you think he's a little old for you?" he said. "He's almost forty-five."

She was tempted to laugh, but she couldn't risk stirring his resentment. "I think I have a lot more in common with someone who's forty-five than I do with a sixteen year old." There was a hint of scorn in her voice.

"You're wrong," he said adamantly.

"How old do you think I am?"

"I don't know." He shrugged his shoulders, but his eyes lit up in anticipation of an answer. "Twenty-five?"

She was touched and at the same time flattered: He reaffirmed her youthfulness and attractiveness. "I'm thirty-two," she said.

"Really?" He couldn't contain his surprise—his eyes grew large, he shifted in the seat, tapped, then nervously grasped, the door handle. "It doesn't matter," he said.

He sounded as if he truly did not care that she was so much older than he was. But she couldn't share her feelings of being flattered, of being appreciated, of being regarded as an object of desire—He wouldn't understand or he would think she was just being silly. Maybe she was. She remained silent, trying to calculate how much difference there was in their maturity and in their physical appearance. He had a few lines around his eyes, even some on his forehead—though not at all deep or creased. He even had some dark patches underneath his eyes. But that was it. Everything else—the texture of his skin, his unfilled physique, his dearth of facial or body hair, even his teeth— which didn't seem to have fully grown in—blatantly indicated that he was still a teenager.

He stood by the open door, the interior light illuminating the space between them. "If that's the way you want it." He allowed his inflection to rise to leave open the possibility that he was posing a question.

He shrugged, shaking his head, as if there was no need for her to answer. His eyes misted over, and he looked away briefly, for a half second.

The obvious hurt in his voice drew her closer to him. She wanted to mother him, but if she reached out to him, she feared she would touch him not as a child but as a lover. "Even if we can't be friends, I do care," she said.

He looked squarely back at her, his eyes glazed over in a defensive mode. He stepped away from the car into the dirt embankment, almost a mock disappointment on his face. "Do you *really*?" A mixture of disbelief and rage rattled his voice.

"Yes," she said. "I do."

His lips trembled. He put his hand over his mouth. His eyes had never been softer or more entreating. He jittered, but took a quick breath, and all his nervous energy instantly dissipated. "I love you," he said.

He spoke as if he had never known anything so certainly. He waited for a moment, searching her face. As she looked at his unruly hair, his blinking lashes which shook, she tried to remain composed, unmoved. Was what she had considered youthful folly and irresponsibility love?

He sheepishly turned and departed down the street toward his house, leaving the car door open.

She should not have been surprised. His admission of love was inevitable. He loved her as she was beginning to love him. She told herself she was right to let him go. She could have told him that she had led him on unjustly—because he was much too young for her—but she couldn't lie. She felt she needed to tell him the truth at any cost. To protect him—from what? Reality? Adulthood? Her? She was lying to *herself*. She did not wish that Christopher were older. She wanted him to stay innocent as he was. She pictured him playing soccer on the field, enjoying power over his peers, perhaps as much as he enjoyed his power over her. Did he realize that he had this power—the power of his smirk, his stare? Could he see that she was so vulnerable she could be spun like a top and stopped with the flick of a wrist? Maybe he was manipulating her. Maybe he could tell that she was the kind of woman who could fuck her husband's best friend and later have the nerve to confess, in order to assuage her guilt.

She was anything he wanted her to be. Even though he had walked away, she felt he was with her more strongly than if he were present. She longed to be with him. With him, she could forget everything: the past, the people she knew, her life. She had her answer: She wanted a lover who was a child.

***

The next morning Brian recollected being awoken in the middle of the night and driven somewhere. He had a foggy notion that Christopher had been with them. Although she could have told him that Christopher had not come to their house, that he had been dreaming, Laney told him she had given Christopher a ride home. She expected him to ask why he had been at their house, but he was not interested in why:

"Why didn't he sleep over?" he asked.

While her surprise at his question settled, she pulled a pre-buttoned Madras shirt over his head and smoothed it on his shoulders. "He just came by to look at the plants and animals in the backyard for his Boy Scout project." Repeating the lie about why Christopher had come almost made it seem more true, but it made her uneasy. "But it was getting late and he had to go home."

"Why?" Brian asked.

Why did he feel Christopher should sleep over? "Why do you ask so much about Christopher?" she said.

He did not hesitate before answering. "I like him," he said, an unambiguous sense of triumph in his voice.

Should she ask him why he liked Christopher so much? Was it indeed such a surprise that her own son would take a liking to him? Was there something about being in the same family that caused its members to have similar feelings of affection toward other people?

When she finished checking to make sure his shoe laces were properly tied, he said, "I wish he would stay for breakfast or dinner one day."

Breakfast? He was not seeing him so much as a friend but as a father figure. To him, Christopher was an adult like her. He did not see the gradations of aging. That Christopher, like him, was still young and growing. Or perhaps he did, and the fact that Christopher was young made him more appealing.

Brian gathered his pencils, placed them in his backpack, and hoisted the pack over his shoulder.

She could feel her discomfort growing and a tightness in her forehead slowly gripping her skull. Confusion, tempered by a tinge of paranoia, was pushing its way ahead of all thought or reason. She welcomed the moment when the moment she did not have to act or think would set in.

He left the room without saying so much as goodbye to her.

After a light breakfast, her headache was gone. *He* loved her, and there was nothing wrong with that. She hadn't responded. She had acted appropriately, like an adult. The beginnings of a smile formed on her lips when she heard his words of last night echo through her: "I love you." She continued to repeat the words to herself, like a mantra, over and over—so much so that he seem to be with her.

As she slinked about the house, she had the strange feeling that she was not following her normal routine. She felt unencumbered, unweighed down by the internal monologues that she played and replayed in her head, which she listened to over and over for signs of something new, something unheard or something not fully understood.

She didn't shower. She felt no need to cleanse herself of something she could neither see nor feel. She looked fine. She had no fear, suppressed or palpable, that today might be her undoing. She had the world open for her to touch, to see, to smell. She was no longer a mere passerby but a participant, a gleeful actor, one who could by virtue of a smile or a glance change the course of events. But if she had a more pronounced will than before, it was only because she believed it to be so and not because anything in her circumstances or her surroundings had changed, only her perceptions of them.

She had a job interview tomorrow. It was slightly after 9 AM when she returned to the kitchen and looked up the number of Evergreen Technologies, the software firm where Dan worked. As she held the slim telephone directory, the memory of looking up the Hendricksons' number and address ebbed in her brain, gently rolling through her and then quietly disappearing as a small wave dissolves against the shore. Edging out that memory was a rising anxiety as she looked at Evergreen Technologies' entry on the page. No address was listed. The company was located in the new industrial park beyond the shopping center, but the one time she had driven through the park, the maze of streets caused her to become lost. An isolating sense of inadequacy crept through her. Working at Evergreen Technologies might be unfulfilling. She would be working in too close proximity to Dan. *Stop dwelling, she told herself.* When she was six or seven, her mother would tell her that worrying would not bring her father back—he used to be away for days at a time on business. Why had the memory resurfaced now?—She had completely forgotten her father used to travel. Had it been Brian's asking about having Christopher over for breakfast or dinner—to take the place of a father who was never here?

Scenes of early home life passed through her mind—a lonely morning at the breakfast table with her mother, an evening at the dinner table, just the two of them. But she interrupted the flow of scenes: Today, she would not be mired in self-analysis.

She took the cordless phone and dialed the number of Evergreen Technologies. A receptionist answered.

"This is Laney Secord. I'm confirming my appointment with Mr. Reditt on Friday." She sounded so businesslike, so sure of herself.

The secretary spoke with a garbled clip, as if quickly finishing her breakfast. "Yes, that's right, at three o'clock. Mr. Malloy said he'd stop by as well. Would you bring an updated resume? We don't have anything on file for you."

"Absolutely," Laney said. "Could I have directions to your office."

After she was given directions and hung up, Laney began to dwell a bit more: An updated resume? What was she to put? Raised a son, painted the living room? She had no accomplishments to speak of. An employer would be leery that her only work experience was a stint as a social worker seven years ago. She cast aside her concerns, determined to create a professional-looking resume.

In the upstairs office, the stack of paper she had printed the other day while researching the myth of Ariadne sat piled in front of the computer. She poked through the papers, observing Ariadne's name spelled in Greek, scrutinizing a thumb-sized picture called "Sleeping Ariadne." She leafed farther, reading that after Theseus abandoned Ariadne, she was kidnapped by Dionysus, god of wine and merriment, and she brought to the island of Lemnos, where she bore him several children.

Laney digested the information: Ariadne had lost the man she loved and married a hedonistic god. Well, there were worse things! She couldn't help but laugh. But as she searched through the papers, nothing more about Ariadne was revealed.

She did not want her own fate be as uncertain, as tragic. She stepped back from the desk and stared forth, as if into a void. The computer, the blotter, the pens and paper did not register. She could have been frozen in time, suspended, were her mind not actively processing the stillness about her. She felt her consciousness not disintegrating, not splintering, not refracting, but rather slowly melding with every thing she barely sensed. When she surfaced from her reverie, she felt less alive, more vulnerable. The walls, the ceiling, the desk, dwarfed her.

As she turned on the computer, the flickering light of the monitor, the digital displays of the operating system which was loading, affirmed that she was emerging from her daydream. She found the file with her resume, last updated when she moved to Plainview. She placed a sheet of bond paper in the printer tray, printed the file, unaltered, and then placed the printed copy atop the papers about Ariadne. She stared at the resume. Tell me about yourself, she could hear Mr. Reditt, whom she pictured as some drab, bald, middle-aged man, ask.

I am thirty-two, I have a son, and lately I have been obsessed with a sixteen year old. Don't you think I am qualified for the job? How much were you thinking of paying? Yes, I can start on Monday.

Her brief interlude with feeling well adjusted, in control, passed. She could see the look in his eyes when he told her he loved her. His Adam's apple that moved, as if he wanted to say something more: "Do you love me?" perhaps. Or, in his adolescent fantasy, did he know that he would not have to ask for a profession of love: It would come naturally, not as a response but as a statement of something which was clearly understood and could only be followed by a tender clasp of the hands, a soft brush against the cheek, or a kiss? She closed her eyes, picturing Christopher in the kitchen on Monday when he had kissed her. He had instantly understood that he liked her and that she liked him.

She opened her eyes and her name and address on the resume melded with the Greek and Roman letters of Ariadne's name on the page underneath. She couldn't argue with the facts, the dates, the places, the names, on the resume. Even in the job descriptions, there was no exaggeration, just pure, unfiltered truth. But it didn't seem to be the summary of her life. Her index finger was lodged between her teeth, between her upper and lower incisors, and she clenched the small mound of flesh at the tip of her finger.

Where had the day's start gone? Such promise, such freedom—all vanished. She bowed her head, cast down her eyes; her feet quietly shuffled away. Her headache was coming back. She thought of calling her father, to tell him the trip to

Santa Maria this July might do her some good. She began to wonder whether Dan was going to say something to Erin about the two of them. Was it really Thursday, she wondered? All the days seemed to be passing in a blur, each indistinguishable from one another. But she felt today should be different, singular. And it was: so foggy out and overcast, devoid of the oppressive heat of the past few weeks. It was an opportune time to take a drive through town, to see Evergreen.

She dressed in a pair of blue jeans and found a short-sleeved blouse to match. When she discovered the blouse's fabric was a linen blend, she put it on anyway, disregarding the admonition not to wear linen before Memorial Day, which was only a couple of weeks away anyway.

Hastily, she scanned her closet for something to wear to her interview tomorrow. She found clothes she hadn't seen in years—suits, skirts, dress coats, even a faux rabbit jacket that Jay had given her one Christmas before they got married. She was never much a fan of fur. She only wore it a couple of times, to satisfy him, to show that she appreciated his giving it to her. Why couldn't she do things to satisfy her own needs? What were those needs?

She was starting to mope again. *Stop*. Yes, she still had a few knock-'em-dead outfits to woo the numbers-crunchers in Accounts Payable at Evergreen. No need to worry.

She slipped out of the front door with her handbag, a leather portfolio, and a note containing Evergreen's address. She planned on paying attention to all the names of the streets in the industrial park, and she would clock her trip. When she left the house, it was 11:22 AM.

As she drove through town, she felt a continuous pull, almost a magnetic force, in several directions—to Plainview High, to the Hendricksons' house. She headed toward the center of town, forcing images out of her mind: Christopher dancing with the soccer ball in the field; Christopher standing like a statue, watching her; Bill walking from her garden with a handful of tomatoes, bending down, their bodies touching. She imagined it was last night, and Christopher was beside her in the passenger seat. She wanted to pluck the stray strands of grass from his shirt. She wanted to hold him, she wanted to kiss him.

She continued through town and approached the new shopping center. She could feel the pull again, this time toward the supermarket. She envisaged the Assistant Manager watching her. She drove onward, keeping her eye on traffic. She imagined Officer Wilkins standing at her front door, Christopher beside him. She detected a pattern: everything, every issue, revolved around Christopher. Bill, Dan, even Brian, all seemed to manifest various aspects of Christopher's personality. Bill was an older version. Dan, the friend who induced shame in her because with him she had betrayed Jay. And Brian, the boy, helpless, dependent, in need of a mother.

As she entered the Franklin Industrial Park, green hills and a broad road—immaculately paved, twice the width of a regular road—welcomed her to an enclave of sedate buildings set back from the road. Every structure was surrounded by a pristine garden.

She pulled out the paper with the address. Ten Briarwood. She stopped at a grouping of white wooden signs that pointed to the right, the left, and straight ahead. Various companies were listed, but neither Evergreen nor Briarwood. She ascended the steep hill. The diamond speckles in the asphalt glittered in the sunlight. She lowered her windows, to allow the breeze to cool the interior of the car. For some strange reason, the overhead light was illuminated. She pressed the button to turn off the light, but the switch was already in the neutral position. The interior lights should have only come on when the door was opened. All the doors were closed. She toggled the switch to another setting, then to a third setting—the on and off positions. Each time the lights remained on. Electrical problems had plagued the car a couple of years ago and had taken months to fix. Every pothole or bump in the road would cause some malfunction. She should have traded in the car at that point, before the warranty had run out.

She passed by a street sign that she couldn't read because she was preoccupied by the interior light. Annoyed, she stopped, looked in her rearview mirror, and backed down the hill. "Briarwood," the sign read. Why wasn't there a listing for Evergreen? This place made no sense. She put the car back in drive and turned onto Briarwood. The road sloped downward and then curved to the left. As she descended the hill, the interior compartment light turned off, annoying her even further.

No edifices stood along Briarwood. She might have gone the wrong way. She proceeded down the hill, twisting around the bend while turning on the headlights to check whether they worked, flicking the radio on then off, pressing the cigarette lighter into the dashboard, thinking about turning on the windshield wipers but deciding not to because she didn't want to damage the blades by having them rub against the dry surface. She was about to turn back when the road took one more dip. Before her stood a modernistic concrete and glass structure, three or four stories high, though there appeared to be only two levels to the building. She drove more slowly to admire the beauty of the architecture, the lines that flowed, escaped, one into one another as if the entire structure were made of a solid piece of concrete and the panes of glass were there solely so that those inside could look out and behold the singularity of the building. A steel sign with green lettering read "Evergreen Technologies."

Although she felt content knowing the route where she had to drive tomorrow, anxiety set in. She had so little information about the position she was applying for. She pictured herself behind a desk with a mountain of paper between her and ringing phones. She could call Dan, but all he would want to talk about was their tryst. As she pictured herself in a maze of paper, her potential new life, which Dan and Erin were arranging, orchestrating, she asked herself: *Is that what I really want?* Or was it merely easier to rely on others to map out everything for her so that she did not have to make any decisions herself? Her whole life, decisions had been made for her by others. Her father had coaxed her into going to college at Boulder. Jay had wanted to move to Plainview. Her friends even talked her into dating Jay. Only her major in psychology she chose herself, sticking to it despite parental opposition. The realizations went further: Her fondness for Christopher sprung totally from within. External factors—other people—or her perceptions of them—caused her to doubt herself. She had lived this way for so long she had difficulty distinguishing between a true desire and her suppression of the desire.

The Evergreen building now looked commonplace. She wanted to return home. She drove quickly down Briarwood, as if in pursuit of something, when suddenly the road stopped in a circle. She proceeded to turn, but the car wouldn't completely make the corner. She effected a three-point turn, the interior light coming back on as she backed up. She drove down the street, toward Evergreen's headquarters, taking another look at the building: Would it look beautiful this time or dull? She couldn't decide. She hadn' t even started the job and already her mind was going in circles: There were opportunities outside of Plainview, there was no need to limit herself. She should return to her field of social work. Evergreen was a first step.

Tell me about yourself, tell me about *you*, she could hear the interviewer asking. Her mouth stumbled, and all she could say were the words: Christopher, Chris. 'Chris': He could be 'Chris', couldn't he? They were 'friends'. No, yes. Her throat, dry, clenched.

There was nothing wrong about seeing him.

She turned on the radio. The volume was too high, but she was thankful it worked. She was traveling fifty miles per hour, too fast for the road, when she reached the main exit to the industrial park. She barely stopped before traversing the street that led toward the school.

Her fears yesterday about driving to the school were unjustified. There was nothing wrong with simply driving by it, to be more familiar, to reconnoiter with Christopher's world. It was normal. Yes, it would normalize everything. Yesterday was an aberration: the discomfort, the police officer, the unwillingness to speak. But not the "I love you."

She was so close, she could simply take a shortcut around town.

It was now 12:15 PM and the sun was coming out in full force. She drove onward. Before she reached the school, she saw groupings of students walking toward the old part of town, where the bank and a few eateries were located. How odd that the students could leave school grounds during the middle of the day, for lunch presumably. They hadn't had open campus when she was growing up.

Behind all the groupings, she saw a pair of students walking hand in hand. As she drove closer, she scrutinized them. Christopher was walking with a pretty blond girl. She passed them, pulling before the bank. She looked in the rearview mirror. They were holding hands. Christopher brushed his free hand across the side of the girl's cheek, letting his hand linger about her face. The girl smiled, said something, and she laughed.

Had he seen her car? Was he acting flirtatious with the other girl to make her jealous? Or were they truly high school sweethearts, as she and Jay had been?

They continued walking down the street, Christopher turning back quickly. Was he checking to see that Laney was still there? They went into an ice cream shop. Before he passed through the door, he looked down the street toward her.

Laney veered into the other lane. She turned off the radio, to head back toward town. Yes, home, was where she wanted to be. Images of Christopher and the young schoolgirl—his sweetheart—flashed through her. She was so petite, so wholesomely beautiful. How jealous she felt. She drove past the ice cream parlor, but could not see inside. She felt clammy. The muggy air was making her claustrophobic. She lowered the power windows, on the driver's door, the window catty-corner to her.

As she passed the industrial park and proceeded down the

final hill before town, the power steering went stiff. She couldn't maneuver the wheel. The brakes didn't respond. The radio went out. She tried to keep the car from veering off the road, yanking the steering wheel so the car would stay its course. She pumped the brake, praying she wouldn't lose control. In panic, she turned the key to shut off the engine. The engine stopped, but the key wouldn't come out. When the car reached the dip at the base of the hill, it slowed down, finally coming to a standstill by the side of the road. She sat behind the wheel, wondering what, how, why. Thank God nothing grave had happened.

After a few moments, she tried to restart the car, to no avail. Not even a click from the alternator. She released the hood latch and stepped out of the car. She fumbled with the stick-like metal bar secured to the engine and managed to prop the hood. The engine was hot, fuming with gas, grease, and oil. She looked at the radiator, patted a hose, then a belt. Nothing seemed out of the ordinary. She poked a metal drum. It burned her finger and she pulled her hand back. She located the dip stick. The oil looked fine. She knew she'd have to re-dip it to check the level, but the problem wasn't with the engine, it was with the wiring. She slipped the dip stick back down the tube.

She found her cell phone in her handbag, but when she tried to turn it on, the battery was dead. Thank you, technology.

She looked down the road toward the shopping center. The supermarket was out of view, but there was a pay phone there and call for help. She retrieved her bag from the passenger seat, checked that she had her AAA card—Yes, that was in order. She turned on the hazard lights, considering locking the doors but deciding not to. Let someone try to get this started. She gathered her registration information from the glove compartment, tucked it in her bag, and started down the street.

As she trekked up the modest incline, as cars and trucks passed, whizzing by, oblivious to her, and the sun bore down, burning the grass by her feet, heating the hard top, she began to feel alone, abandoned even. The memory of that first night alone after Jay had died resurfaced: her sitting by herself in the living room, staring into oblivion, the pictures and fireplace and curtains and carpet, all of which looked inconsequential because he was gone, not away on a trip, but permanently from the earth. Afterwards, she had had no sense that his presence was with her in the living room. She looked at the sofa, the chairs, the painting of the sea scape over the fireplace. He wasn't there, not in any form imagined or real. She searched for his ghost for days and days, leaving the cap off the toothpaste tube as he would, cleaning her hair from the bathroom counters, about which he complained, peering at his socks—the dress ones in a separate drawer from the athletic ones—and so on until she gave up. She did not believe in ghosts. So he did not return.

Now, as she walked along the street, she was reminded of her detachment from all about her. She, herself, I, all invisible. She could be walking and disappearing at the same time, and there would only be her car, the witness reluctant to come forward, with its hood open and lights flashing.

9

When Laney reached the supermarket, she stopped at the pay telephone near the exit and dialed the service number for AAA. The AAA operator told her a tow truck would arrive within half an hour and that Laney should wait by her car.

After she hung up, the Assistant Manager of the supermarket, wearing his uniform of a crisp white button-down shirt and black slacks, rushed toward her, giving her a broad smile.

"Didn't I see you shopping here yesterday?" he asked.

Because of his exotic looks, she had expected him to have a foreign accent, but he did not. "I don't recall," she said, aloofly.

He looked older than when she had seen him the other day, in his forties rather than his thirties. His skin was drier, more creased around the eyes and lips, cracking almost, and it was not so dark or velvety but had a brownish, soiled hue. Why had she found him attractive? There was nothing at all special about him. She began to feel uncomfortable.

"Are you new in town?" he asked.

She did not wish to further their conversation. "No, sorry." She gazed at the parking lot, toward the street.

"I just moved here from Detroit," he said.

She gave a polite, though quick, smile. "Welcome to Plainview then. I have to be going. I have someone waiting for me."

"Your friend?" He was referring to Erin.

Laney gave him a nod that indicated little interest, then she started down the sidewalk.

"Come again," he said.

As she made her way through the parking lot, she could sense him watching her. Was he talking to her simply to be cordial or was he going to ask her out on a date as well? Why would she care where he was from? She should have never thought of him for even a moment.

She weaved through several cars so that he would lose track of her. What was she doing—hiding? Why did she go back to the school? Didn't she know that men pursue women as sport, as a challenge? With boys, it was no different. Christopher had already moved on. He had a girlfriend. She was just a brief diversion for him.

When she returned to her car, a tow truck was already parked beside it and a mechanic was attaching cables to the chassis. The mechanic was a young fellow, maybe twenty-five, of Middle Eastern descent. His navy outfit ballooned over a thin frame. Plainview was indeed becoming more diverse—first a black man at the supermarket, now a Middle Easterner—such contrasts to the mostly white Midwesterners that were prevalent in town.

As the mechanic secured her Volvo to the tow truck, she wanted to ask him why he had chosen Plainview, but she resisted. He was busy. He might misinterpret her question as an advance. She was not looking at him out of interest, no. He merely looked different, unusual, so thin, and yes, truly from a foreign land.

When he finished, he took her AAA card, wrote down her membership number, then had her sign an invoice. "Do you need a lift?" he asked.

"Yes," she said. "I live at 11 Heather Lane."

"The shop's as far as I can take you."

Let down, she put on a brave face. "No problem," she said,

immediately recalling Chris's words— "No *problema*" of the other day. She was starting to talk like him. She had to exorcise him from her mind. She could move on.

In five minutes they arrived at Hank's Garage in the old town center. She never stopped for gas here, preferring the new station near the supermarket, with its bright lights beaming from an attached convenience shop. The inside of Hank's, with its smells of grime and gasoline, confirmed her suspicions that it was a grease pit.

She sat on an aluminum chair in a tiny office with her back against the window. Her car was in the adjoining repair area, hoisted on a hydraulic lift, being subjected to a variety of diagnostic tests. While she waited, staring at the squiggle on the chalk board, watching the second hand click around the face of a clock, she began to plot how to get home if her car could not be readily fixed. Erin would have to pack up the kids to come get her. What an inconvenience that would be. She could take a cab. A cab would be the surest, easiest solution.

In the rear of the garage, there was an old car, a relic, similar to Bill's. He would probably be glad to pick her up. He was virtually her only other friend—Virtually?—Who was she kidding? She had no friends other then Erin. No, a cab was the easiest solution.

She picked up the newspaper sitting on the edge of the desk. On the front page of *USA Today*, in the lower, left-hand section, an article with the headline "Teacher Arrested for Affair with Student" caught her eye. She read, almost in disbelief, of a thirty-three year old Florida math teacher who had had a two-year affair with one of her male students. They had had trysts in motel rooms, starting when he was fifteen. The boy told his friends about the affair, about having sexual intercourse with her. A parent found out, and the police arrested her. Above the article, there was a color picture of the woman, handcuffed and shackled at the waist, wearing a navy jumpsuit, appearing in court, her hair disheveled, her face drawn, vanquished.

The caption underneath the photo read "Ms. Martin, 33, being arraigned. Her trial is set for September."

The woman bore an eerie resemblance to Laney. They were approximately the same age, both had blond hair, though the woman in the picture had dark roots showing. Each was attractive and svelte.

Laney's chest started to pound, and she felt as if she could not breathe. Here was... another *sick* woman, who had actually had sex with a boy. Pity seized her, causing her to become squeamish on the chair. No, there had to be another fate. There had to be more to the story.

Hank, the rotund and balding garage owner, entered the office, and she placed the paper back on the desk, unable to stop looking at the picture of the woman.

"We already found two shorts in your car, but we haven't finished going over the entire electrical system. Chances are, you're going to have more shorts. I've seen many of these cases, and they're tricky to fix. If you want, I could junk your car. I could probably get you eight or nine hundred dollars for it."

"But it's only eight years old," she said. "It doesn't even have a hundred thousand miles on it."

"With this kind of problem, it's only worth its parts. Or maybe some kid would want it."

A kid? Christopher? This could be his first car. She looked at the newspaper. No, she couldn't give him anything. Legal problems could result. There could be nothing traceable between them.

She could get more money for a trade-in—She had no doubt her car was worth at least $2,000, maybe more. The monetary aspect ruffled her, but she didn't want to deal with buying a new car the day before her interview. She needed more time, a week, a month maybe, just another day. "How much will it cost to fix?" she asked.

"I estimate three to four hundred. I can't be more exact. It all depends on the extent of the problems."

"Will it be ready by tomorrow?"

"We'll try," he said.

As he filled out the paperwork, Laney's eyes drifted back to the newspaper. She did not want to become that woman. No, she did not love Christopher. She was an adult, with the ability to make any decision she wanted. She was going to get a job tomorrow, she was going to a dinner party Saturday, she even had a date with Bill. She couldn't even call him by *his* name anymore—not 'Christopher', surely not 'Chris'. In her mind, he was merely 'the boy.' The old car in the corner caught her eye. It would serve him right that she call his father. Bill was a friend, an adult as well. There was nothing wrong in asking him for a ride, in continuing their friendship.

"Do you mind if I use your phone?" she asked.

"Go ahead," he answered, pointing to it.

She took a breath. Yes, this was the right thing to do. She was doing nothing wrong. She was not doing this out of vengeance or spite for having seen Christopher with another girl, or because she felt bad about her car, or her inability to deal with the supermarket manager's interest in her. She simply needed a ride home.

She dialed, and Bill answered. "Hi," she said sweetly. "...I'm doing well, thank you. I have a favor to ask. My car just broke down, and I could use a ride home... Hank's Garage... Yes, exactly... Great, I'll see you in fifteen minutes."

As she sat back in the aluminum chair, she closed her eyes and could picture herself at the Hendricksons' house, eating dinner. It was a strange vision. Brian was there along with Bill, and they formed a normal, happy family. She had a sense that the peaceful idyll in which they lived would not last. Christopher came into the picture, and he and his father were two towering figures over her and Brian. Then a policeman came and took her away, leaving Brian behind. She dozed off and was later awakened when Bill tapped her on the shoulder. She didn't know whether she had dreamed about living with Bill and Christopher and being arrested or whether she had actually thought about it and then slipped off to sleep. Yet when Bill, standing beside her, touched her, she had the distinct recollection of being stirred from sleep by Jay's doctor at the hospital and being told that he was dead. At the time, she believed that the doctor had told her that she was dead.

10

"I really appreciate your picking me up," she said to Bill as they drove through town, the sun having now come out blazing, shattering the cloud cover.

"It's the least I could do after you gave Chris a ride home last night."

How did he know that she drove Christopher home? Did he see her car parked on the street? *Try not to react, she told herself.* "It was nothing."

"He apparently didn't think it was a big deal either. He didn't mention it before he went off to school. Bobby Wilkins called from the Police Department. He told me he found Chris snooping around your back yard."

The police called him!—What else did Officer Wilkins tell him—that she was at the school? She couldn't panic. She repositioned herself in the seat, becoming more aware of the steady whine of the Galaxy's engine. "I meant to call you myself. Chris said he had a Boy Scout project to work on."

"He told me he was going to the movies."

"Boys that age will use any excuse to get out of the house."

"It *is* odd he was in your neighborhood," he said.

"He was interested in that swampland across the street. It's unusual for Colorado."

"But he knows better than to go out in the dark alone, when nobody knows where he is. He doesn't know the area."

"Kids have no fear," she said to allay his suspicions.

"Did you know he was coming to your house?"

"No, but I didn't want the officer to become alarmed, so I offered to give him a ride home myself."

"How could you with your son?"

"My mother was visiting, so she was able to watch him." The lies were being compounded, but she didn't know how else to handle his questions.

"I'd like to meet her."

"She left this morning." She was afraid her tone, high-pitched and overly quick, was giving her away.

As they approached the road that led in two directions, one toward Laney's house, the other to Bill's, he slowed the car. "Do you mind if we stop at my house? I have something for you, if you have time."

She twisted her watch. "I really need to be getting home. I have to get started on dinner."

"It will only take a minute," he answered

She winced.

"I promise," he added.

Because he was doing her a favor, she felt obliged. What might he have for her—She was intrigued.

They drove down the idyllic country road, the crisp spring breeze flushing her face and hair. Her distress over her car breaking down diminished. She would be able to solve the problem. In driving with Bill, she had a sensation of doing something new, of countering the routine she had fallen into. The change of scenery, so refreshing and invigorating, relaxed her, and because Bill brought up nothing further about Chris, she sensed trust had formed between them. Yet she still had doubts about his past, their family history, Bill's suspicious attitude toward Christopher visiting her house.

"Does Chris ever see his mom?"

"Yes, all the time."

All the time? Then why was Chris so reluctant to talk about her? "I got the impression he never saw her," she said.

"You did? Well, no. She lives kind of far away, but we have a good relationship. The divorce was better for all of us." He was speaking in platitudes. His tone, though masked, was defensive.

She could pry just a bit more: "Chris didn't have a hard time with the divorce?"

"He's climbed up to Eagle Scout faster than anybody. When he sets his mind to something, he goes all out."

He was again avoiding the issue. But she feared that if she pressed for more information, too overtly, he would become suspicious of her interest in Christopher. She had to be cautious in her approach. "I'm sure he has many girlfriends."

"They seem to like him. I guess he has a chip off his old dad." He winked.

The facial tic caused her to recall how Christopher had winked at her in the kitchen. Christopher had indeed picked up certain mannerisms from his father, mannerisms that were now blurring.

They passed the spot where she had pulled over with Christopher last night. She became uneasy. She could not break free of him. She looked at Bill and saw the string of similarities between them: the way they moved their hands, the way they carried themselves—indistinguishable but for the fact that Christopher's movements were fraught with nervousness and tension. Being with Bill, she felt she was with Christopher. Though last night, she had no sense that Bill was with her in the car. Brian, too, was barely there. There was only Christopher, alternating between brooding and being tender, believing that everything was a choice between life and death. She either loved him or hated him. Bill was devoid of such intense feelings. Being older, he more secure with himself.

She heard Bill chuckle and noticed that he was watching her. "You remind me of Chris—staring off into space like that. What are you thinking about?"

'Chris'—she too might be able to call him that.

"I'm just nervous about my car," she said. "I might have to buy something new."

"Do you need to borrow some money?"

The question struck her as odd: She probably had three, four times as much money as he did, but he acted as a good friend, even if she didn't know everything about him. He was giving her a ride—Who else would have done that? If Erin had come, she would have let Laney know that she had gone out of her way. Would Erin lend her money, or her mother? Of course, but there would always be issues of control, increased interference in her personal life. Bill was proposing no such arrangement.

"You don't have to pay me back right away," he said. "I know you're good for it."

"Thank you, but it's not the money. My husband and I bought that car together. I guess it's finally time to let it go."

He looked at her, wincing as the sorrow she was trying to mask overtook her. "If you need anything, just ask," he said, placing a hand on her knee. She could feel herself slowly surrendering to the feeling that he liked her and that she felt more comfortable with him than any man since Jay had died. Being with him reassured her. She felt like a young girl in the presence of an all-knowing, all-loving father.

They were almost at his house, and his hand rested still on her knee, as if it belonged there. Slowly, she lifted her left hand and put it atop his. "Thanks for your help," she said, grasping it. She kept her eyes on the road a short distance ahead of the car.

11

When they reached Bill's house at 11 Grove Street, she stepped out of the Galaxy and looked precariously down the street. Just last night she was in her car with Christopher, afraid to drive too close to the house. Still unsettled by his words, "I love you," which echoed as if he were right beside her, repeating them, she expected at any moment to see him walking up the driveway, asking what she was doing with his father. He would repeat his stern warning—*Don't See Him*. She tried to shake Christopher's presence, but his connection to this house, with its roof in need of repair, the grass that shot up in unruly patches, left her anxious.

As she made her way down the sidewalk, Butch, the Hendricksons' German shepherd, started barking and ran over to greet Bill. He jumped repeatedly while Bill moved a hand in the air to tease him. He cantered over to Laney, sniffed around the side of her calf, and wedged his nose into the hollow of her knee, as if he picked up some intriguing scent.

As she petted the dog, trying to keep him off her, Bill entered the house and disappeared down the hall, to the kitchen. "Make yourself at home," he called back.

She went inside, the dog eagerly nudging against her. She was instantly reminded of the other time she had been in the house: the medicine cabinet in the unkempt bathroom, the open hamper with Christopher's underclothes exposed. She stood frozen, unable to quell the memory until Butch whimpered, wanting attention.

She proceeded down the hall, stopping at a frameless Polaroid of Christopher tacked to the fading wallpaper. In the picture, Christopher, no more than eleven or twelve, was holding a fishing pole and a fish, a trout or bass, attached to a chain. The fish was about the size she would find in the supermarket, not too large, though to a boy it probably seemed enormous. He looked proud. A goofy smile was plastered over his face. One of his front teeth was chipped. He was so young in the photo, his face and body undeveloped.

Her curiosity turned to unease. How could she view him in intimate terms? Her stomach turned.

Now, as she looked at him in the photo, so innocent, so young, so boyish, he was undeniably 'Chris'—an immature, happy-go-lucky kid with a Scout's interest in nature and a blue-collar dad, not a refined young gentleman who would soon have the world of college with its possibilities of a future opened to him. 'Christopher,' not wanting to be reminded that he was once a boy, would have taken down this picture. 'Chris,' still fascinated by boyhood pastimes and clinging to his accomplishment, cherished it.

Bill was standing by the entrance to the kitchen. There was no door, just a frame with molding and the back plates of hinges, painted over. Carrying two glasses of lemonade, he handed one to her. It had to have been obvious that she was looking at the photograph, but she could think of nothing to say except, How long have you been watching me? She knew better than to ask.

"Do you like to fish?" he asked.

"I used to go with my father when I was little, but I haven't in a long time."

"Maybe one of these days we'll all go."

Like a family, she thought. *Don't you know how uncomfortable that would make me feel? Haven't you figured out that I have feelings for your son? No, you haven't a clue.*

She did not answer Bill, continuing to look at the picture on the wall. *My feelings for Chris will pass, too. This is not love. This is mere infatuation, a shared sickness.*

"Let me show you out back," he said.

She became apprehensive. What did he have out back for her? A gift? Why? Now, she might be expected to reciprocate, perhaps this Saturday when they went to Erin's for dinner. A deepening of their relationship would inevitably result.

As he walked to the front door, her body moved in pieces after him, a foot on the hardwood floor, a hand disjointedly flowed through the air, her head tilted side to side, a bit askew like that of a marionette. Her instincts told her to say she had to be returning home, but as they went inside, the fresh air was a relief from the cloistering solitude in which she had come to find too great comfort.

They walked around the garage. Had he invited her over as a pretext to spend time with her? Or perhaps he was going to ask her to be the custodian of something—some surprise for Chris.

He stopped at the side of the house and picked up a cardboard box. He was going to gather something from the garden. How foolish she was to think this had anything to do with Chris! *She* was the one living in a fantasy, who had an adolescent crush, not Chris.

She followed Bill to the back yard, where a tall wire fence spanned from one end of the lawn to the other. The fence was covered with green tarpaulin, preventing her from seeing inside. He made his way through the chain-link gate, putting down his glass of lemonade on the ground before he passed through. As she closed the gate behind her, she saw a pair of fishing rods propped against the back of the house, next to a white bucket. Reminded of the photograph in the hallway, she felt uneasy and saddened. She could not be like that woman in the newspaper. She could not allow him to have power over her. He already had a girlfriend his own age. She could move on with her life, too.

***

The garden was pristine, and there was not a weed in sight except for heavy brush at the far end toward the woods. The plants were spaced apart with mathematical precision. Before all the vegetables, several rows of spices—rosemary bushes and lavender—billowed in the gentle breeze. Bill was certainly not an amateur gardener, and this intrigued her.

He meandered past a row of young beanstalks budding from wooden poles through the center of the garden, toward a scarecrow made of straw. It had a blue sheet for a dress and it was brandishing a tall stick with a tennis ball stuck at the end. As she walked closer to Bill, she noticed that ears of Indian corn served as the scarecrow's arms.

"Chris made her," he said.

She looked at it again briefly and made her way around it. How odd that the scarecrow was female, an adult female, sporting make-up and a dress. Was Chris searching for some sort of mother figure?

"Chris hated his math teacher, so he made her into a scarecrow to scare away all the birds."

She chuckled, but she ruminated over the implications of what he had said: Chris had a conflict with an older female authority figure, but was it based merely on dislike—or like? Why did he go through all the trouble to make a scarecrow of her? What a childish reaction. Yes, very childish, and how ordinary the scarecrow was—There was nothing special about it.

Bill gingerly stepped over some zucchini plants, placed the box on the ground, and squatted beside a large leafy green plant. "With the way the weather's been, I can't keep up with the squash. It normally doesn't grow for another month or so. But the new fertilizer I've been using is really doing the trick."

"Your garden is absolutely beautiful," she said. "I feel so embarrassed about mine. It's such a mess."

"It just needs a little TLC," he said.

"Don't we all?" *Where did that come from, she wondered? Her being so natural, so at ease, so herself, with him?* Perhaps the hot sun, the ambience of the garden, was calming her nerves.

He proceeded to scavenge the leaves and vines in search of the best specimens. A few he tossed toward the rear of the garden, where small stalks of corn stood before the brush. She helped by taking the vegetables and putting them in the box. How generous he was to give her so many. Sometime between marrying Jay and his death, she had forgotten what a true friend was. What did it matter that he was concealing some information about his past, his relationship with his ex-wife. They were divorced after all—It was right of him to minimize her role in his life.

As he picked, she found herself examining his shoulders, his hair, the back of his neck. She began to compare his features to Chris's. Bill was broader, heavier, more of a sturdy oak than a sapling, but she could see similarities of pallor, size, and proportion. The more she observed him, the more she became beguiled. Even his tanned, weathered complexion—signs of experience and hardiness—she found appealing. The glint in his eyes, the cocksure smile that he periodically flashed her, made her feel appreciated. She was glad to take her mind off her car repair, the job interview, Chris.

When he finished picking the zucchini, he walked toward the tomato plants. Two days ago she had been in her kitchen with him when he dropped a tomato to the floor, and their limbs had touched. Now, they were repeating a sort of ritual, the garden becoming their common ground. Even though there was little room in the aisle, she knelt beside him to help pick some tomatoes. She became conscious whenever his hand grazed hers or when his elbow skimmed her arm. He would look at her. Then just as quickly he would look away. This sign of nervousness, rather uncharacteristic of him, drew her closer to him. As the minutes passed, she began to view him not as Chris's father but as a man in his own right, an attractive man, who had a mysterious passion about him.

The heat was bearing down. Her jeans were soiled at the cuff and knees. When the box was filled, he helped her organize the pickings. "Did you talk your friend yet about Saturday?" he asked.

"I'm sure it won't be a problem."

"You didn't seem so sure the other day. I was surprised you invited me. Why did you?"

His honesty caught her off guard. She had invited him to Erin's dinner party to try to conceal her interest in Chris, but now she was interested in getting to know him better. "It seemed time for me to go out and start dating again," she said.

"But is it *me*, personally, who you're interested in?"

Again, he was being persistent, but because of his honesty, his sincerity, she was not annoyed. She felt his insecurity was the result of mixed messages she had sent him. "I called you, didn't I?" she asked. "There's no one else." As she said this, the words almost seemed true.

Bill seemed relieved, releasing a breath, letting his hand fall into his pocket. But a blanket of anxiety descended over his face. "I haven't been with anyone since my wife either. I've dated other women, and have wanted to re-marry, but it's hard when you have a teenage son. Does the fact that I have Chris bother you?"

Her shoulders tensed, the muscles in her neck contracted. He didn't seem to have a clue of the triangle that had formed about him. "No. He's your son. Of course not." Again, as she spoke, the lies became truer for her. Her feelings for Chris *were* shallow.

"I think he likes you, too."

He does?—She couldn't show her excitement.

"Apart from his mother, he hasn't had too many women in his life. You're a good influence on him."

"You and your wife didn't have any other children?" she asked.

"We tried..." he paused, for too long, "... but she was infertile."

She lost her fertility?—How incredibly odd after being able to bear a child. And what a strange word to use to refer to an ex-wife: 'infertile.' So impersonal and formal. How difficult was their breakup, and why did he view her in such distant terms?

"Trust me, it wasn't me," he said, winking. "No blanks in this arsenal."

She laughed, but his statement— 'no blanks in this arsenal'—such a cliché and so uncharacteristic of him to be so familiar—caused her to cringe. And those words, 'Trust me,' made her wary. 'Never trust anyone who says, "to be honest," "to be frank," "trust me," '—her father used to say.

Why was he withholding information about her? Were they attempting a reconciliation? He might be trying to make her think he was uninvolved.

The sun reflected the salt-and-pepper of his hair. He was quite attractive, in a gritty, hardened way. As he crouched beside her, her eyes gravitated beneath his beltline, to the vee of his pants, where the fabric bunched up and shifted as he moved. How long it had been—too long—since she had looked, truly looked, at a man. How foolish she was to have been seduced by Chris's boyishly long lashes, his perfect hairline, his smooth, unwrinkled skin. Bill's imperfections were real, the product of years, of knowledge, of life. His arms were much more muscular, more fully formed, hardened, stronger, than Chris's.

"Is that an arbor?" She asked, pointing to a white, trellis-like structure at the far end of the garden.

"It is. The previous owner of the house built it, and every year the grapes come back without my having to lift a finger."

She sauntered over to the arbor, where large, green leaves and twisting vines draped over and through the trellis. Underneath several of the leaves, she noticed clusters of green grapes burgeoning forth.

He came up behind her. "This variety tends to ripen in late summer."

Overhead, a flash of purple caught her eye. "It looks like some have already ripened," she said, reaching upward to the top of the trellis. She moved the leaves to show a cluster, fully ripened, with large, meaty fruit hanging down.

"And it's only May," he said in surprise.

"We've had an unseasonably warm spring." She couldn't reach the fruit, so he helped by leaning in and picking one of the bluish-black grapes. He rubbed it against his shirt, at his chest, to clean it, and proceeded to eat it. "It takes good," he said. "Nice and sweet."

He reached up and grabbed several more, handing her one, which she promptly wiped off and ate. He continued to pluck from the cluster, eating one grape after another. One was so hardy that juice dribbled down his chin, and she reached forward to wipe it.

He watched her hand for a moment. Then he leaned over and kissed her. She remained calm, as if she had expected the kiss. A vision of Chris surfaced, only to be quickly swept away by memories of Jay. But soon, all thoughts of Jay receded, and when she tried to retrieve them, to revive even his face or eyes, the fragmentary images would not congeal but evaporated. She was left in darkness. She had no desire to pull away. She placed her hand on Bill's face and felt his fine shadow of stubble chafe her palm. She became lost in the sensation of his tongue, his lips, his fingers tracing her spine. He pressed against her, pushing her against the ground. The prickly leaf of a vine scratched her arm, while he kissed her neck, her chest. He cupped his hands around her breasts, then he proceeded to lap, almost even nibble, her nipples.

He undid his pants, hesitating. "Are you okay?"

"Yes." She held him tightly and felt his large frame sink against her, realizing that this was not how she had imagined her first experience after Jay would happen, outside, in a garden, under the hot sun.

He thrust inside her, mercilessly, as if he didn't know—or care—that she hadn't had sex in three years. He grabbed her by the shoulders and jabbed his pelvis at her, as if pounding a piece of meat. She was afraid she was hemorrhaging—but no—she was merely opening wider to receive him. She felt herself becoming smaller under him. The weight of his body, the hair on his chest, stomach, and cheeks, smothered her. His mouth traversed her body, rapidly and skillfully.

He had a trio of grapes in his hand, and one rolled loose, onto her breasts, as he thrust into her. He instantly seized the grape, hungrily took it into his hand, and withdrew from her. He ate it, then placed a smaller one between her lips. He kept the largest grape in his palm. She closed her eyes and after a moment felt something—his mouth, his fingers, the grape?—between her legs. She squirmed, opening her eyes, watching his head bob, buried between her thighs. For several minutes, he darted his tongue, swirling it between her legs, lapping up the juices—her own, his saliva. She couldn't tell whether she was feeling her own inner membranes, his tongue, or seeds, fruit! He rammed his penis into her, mashing whatever was inside of her, fucking her even more ferociously, as if determined to obliterate any trace of pulp. She squeezed and contracted, as if to help him rid any last vestige of meat or skin. But she felt ecstatic gripping his cock, enjoying not the mild sensations of intercourse that she had imagined and avoided for too long, but the unbridled, lustful fuck that he was unleashing upon her. As the sun sweltered down on them and his sweat dripped over her breasts and belly and the bed of dirt shifted and scratched, she held on to him as if she were on a precipice, with nothing beneath her. She feared that if she let go, she would fall, spinning, into a kaleidoscope, a cornucopia, of colors—greens and reds and yellows and browns—from the leaves, the vegetables, the earth, as if they and she were part of a never-ending abyss.

12

It was still early, 2:30 PM, when Bill dropped Laney off at her house. She had told him that she needed to return home to prepare dinner, and after their rendezvous in the garden, things had become so easy between them he didn't object.

His Galaxy floated over the road. Cool breezes took the edge off the sun. When they laughed about the dirt in their shoes and clothing, there was a hint of pride in their voices. They had done "it." How easily she had performed the requisite squeezing, the holding, the arching. An unbridled sense of accomplishment, of tackling some long-ignored onus, permeated her. She had broken a limitation she had imposed on herself. She should not have waited so long to have sex. She had not betrayed Jay's memory. On the contrary, she felt more free, less tied to the notion that she had to remain celibate. Her mind and body relaxed, she could now recall so easily and clearly those mornings, Jay's preferred time, when she and Jay would fuck.

When it was time for her to step out of the car, an uncomfortable silence crept between them. She didn't know what to say: Thank you, That was fun, What exactly did you do with the grapes? You devil, See you soon. Now that she had actually fucked him, on the spur of the moment, without thinking of the complications—or perhaps, having convinced herself that there were no complications, she was afraid that their relationship had reached a point where he was certain to tell Chris what had happened.

"Bill, could I ask a favor of you?" she asked.

"Sure. Anything you want."

"Would you mind not saying anything about this afternoon to Chris?"

His brow raised in surprise. "I wasn't planning to. Why?"

She should not have said anything. Now, she had piqued his suspicions. "We just met, and I wouldn't want word to get around."

His brow settled. "No problem. I know, life in a small town. But I'm old fashioned. A gentleman never tells. Not even in Plainview," he winked.

"Thank you." She lightly put a hand on his arm. Then he kissed her. The kiss made her uncomfortable. It was not an act of passion, as their interlude was, but one of affection, if not love. As he held her and looked into her eyes, she was forced to demonstrate some sign of love in return, but she could think of nothing to do or say to honestly convey her feelings. So she simply said goodbye.

"Don't forget the vegetables." He pointed to the back seat, at the half-filled box of offerings from his garden.

"Yes, thank you again," she said.

As she made her way to the front door, Bill, who had parked in the driveway, waited, old fashioned, for her to step inside. "Good luck with your interview tomorrow," he called out.

As she waved—how many times did he have to say goodbye to her?—further doubts raced through her mind. Why had she slept with him? Weren't they on their way to becoming friends, not lovers? Had they used sex as a way not to communicate with each other?

She had no answers. She told herself everything was fine.

She moved hesitatingly about the house. No, an answer came, she should not have made love to Bill, there was a connection to Christopher. She had used to Bill to become closer to him. No, stop fixating. Then: Bill was too old for her—a twelve-year age difference. But while sleeping with him didn't seem entirely right, it wasn't *wrong*.

She showered, to rid herself of the dirt from the garden. When she looked at her naked body, she was mesmerized by its unmistakable beauty. None of the small, nagging faults caught her eye—the faint stretch marks where her buttocks creased into her thighs, the stomach which protruded more than it used to, the left breast which sagged downward, to the side, and was larger than the right. No, it was completion, perfection, that she saw: the luxuriant hair, the fresh skin, the doe-like, blue-green eyes. Yes, yes, she thought!

With a towel wrapped around her, she danced, listening to music, thinking how fulfilled she felt. How refreshing it was to have had someone else pleasure her. If only she had allowed herself to, she might have had an orgasm. Yes, it was only a matter of permission. The sex was fine, good.

The phone rang, and she answered it while toweling her hair. "Hello—" Her voice was perkier than usual.

"Hi, Laney." It was Bill. He didn't wait long to call.

"I just wanted to make sure you were all right," he said.

"How sweet. Thanks." She was about to hang up.

"Laney?"

"Yes?"

"I know it's early," his voice paused. "I just wanted to say I love you."

Any remnant of joy was lost. How naive he—and she—

both were. They were deluding themselves. This could not work. Still, she made a joke: "Was I that good?"

He was silent. "You were." How serious he sounded.

She laughed. "You weren't so bad yourself." *Why was she forcing this compliment?* "I'll talk to you later, okay."

"Okay, bye," he said in an almost sing-song voice. His disappointment was barely camouflaged. He was trying to make it seem that he was not pressing her, but she felt the nudge: *"Maybe next time," his voice said, "you'll tell me you love me, too."*

She hung up the phone. "I love you," he had said. When Chris had said he loved her, he had not expected her to say anything in return. There was a matter of factness in his voice. The statement for him was almost an emancipation: He was freeing himself. But Bill's declaration, disguised as a confession, suggested dependency. He was *less* free as a result of his so-called love. No, she did not believe it was love. His motives were grounded in want, in need.

Despondency threatened to set in again, and as she looked at the king-sized bed, the size Jay had insisted on even though she had felt it would be too large, the first twinge of betrayal of his memory surfaced. She felt as she did when she had slept with Dan, when she had tenaciously clung to her side of the bed for days. Afterwards, she had tried to confess her feelings of isolation to Jay, managing even to elicit his assurance that he loved her. But she did not feel that love as unequivocally as when they had first met. Now, in looking back, she began to wonder: Had she stopped loving herself? Everybody seemed to believe he loved her: Jay, Bill, Chris. They had found a way, even though she could not.

She had to get dressed, but her usual loose-fitting clothing didn't look right to her. She had reached a crossroads. She had just made love to a man for whom she had conflicted, mostly carnal feelings. Now that she had allowed herself to be intimate, she saw clearly that her retreat into abstinence, her decision not to pursue relationships, were ways of keeping herself apart from other people. The loose clothing had the same sheltering effect. Her beliefs about herself were shattering. She was like anybody else, capable of erring, miscommunicating, being false, hiding to conceal her true nature.

She came across the shorts she wore on Tuesday when she had gone to see Chris. She had berated herself afterwards for wearing them, but now they looked fine. She put them on. She imagined how Chris would have reacted to her if he had seen her in them. Would he have led her to the garden, and would she have made love to him? Or would she have sought out denials, and if they failed, recriminations? Could she have imagined, while Bill caressed her, that she was with Chris, that *he* had placed a grape inside her? Yes, for a few moments, he did come into her mind, but she had dismissed the thoughts, believing she was only trying to sabotage the experience. That was what she was doing now. *Yes, she repeated herself, the sex was good.* There was no sense in belittling her accomplishment. She had broken through the last barrier, the last thing that was holding her back: sex. She could feel good about herself.

She changed into a sleeveless silk top and jeans that she had given up on years ago, because she thought they were too tight. This afternoon, they made her feel feminine, wanted.

When Brian came home from school, he immediately went upstairs with his surprise for Mother's Day. Although he had asked her not to look, she could not help but catch a glimpse of unstained, blond wood, carved into an odd shape, pointy in places and rounded in others, all of which suggested an Indian totem of some sort. It seemed a bizarre gift for Mother's Day.

He returned to the kitchen while she was making dinner and asked, "Was Christopher Hendrickson here today?"

She felt anxious. Had he seen Chris this afternoon at the bus stop? "No, why?"

"I thought he might have come back."

"Why?"

"I don't know," he replied.

The knife went unsteady in her hand. "What do you mean, you don't know?"

He leapt to the counter, stuck his hands in the box of vegetables, and grabbed a tomato.

How mysterious he was acting.

She took it from him, brought it to the sink to wash it, and handed it back. Should she ask something more about Chris or let the subject go? If she persisted, it might only encourage him.

He sat on the stool and watched her prepare the spaghetti sauce using the fresh tomatoes Bill had given her. He stared at her for several moments, at her arms and face. She began to feel apprehensive: When would he bring up Chris—Christopher— again? She smiled, uncomfortably. "Are you getting hungry?" she asked.

"How old do you have to be to drive?"

There he went again. "Sixteen. Why?"

"Does Christopher drive?"

Why did he keep asking about Chris? And why was he being so evasive? "I don't know," she answered.

She had forgotten to take the stems off the tomatoes already in the saucepan.

"How does he get everywhere then?"

"He probably walks or takes the bus. Or his father drives him." She left the stems in. She could fish them out later, if need be.

"Why didn't his father pick him up last night?"

He was sending her into a whirl. Why was he bringing up last night? He should have forgotten about the ride. "It was late, and we didn't want to bother him."

"And his mother?"

She didn't want to delve into Chris's family history. "Brian, is something on your mind?"

"No," he shrugged. "But if you married Christopher, I could have a mother, a father, and someone to play with."

Marry Chris—Why was he talking such nonsense? Had someone planted the idea in his head? "Chris is too young for me. He's just a boy."

His eyes bore into her. "What about his father then? If he doesn't have a mother, he could use you."

Use? Is that what she was teaching him? "You don't marry someone just to give someone parents. You marry someone because you love the person." Her voice rose in pitch, but she steadied it.

"But I heard you in the car, last night."

Her body stiffened. "What did you hear?"

"Stuff." His tone was innocent and beguiling. His voice was almost too innocent. He locked his hands together.

He was awake? He had overheard them? She had checked the rearview mirror—repeatedly—to make sure that he was asleep. Why had he waited until now to say something? "What stuff?" she asked.

"*You* know." His stare was hard, unshakable. His face smug.

He *had* heard everything. When she had put him back to bed, he was breathing as if he were sleeping, tossing in her arms, grumbling, all the while *pretending*. Her panic deepened. Had he told anybody else—a classmate, a teacher? "Honey, you misunderstood. Chris and I are just friends."

"But why did you let him walk away? He could have slept over." He spun around on the stool, and the room seemed to spin with him. He was tormenting her.

The pasta sauce was bubbling to a boil, burning at the sides of the pan. She turned down the gas. "He has his own family. All he did was thank me for giving him a ride home."

"I dreamed the whole thing?" he said, his eyes wide, becoming whiter, while a beguiling smile appeared on his lips, fainter and fainter, until she was unsure whether it was really a smile or just his usual expression.

Her stomach twisted in a knot. Had someone told him to pretend he didn't know anything? The principal, his scoutmaster? The police? What if he were to tell somebody? What if Officer Wilkins were to stop to question him? Brian couldn't—or wouldn't—keep his mouth shut. The whole town would know. *Her* picture would be in the paper. Her parents would find out. She would be mortified. She was becoming paranoid. "You must have been dreaming," she said.

The smile grew, becoming self-satisfied, self-contained, as if it had a will of its own. Was it gone or still there? The more she looked at him, the more he looked like some stranger's child.

"I'll go to my room now," he said, as if someone had ordered him to.

"Honey, you don't have to go." If she said anything more to him, he might become more suspicious. He would dwell on the subject, as she would.

But perhaps he sensed that she wanted him to leave because he went away without so much as glancing at her.

Perhaps she had already cast doubt in his mind. Yes, he had gone away confused. It was better to try to keep him quiet.

13

The next day, Friday, Laney was startled awake. Brian, frenzied, was shaking her. "Mom! Wake up!" His voice was pleading and desperate, his movements frantic.

"What's the matter?" she asked groggily. Her dream—she had been... not making love to, but fucking—Christopher—ferociously—in the Hendricksons' garden—would not loosen its grip on her.

"I'm going to be late for school!" Brian shouted.

She looked at the clock on the nightstand. He was right. She had forgotten to set the alarm and had overslept. The bus would be arriving any minute, and Brian was still not dressed. If he missed the bus, she would have no way of bringing him to school because the Volvo was at the shop.

She hastily dressed him, and, having no time for breakfast, rushed him to the bus stop, apologizing all the way for almost making him late and cursing herself for not being as good a mother as she should be. But her dream, vivid and realistic, still captivated her...

She and Christopher—he was Christopher again. Now, because she was imagining him—they were standing in the garden, she was holding onto the arm of the scarecrow, and he was fucking her, so hard, holding her up. At one point he leaned over her arm. She thought he was going to kiss her arm or hand, but instead he started eating the ear of corn—the Indian corn!—which served as the scarecrow's arm. He kept nibbling away, and several kernels fell out of his mouth, soiling his Eagle Scout uniform.

It was a dream, she told herself, Let go. But she kept thinking of the kernels of corns popping out of his mouth, like flies, as if he were dead. She had to face reality—Brian needed her reassurance, but he glided before her onto the bus as if he too were some imaginary figment. The bus zoomed by, the driver and kids seemingly unaware that she was there herself.

She had to relax. She shouldn't be hard on herself. Her interview was today, and it was important to keep her head clear. To veg out, she tuned the TV to the *Today* show while she ate breakfast. Savannah Guthrie was hosting a segment about the increasing number of women in their thirties and forties—single women, mostly professional and with good incomes—who were having children out of wedlock. Several were artificially inseminated through anonymous donors. Then, a pair of women appeared who said that their pregnancies were accidental, but they opted not to have an abortion. "It was a mistake sleeping with him," the woman said. "I knew it at the time and I knew it afterwards. But what came out of it was beautiful."

"Does he know that you had his child?" Savannah asked.

"No," she answered. "He has no idea. I don't think he would want to know either."

Laney felt a cramp. An intrusive fear crept through her... What if she were to become pregnant? Bill had not used a condom. She should have insisted. The cramp tightened its pull on her. She could not eat any more.

Nauseated, she went to the upstairs bath. She leafed through the instruction pamphlet of her birth control pills. "Take one pill per day. If a dose is missed, take only the regular dose at your usual time. Missing one pill will only minimally affect your chances of becoming pregnant."

What did 'minimal' mean? A pregnancy was a pregnancy. She and Jay had conceived Brian practically on the first try.

She read the instructions further. There was a warning not to exceed more than one pill in a 24-hour period. Doubling up was unnecessary because the medication stayed in the body at all times.

She was being paranoid. She had been taking these pills regularly. One sexual episode was not going to undo years of almost fanatical celibacy. She took a single pill, her daily dose, but she quickly chased it down with a full glass of water as the instructions indicated.

The water made her feel queasy, and she went to rest on her unmade bed. She could not be nervous at her interview today, even if the meeting was only a formality. Dan had told her they'd be discussing salary, benefits, job duties, schedules. Job duties: She could barely manage to get her son to school in time.

She called Hank's Garage to see when her car would be ready, her intention being to take a cab there and then drive home to dress and gather her paperwork. Hank told her, gruffly, that the car would not be ready until 11 AM. She had to revise her plans: She would dress for her interview, take a cab to the garage, then head directly to Evergreen.

For her interview, she put together a conservative outfit— navy blazer with a low-heeled shoe, a cream blouse, and a matching skirt. She could have worn pants but she did not want to relinquish her femininity. She put on stockings that complemented the color of her legs, nothing too dramatic but nothing raw either. She painted her nails in a beige enamel that matched her blouse and dried them using the cool setting of her hairdryer. She wore the gold Concorde watch that Jay had given her their first Christmas together. At the time, she was stunned at how expensive his gift was. She later found out that in order to buy the watch he had saved for six months from his after-school job.

She sat before the dressing table mirror. She looked fine, she told herself, *too* good. No wonder Christopher had found her attractive. The other young girl he was with didn't—and would never—compare.

My name is Laney Secord and I'm looking to join a company where I can make a contribution. She repeated it several times, trying each time to sound less false so that the interviewer would not see through her. Then she coated her lashes with a clear mascara and dabbed her lipstick so that the blend was smooth, perfect. She would be a vision of perfection.

At 10:40 AM she called Hank's Garage to make sure her car would be ready. She was put on hold. Finally, Hank picked up. "We found a half dozen shorts in the electrical system," he explained, "and there might be more. With these sorts of problems, unfortunately I can't give you any guarantees."

"Could I drive it?" she asked.

"As long as you have a tow truck nearby. Listen, I told you I can junk it for you. Get you $800 or so."

Hadn't he told her yesterday that he could give her a thousand dollars? She felt the garage was trying to take advantage of her. The car had to be worth more.

"Let me think about it," she said, hanging up. She would have to take a taxi to the interview. But what else was she to do? She really didn't want to bother with a cab, because she would have to have it wait for her during the interview, and if someone from Evergreen saw her leaving in a cab, it might look odd.

After gathering her papers, she took the box that contained the produce from Bill's garden and broke it down, stomping it under her heels. She took it out back and placed it in the garbage can—the recycling bin she never used. In the garden, an overgrown weed the size of a small tree had inserted itself where corn was planted. An unsettling feeling began to develop inside of her. Corn: Her dream of having sex with Christopher returned. She could almost see him standing there among the weeds, waiting, beckoning, his uniform immaculate, his air inviting. "Just a little corn," he sang. Yes, she needed him to fuck her!

The monstrous weed, the wee stocks of corn, once blurred, came into focus. She was imagining. Why did she have such a hard time accepting reality, dealing with it? She hadn't made love to Christopher, only dreamt of it. It was Bill she had had sex with. The garden had reminded her and was stirring her guilt, her lust.

Bill would never have allowed such a weed in his garden. How different she was from him. She had misled him. She had used him, for her pleasure.

She stepped off the grass, checking over her shoes, and returned to the kitchen where she fetched her bag. She found the pizza wrapper with Bill's number on it. She had to make everything right. She had to be honest with herself and with him—as much as she could be. She had no desire to hurt him. Before he was misled further, before she went on her interview, she would tell him the truth.

Besides, she whispered to herself with a glimmer of a smile, she needed a ride.

***

Bill arrived a little over half an hour later, more than happy to give her a lift to Evergreen.

When she let him in, he attempted to kiss her on the lips, but she turned so that her cheek caught his mouth. "I don't want to mess my lipstick," she said, half-believing that she was sending him a message.

She detected the scent of aftershave on his face, strong and pungent, and she tried to discern whether this was something he put on especially for today. He was still wearing his black cowboy boots. He probably slept in them.

When she turned, he put a hand on her arm, grasped it, and took his other hand from behind his back. He offered her a small bouquet of flowers—petunias and daisies surrounding a single red rose. "I had just come from the florist when you called," he said with an ironic, saccharine tone. "I was going to drop them by later. Serendipity," he said.

Another word from him she didn't expect to hear. Sometimes when he spoke, he seemed a different man. She began to think: They were not so terribly mismatched. He was educated, he could use the word "serendipity" casually, even though she knew its meaning only in context. Why did she think she was better than him? Because she happened to have more money? Was her feeling of superiority a protective device? She had to realize she was no different from anybody else.

She took the flowers, blushing, looking askance while walking down the hall to the kitchen. She felt a thorn jab into her finger as she tried to think of the words to say to him: 'Bill, I'd like to be friends, but...' Wouldn't the friendship, like the romance, always be uneasy and false?

"You look so fabulous there's no way they can't hire you," he said.

She set the flowers in a vase, arranging them, delicately, loosely, trying to concentrate on her interview responses. *I am highly organized. I possess outstanding communication skills. I can juggle many tasks at once.*

The reflection of her watch in the granite counter gleamed, contorting itself as she moved her wrist, such that the sparkling dial resembled one of the badges of Christopher's uniform. Bill was quietly watching, but she imagined that he was not behind her, that it was Monday and Christopher, in full uniform, had come to the door, flowers in hand. In her re-creation he was eighteen, nineteen, twenty. He was returning after a long absence, because he had missed her. They were resuming a commitment to each other that didn't need to be expressed in a kiss or a touch but merely by cooking dinner and being together. Silently, she would pace around the kitchen while he sat at the counter, admiring her, and in their silent choreography there was no need for a yesterday or a tomorrow because they had the present to claim as their own.

"Laney," Bill said, placing his hands on the counter across from her. "I want to ask you something. This may come as somewhat of a shock, but I'm going to go out on a limb. That's something I've tried to instill in my son—risk-taking."

She sensed this was a rehearsed speech.

"I didn't plan on this," he said—

Although it sounded as if he did.

"I'd like nothing more than for you to marry me," he said.

She wanted to reverse time. He could not be—he was—and she had to stop him before he made a complete fool of himself, before she said something that *he* would regret.

She slinked onto the stool at the counter. "I'm at a loss for words."

"I'm a new man since I met you."

"But it's only been a couple of days."

"Four," he said.

"Okay, four. But how is four days enough time?"

"Haven't you ever met someone and known instantly that you liked him?"

Immediately, she thought of Christopher: He had said the same thing to her the other night. "I can't decide so easily. Marriage is a life-long commitment."

"We have a lot in common."

What exactly did they have in common, she wondered? An interest in his son? She wanted to say, How can you spring this on me, Why couldn't you have given it more thought yourself, and *No, I can't marry you.* She took a breath. She needed to be mindful of his feelings. She couldn't risk an eruption. Believing she had found a clever way to convey her shock and at the same time discount his offer, she continued to arrange the flowers and, in her sweetest voice, said, "You're really serious, aren't you?"

His eyes blinked in rapid succession, as if he had done a double take, but he appeared unaffected: He had misunderstood, misconstrued, her subtle jab.

Perhaps she had been too subtle. What did she have to say? *You're crazy!*

"I know what you're thinking," he said. "It's not what happened in the garden. I'm not *that* old fashioned."

He had misread her—he was always misreading her. Couldn't he see that *that* was the problem? She should have known this might happen before she let him fuck her, before she let him put that, that grape—She didn't want to think about it.

"Bill, don't take this the wrong way, but I hardly know you."

"Don't be silly."

"I'm not being silly. There's a lot I don't know about you. For instance, where does your ex-wife live?"

"In Denver," he said rather absentmindedly.

Previously, he had said she lived 'far away'. Denver was only a half-hour to the north.

"Has she remarried?" she asked.

"As a matter of fact, she has."

'A matter of fact'—another one of those phrases her father had taught her to mistrust. Similar to 'in fact,' 'point in fact': He's covering for something.

"How does Chris get along with her new husband?"

"Very well, as a matter of fact."

A matter of fact: again.

"Laney, why does this matter to you?"

"I'm a social worker by training. I'm very interested in how families work."

"I didn't know that."

"See, there are things you don't know about me either."

"But the more I learn, the more like." He caressed her cheek with a hand, and he leaned in, to kiss her.

She gently pushed him back. "Bill, I'm not ready for this."

He interrupted her: "Don't say that. This is just a shock. But we know each other well enough, don't we?"

"No," she said. She felt relief. She had said No. That was her answer to his question and to his proposal. A sense of power overcame her, as if she had triumphed. But when Bill spoke—so quickly, not giving her the opportunity to explain further—it was clear that the victory was fleeting:

"Give it some time then. I'm not asking you to be impulsive like me. I just want you to be my wife."

Wife: the word sent chills through her. If she were married to Bill, she would become Chris—No, that word sounded revolting!—Christopher's—mother. How would she be expected to act with him? She would have to wash his clothes, cook his dinner, watch as other girls came to the door to date him. She would have to pretend nothing had happened between them—that their kiss in the kitchen was an innocent act of affection, as between mother and son. That they had had no yearnings for each other. That his declaration of love had been not carnal but filial.

Bill put a hand atop hers. The memory of Christopher's hand touching hers, in this kitchen, on the same countertop, invaded her. The boy who wanted a kiss, whom she did not stop but told to leave—because she wanted the kiss also—seemed to be touching her at this very moment, and as she watched his hand, his roughened skin, his large, strong fingers, the smattering of hair on his knuckles, she sensed this is what Christopher's hands would one day look like.

She should not respond to Bill as if he were his son. She should not allow thoughts of him, the excitement she felt when she was with him—the nervousness, the paranoia—to color what was happening. She loosened her arm from his hand and stepped toward the counter, to get her handbag

No, Bill was not proposing marriage, he was proposing a lie. He had no clue. Is that what she wanted, a sense that she had managed to fool a decent man, and that she would go to any length to be near his son? Was that the only reason she did not tell Bill she did not need more time—because by keeping Bill close, Christopher would not be far away?

"Perhaps I should have given it more time myself," he said. "You have a job interview. No worries. You'll either marry me or you won't. Will you just promise me one thing?"

"What is that?" she asked.

"That you'll be honest."

She winced. She was about to say, "Of course," but she held the words back.

***

During the ride in Bill's Galaxy to Evergreen Technologies, there were several moments when Laney could have explained to him why she could not marry him. She was not ready for marriage—a lie. They needed to get to know each other further— a more egregious lie. She could have steered closer to the truth—that they weren't right for each other. This would have been the most convenient way to handle the matter. But his request, for her to be honest with him, which came almost as an admonition—Did he know something? Was he really misreading her?—gnawed at her. She had to find a way to tell him she would not, she could not, marry him.

"You're quiet," Bill said.

"I was just thinking of what I'm going to say at the interview," she answered.

His hand gently found her knee. He was always touching her!

Caressing the inside of her knee, he said: "You really do look beautiful. You're the most beautiful woman I've ever been with. Chris would be lucky to have a mother like you."

Though uncomfortable, she remained still. How horrible it would be to be married to Bill, with Christopher looming in the house, watching her every movement, seething with anger and jealousy, until finally, he could tolerate the situation no more and he would flee the house. Her punishment: a penance with Bill. Why couldn't she just tell him? Why should she even take the proposal seriously—perhaps he proposed to every woman he knew after four days! Especially women he had fucked with grapes!

She felt queasy. She couldn't be Christopher's mother—his stepmother—She cringed at the thought. Critical thoughts were storming her, demanding perfection at every pass, scrutinizing and cajoling and scolding, chasing her, possessing her. For once, she was grieving not for Jay, not for Brian or herself, the wife, the mother, but for the life she was not leading—being in a healthy relationship, having friends who cared about her and whom she cared for—all of which she had forsaken out of convenience—out of guilt—out of fear—no—out of desire. She could not let this gloom win. She had to take concrete steps—small, measured, calculated—like this job—and then everything she wanted would fall together like the pieces of a puzzle.

They arrived at Evergreen's headquarters. The interview would be a breeze, she reminded herself. Re-entering the job force would mark the end of her solitude.

Bill stopped his car in the lot before the building, told her to knock them dead, and said he'd be back at 2:30 to pick her up.

She reached Mr. Redditt's office just before one. The secretary greeted her, asked for her resume, and Laney fished one out of her portfolio, not completely satisfied with the version she had come up with, but she doubted anybody would look at it much anyway.

She took a seat, sorting through a stack of magazines, all computer related, set on a white table in front of the sofa. The waiting area had the antiseptic ambience of a dentist's office. A slender woman a few years younger than Laney, attractive, with auburn hair and flawless skin, entered the room, introducing herself as Julie Crowley, the office manager, and she led Laney to a conference room beside Mr. Redditt's office. While she scanned over Laney's resume, Laney asked when Dan and Mr. Redditt would be joining them.

"I usually do the first round of interviewing," she said, continuing to peruse the resume.

Dan had told Laney he would be there to make sure the interview went smoothly. Why had he misled her?

"So, tell me about your experience in the technology sector," Julie asked.

In quiz-like fashion the questions piled on: "Do you have any knowledge of networking solutions products?" "What do you know of telephony software?"

Telephony, did she say? Did she mean 'telephone'?

"What do you think you can bring to Evergreen Technologies?" Laney's answers consisted mostly of camouflaged "no's," "I don't have any, but..." The minutes churned. She desperately wanted to leave. Julie's fingers clenched together while her thumbnail scraped the underside of a fingernail. At every answer, she looked at Laney with a surprised expression that barely masked her puzzlement, pausing for no more than a millisecond before moving on to the next question. Periodically, she glanced at Laney's resume with an even more profoundly perplexed look. Laney wanted to shift the interview so that she could ask questions such as, "What exactly is this job I'm applying for?" It certainly didn't sound entry-level to her: *telephony*.

The opportunity never came, and, fifteen minutes after she had sat down, the meeting was over. "We've just begun interviewing candidates, so thank you for coming," Julie Crowley said in an almost friendly tone. Laney was led to the waiting area and courteously wished a nice day. The secretary looked up from her desk. Whether she was smiling, Laney was unsure.

Laney felt herself being pulled, as if in a vacuum, down the hall, into the elevator, and through the lobby. It was as if the building was kindly showing her outside, not because it didn't like her or want her, but because she didn't belong there. The sting of being so summarily dismissed irritated her. This was business. Despite the modernistic, artful facade of the building, it was a place of numbers and technology.

She felt as though the building was staring down upon her, unconcerned, unforgiving. *I am not of this place, she told herself. I was born of a different creed. I do not believe in mathematics or science. I believe in the human spirit.* Her spirit needed nourishment, but she could not find it here. She knew this all along, but still she came. She was traveling in circles. She could see the way out, she knew it existed, but she didn't know how to get there.

She stood near the entrance of the building. Forty-five minutes before Bill would return: There was little she could do but wait. She could go for a walk, but her heels were uncomfortable. She could go back in and try to see Dan to ask him why he hadn't stopped in during the interview. If he had, he would see how quickly she had vanished. That would serve him right. He had done her a favor in securing the interview, but he had let her down. She never even found out exactly what the job was. The situation was all wrong. She should have expected nothing less from him. She should not have come. She had no one to blame but herself. *Yes, take responsibility, Laney Secord. Do not care what others think. Do what makes you happy.* Such went the voices inside her head, such strong, dictatorial voices. But her movements—tentative, cautious, and slow—belied them.

As she sat on the bench near the edge of the parking lot, she could feel contractions at her temples, a pull, and she realized she was on the verge of crying. She *could* hold back the tears. She would not let Julie Crowley, Evergreen, make her cry. The defeat was slow in coming, but it wouldn't relent. The pinching at the corners of her eyes continued. Blink the tears away, just blink, and already she could feel her mascara running. So much for her vision of perfection. Don't wipe, or it will smudge. She reached into her bag for a make-up mirror—She had none, nothing but tissues. Such a charade, a farce, her life had become. But couldn't this be a day, the week, to assert control? Were these growing pains, these pinches and pulls?

She opened her portfolio, looked at her resume, and thought, yes, this was her. There was nothing wrong with her resume. It was not some strange fabrication but parcels of my past. Places she had been, people she had known. Evergreen was going to reject *her*. Her working life would have to take a different start. The only blessing was that she wouldn't have to explain to Dan and Erin why she didn't take the job. Evergreen didn't want her. Why should she explain anything to anybody anyway? Couldn't she live free, unencumbered? What was holding her back? *Who* was holding her back?

She stood, examining the clear blue sky, the lush mountains east of the industrial park, the trees towering down from the range, which reassured her. Nothing could move those trees. An iron and brass plaque next to the bench announced that the Evergreen Technologies edifice was called the Gateland Building. The building was dedicated to the Utes, the indigenous peoples of Colorado. On the plaque there was a silhouette of tribal peoples—chieftains in head dresses, tomahawks reared, beaded belts and moccasins. Women with children—faces painted black. Laney looked closer at one of them. Wispy hair streaked gray and platinum. Eyes round and sad. Skin rosy but parched. The woman could have been her mother. In thirty years, she herself might look like that. She glanced at her watch, but before the time registered on her, she noticed fine wrinkles had formed on the back of her hand. Her skin was looser, more aged than it once was. She was getting older. How could anybody want her? She had passed her prime. No wonder Bill had proposed. She was more suited to him than to Christopher.

She looked up at the rolling hills beyond the interstate. Who in their wildest dreams could have envisioned what Plainview would become? It would change, for the better, while she would simply dissolve, into ash, to feed the land.

She heard footsteps behind her, and when she turned, Dan, his shirt partially untucked from his dress pants, was approaching. "I'm glad I caught you. How did it go?"

"Fast. Real fast. I was totally humiliated."

"I'm sorry, I meant to drop by. I was just too busy. Listen, I talked to Eric Redditt, and he'll meet with you directly."

"That's okay."

He looked surprised.

"I appreciate your help," she said, "but this isn't a job for me." If the people at Evergreen could be this cold, if she did not know exactly what the job entailed, if she were not going to use her training—her people skills, her background in social work—then no amount of persuasion could force her to take the job.

"It's tough out there," he said. "There aren't too many jobs in this area."

He was pushing, and because she knew him well, she felt she could answer him in a forthcoming fashion: "Why does it matter to you whether I go back to work? It's just a job. I don't need the money."

"I want to help. I thought that's what you wanted."

Take matters in your own hands. Do not allow him to do to you what the interviewer had. Confront him, she thought. "No, it's more than that. You're trying to make it up to me. To pretend nothing happened between us."

"I want to come clean. Erin is going to ask. I know she will."

She looked away, toward the parking lot, bordered by a fringe of trees. They formed a straight line, a wall. She knew he would not be able to keep their affair secret.

"There have been other women beside you."

She was not surprised, but she tried to minimize her reaction. This was not her problem. It was a one-time affair for her, not a pattern of behavior. She had suffered more than enough guilt.

"I've tried to stop," he said. "She needs to know."

Laney felt he would be making a grave mistake, but she felt powerless to tell him. "This isn't something a woman wants to hear after ten years of marriage."

"I know. But I can't help it."

Erin loved him so much, perhaps too much. Their marriage seemed perfect to the outside, but it was crumbling from guilt, just as her own had. "Did Jay know what you were doing?" she asked.

He looked down at the sidewalk, ashamed. He slowly nodded his head, to indicate yes.

Although she watched him, she became mired in her own thoughts, in her own sense of guilt and betrayal. Because Jay had known about Dan's many adulteries, perhaps he had not blamed her wholly. "If you want me to tell Erin, I can't," she said. "Don't mention me, please. This isn't about me. I need to put this behind me, for once and for all. I'm not going to relive back pain, for you, Erin, or anybody."

He looked stunned.

"And I never want to talk about this again. Or God knows what I will do." She started to walk into the parking lot, as if going to her car. She felt she had managed a small victory by salvaging the most she could of the situation. She had balanced her concern for Erin's feelings with Dan's need to tell all. She was tempted to look back at Dan, to make sure he was not following her, but she refrained. *Let him go, she thought. I made my mistakes. My penance is done.* When she did finally look back, Dan had already gone back into the building.

She continued to walk through a row of cars, to the rear of the lot. She felt a shortness of breath. Dan was gone. A significant burden had been lifted from her. She was not the only woman Dan had cheated with, and Jay knew. In giving Dan permission to tell the truth, she eradicated the power the secret had held over her. She began to see how her guilt had prevented her from growing. Why couldn't she, three years ago, simply have accepted it? Instead, she had denied her feelings and, in turn, the possibility of other relationships. It was so clear to her—it was always so clear, but now it seemed incredibly stupid that a rational, sane person could treat herself this way. She applied this same reasoning to her current predicament, that of Bill and Christopher. She had denied feelings for Christopher and ended up sleeping with Bill, a foolhardy choice. This was not something that she could blame on booze or youthful folly. She *did* have feelings for Christopher. She *was* attracted to him. She needn't feel shameful or unsavory. She felt a stab, a scream, of triumph. She looked at her watch. She still had a half hour before Bill would arrive. She had to tell him she couldn't marry him. If he was hurt, then so be it.

She noticed the skin on her hand again. Her other hand had similar wrinkles. This watch was nearly as old as Christopher.

She saw Bill's car at a distance driving along the wide street toward Evergreen's headquarters. It was traveling faster than the rest of traffic. Concerned, she waved to him so that he would see her at the entrance to the lot. The car slowed, but the engine continued to rumble loudly, the hood vibrating. When the car finally stopped, Laney stepped forward. In the passenger seat, looking straight ahead and not at her, sat Christopher.

Thrusting the passenger door open, Christopher burst out of the car. He was wearing a loose-fitting short-sleeve pullover shirt and baggy jeans, underneath which his body was barely discernible. He positioned his head toward the ground, not permitting Laney within his line of vision. A vein on the side on his neck throbbed as it twisted up into his jawbone. He did not lift his eyes as he flung open then closed the rear door. She smiled at him, he would not look. The front passenger door still open, Bill leaned over the seat. His face looked sullen and perturbed. The lines around his eyes—both underneath his eyes and on his temples—seemed strained, creased deeper than before, as if the lines were desperate and wild.

Bill's hands tightly held the gleaming chrome and leather steering wheel as he looked into the rearview mirror at Christopher. "Mind your manners. Say hi to Laney."

Christopher's eyes barely lifted from the back seat in front of him, but she could see that they were red and watery. He had not been crying, but he was angry. "Hello, Miss Secord."

He was being so formal. "Hi," she said, her voice weak and tentative.

Had he gotten into trouble at school? Why was there tension between him and his father? Did his mood have anything to do with her? She had a terrible intuition that he knew about Bill's proposal.

"I didn't think you'd be out so soon," Bill said.

She stepped into the car, checking the stockings on one of her legs for runs. There were none. Not that it mattered: She was free to look as unkempt and disheveled as she liked, but she felt the need to maintain a sense of propriety and decorum.

"Did you get the job?" he asked.

"No," she answered.

"Not enough money?"

"No. Not what I want."

14

When they arrived at her house, she thought of claiming—to avoid having both Bill and Christopher in the house at the same time—that Brian was sick. But he was still at school, and in less than an hour the bus would drop him off and he would be home, surely showing no signs of illness. Instead, he'd probably be excited to have company.

So she asked them, out of courtesy, if they wanted to come inside. During the ride Christopher had been so quiet, edgy and morose, and she and Bill had barely made small talk, that she hadn't expected them to take her up on the offer. But Bill, trying as best he could to pretend that there was nothing wrong, said yes.

He stepped out of the car, while Christopher stayed inside. Before he closed the driver's door, Bill looked at Chris and said, "Are you coming?" His tone was begrudging. His paternal pride had been wounded. She felt he was rounding him up merely to make a good impression on her, his potential new wife, a potential new mother. His scolding grimaces, though, were making her edgy.

What had come between them? Did Christopher know that his father had asked her to marry him? Was he jealous and resentful of his father because she was spending time with him? Or did his tense demeanor—she hoped—have nothing to do with her? Something may have happened at school—an altercation with a fellow student, a poor grade on an exam— something an adolescent would magnify out of proportion and take out on those around him.

As Chris opened the door—he was becoming a Chris again, not a boy but someone she felt comfortable with, like an old college pal—his knees and baggy pants swung to the side, his entire torso bounding through the door in one swift motion. He jerked his head downward so that he would not have to look at her.

She stood near the steps to the sidewalk, not wanting to walk farther. Any more of his sulkiness would be excruciating. She sensed that anger was boiling inside of him, and the only outlet would be the inevitable explosion. Having him return to her house, distressed and disgruntled, with Bill, was shattering the fantasy she had played for herself that they would get to know each other further, that they could sit and laugh, that there would be no tension between them—no yearning—only fulfillment—fulfillment of mind but also of desire.

Bill entered the house first. Chris lingered behind her on the sidewalk. From this angle, he was taller than his father, but more wiry and leanly built. But he did not walk with the certainty of a man. He was gangly, his feet hitting upon the sidewalk and lifting up sharply, as if struck by hot coals. Wanting to reassure him in some way, she gently put a hand on his shoulder for him to follow her down the sidewalk. Instantly, his lean frame stiffened under the pullover. She looked ahead to see whether Bill noticed the reaction, but he had already made his way into the hall and was walking toward the French doors that led to the living room.

Chris continued forth, passing by her. He was not the same boy who had come to her door this past Monday. He was not nervous or shy, or even cockily confident. He was apathetic, like a spoiled child.

"Why don't we go to the kitchen," she said flatly.

Without turning, he made his way from the foyer to the hall. His pants hung over his sneakers, slipping from his waist, but his hips held them. He was emulating the look of rappers he saw on television, but the look didn't fit him. Surely, she thought, he would look better in something more conservative, such as a Ralph Lauren polo shirt, more tailored khaki slacks. What was happening to him? Was he trying to impress that girl at school, adopting a style she favored but one that didn't suit him?

She watched him stride down the hall, taking exaggerated but slow steps. Because he was ignoring her, she felt they were strangers. She stared at his back—the back of his head, his legs—and realized she liked them as much as, if not more, than his eyes, face, and hands. They were alone in the hall, but he would not acknowledge her. Then the thought occurred: perhaps he was having as difficult a time dealing with his feelings for her as she was for him. That was why he became stiff when she placed her hand on his shoulder. Yes, he cared for her, he still "loved" her. A sense of approval filled her, quickening her step.

Bill was still near the living room. She cleared her throat, but Chris would not look. He inadvertently brushed against the ficus tree in the hall, almost pushing the branches out of his way, and her encounter with Bill in the garden, under the green foliage, where the plants got in their way, invaded her. Did he know that they had had sex? No, "a gentleman never tells," and still, he might have learned of it, somehow, or merely suspected it.

Bill drifted back down the hall toward them. "You have such great taste," he said, affectionately putting a hand on her arm. "I should have you help with my house."

Laney felt uncomfortable. Chris's eyes were watching his father's hand. Modestly, she said, "Thank you."

"Did you do all the decorating yourself?" he asked.

She lifted her arm in a subtle gesture so that he was forced to remove his hand. "Mostly. My mother and Erin helped." She opened the kitchen door. "Chris, what would you like?"

He looked confused. His gaze lingered over her chest.

"To drink?" she clarified.

He stammered. "Uh... a Coke, I guess."

"Here, come on." She put a hand on the side of his shoulder, and the tension that had, moments ago, gripped him seemed to dissipate. Something had altered his mood. Then, upon entering the kitchen, she glimpsed on the rosewood console against the wall the solicitation sheet that he had left behind on Monday. She had never returned it. It was folded, and the part with the note about Henry Miller faced upward. It apparently had reassured him to see it.

Chris seemed to flash a quick smile at her—his eyes danced— *Did he smile?*

"You must be disappointed about the job," Bill said, walking toward the center island, Chris right behind him.

"I'm sure there'll be others," she said, proceeding to fetch the drinks. "What would you like?"

"Oh, Coke's fine," he said disinterestedly. "Why don't I finish up in your garden. You have a lot of vegetables that should be ripe now. Especially with the rain last night."

He wanted to be so helpful, helpful to the point of annoyance, but she did not stop him. If he stepped outside, it would give her an opportunity to speak with Chris in private. "Sure," she said. "The lock's a little tricky, remember?"

"Yes, I remember." His tone was suggestive, almost flirtatious, as if he were referring to their interlude in the garden.

Did Chris pick up on his father's flirting? What exactly did he know about his interest in her?

As Bill departed through the sliding doors to the deck, Laney poured two glasses of Coke, one for Bill, one for Chris. She didn't want anything for herself. She set the glasses on the counter while Chris—he seemed completely like a Chris now, a relaxed, all too familiar friend eager to help—watched his dad descend the cedar steps of the deck leading to the backyard. Bill unlatched the wire latch on the makeshift gate to the garden and walked inside. The sun was shining, and Laney knew that he could see only the corner of the kitchen near the deck because of the reflection on the doors.

She was relieved to be alone with Chris. After Bill's proposal, the interview, Dan, she was finally with someone who was happy merely to be in her company.

She walked to the other side of the island, stopping opposite him. He hadn't shaved—he had a patchwork of faint blond whiskers dotting his chin and cheeks. From the spotty, uneven growth of hair, it looked as though he shaved only once a week. Christ, he was beautiful. The moment she had seen his razor in the bathroom returned, and she wished she had touched the razor then, run her fingers over it. Now, she could hand it to him or drag it, herself, across his face. She would drape the towel around his neck and pull him, wet and foamy, into her.

"You're not going to marry him, are you?" he said, his voice aquiver as if he was afraid both of the possibility that she might and of the words he was uttering.

He knew about the proposal. Why had Bill told him—and why hadn't he told her that he had?

"Why does he think you like him?" he continued. "You don't, do you?"

"Of course I *like* him," she said defensively, emphasizing the neutrality of the word 'like.'

"You wouldn't sleep with him, would you?"

So he didn't know about the encounter in the garden.

"You can't marry him," he continued, his voice ringing louder, becoming stronger, fiercer in edge. His feet tapped as if he were a boxer readying to fight.

No, only the prospect of her marrying his father terrified him. Still, her guilt over having had sex with Bill prevented her from answering.

He stepped around to her side of the island, the fabric of his pants crunching upon itself. With an excited look in his eyes, he placed his hands on her arms. "I want you," he said.

He towered over her, by several inches. He was taller than Jay, so much so that she felt she was not in the presence of a boy but a man. He leaned down to kiss her, but she pulled back. "What?" he said.

"Your father's outside."

"You don't want *him*, do you?" He briskly straddled his legs apart and stretched them around her, so that she stood between them, ensconced in the bunched fabric of his pants and his loosely laced high tops. "You're too good for him."

He reached into his pocket, digging deep down so that his hand almost reached his knees. What was he doing? Then, he took out a roll of Lifesavers, putting his thumb behind a candy, to offer her one. She shook her head. He proceeded to pop a candy into his mouth.

She began to feel slightly giddy. With boy-man elan, he was charming her, and she sensed that the wall between them—their difference in years and maturity—was slowly crumbling. But with Bill outside, she could not allow herself to succumb to his advances. "I'm not going to marry him," she said.

"No, you're not going to marry him," he repeated, his eyes still, as if hypnotizing her.

She looked out the sliding glass doors. Bill was not in sight. Chris's eyes roamed over her face—stepping from her eyes to her cheek to her mouth in a sort of dance.

She clenched her throat, swallowing. Then she leaned forward, closing her eyes, and kissed him. His nose jutted against hers—she tilted her head, but he grabbed her, mashing his face into hers, thrusting his tongue into her mouth, grabbing her by her waist, pulling her into him, forcing his pelvis against hers. She could taste the cherry lifesaver on his tongue, and she swirled her tongue against his, taking the candy from him.

As he pressed against the small of her back, he glided a hand, twitching and clammy, behind her legs up her skirt. She absently swallowed the Lifesaver. Feeling herself becoming not moist, not damp, but nearly gushing, she opened her eyes, and over his shoulder she watched the deck, the stairs leading down below, the edge of the garden. Bill was standing by the gate, putting vegetables on the ground. She pulled away from him, but he held her.

"He's outside," she said.

His belt buckle pressed against her stomach while his hands undressed her. No, this was not the first time he had been with a girl. She detected he was looking at Bill. Her body pulled back.

"We can't do this," she pleaded.

He brazenly lifted his shirt, holding it up by his chin, watching his father, exposing the waistband and corralled fabric of his boxer shorts. Her eyes fell upon the snap of his jeans and, underneath the scrunched denim, what looked like a small erection.

Bill was walking away. Her line of vision became obscured. Did he go back into the garden or was he walking toward the deck?

"He's coming back," she said, frenzied.

He stepped forward, unzipping and unsnapping his jeans.

Her eyes were on the steps of the deck outside. She shook her head. Tears were forming. His jeans and belt fell to the floor. He bent to slip down his boxers. When he stood up straight, she was besieged by his large penis, pointing at her, pressing her, throbbing against the top of her thigh. She could not move. Her eyes quickly averted, and she saw in Chris not the slightest pride or bemusement, but a self-conscious, almost embarrassed expression.

Bill was back in the garden. Christopher drew her toward him, with little finesse, lifting her skirt and positioning his legs between hers. He had a thick thatch of pubic hair, but he was so smooth everywhere else. He tried to enter her, clumsily. But he persisted, using only enough pressure so that she would receive him. As she held onto his sides, feeling the tautness of his flesh, she could feel herself rising on her tiptoes. Sensing her resistance, he put his hands around her waist and rollicked her from side to side. He carried her to the counter nearest to the window, laid her against the counter while he fumbled with the buttons of her blouse and her bra. He began to fondle, to kiss, almost seeming to nurse from her breasts.

He looked outside, straining to locate his father. "Where the hell is he?" he asked.

She became frantic. As he continued to push up into her, withdrawing and re-entering, arching his back and twisting his hips, she could feel herself expanding and contracting, pulsing and pushing and squeezing. "We have to stop," she said, but he craned her head. She tried to turn away, but he wouldn't allow her to. He was forcing her to look out the window.

"Look at him," he said. He pushed her head, holding his hand against the side of her face, forcing her to stare at Bill.

Watching right alongside her, his cheek against hers, he thrust at her, harder and faster, and her thighs were slapping against the counter, and she had to grab the edges of the countertop, so she wouldn't fall completely into him. Soon she could feel herself splitting in two, becoming wet. Uncontrollably her juices oozed over his cock, down her legs, into her stockings. She was coming, she couldn't stop, and he wouldn't stop, pushing his way into her, clamping onto her wrist, against her dress watch, pressing his cheek against hers as he made her watch Bill in the garden.

As she gave up pushing against his head, Chris looked away from the window and stopped fucking her. He moaned "Fuck him!" and grunted, his hot cum spilling from her. When she looked behind him, Brian was standing in the doorway to the kitchen with his hand over his mouth. All the pleasure she had experienced instantly vanished. She had completely lost track of time, forgetting that he was due home from school. She tried to turn Chris's head, but he wouldn't look. He was still looking outside, at his father. She pulled his head toward her, and he leaned in to kiss her on the lips, but she pressed a hand on his shoulder. "No," she said.

He turned, saw Brian, and hastily pulled up his jeans. "Oh, shit," he said.

She straightened her skirt, hastily buttoning her blouse, leaving her brassiere unhitched. "Honey, I didn't hear you come in."

His eyes were bulging. "Mom, are you okay?"

"I'm fine." She went to the doorway, wiping the perspiration from her face. Her makeup was running. "Let's go get washed." She led him to the hall.

"What were you and Christopher doing?" he asked.

"Nothing. We were just pretending."

She led him to the powder room, standing him on the stool so he could reach the vanity. She turned on the faucet and slipped the bar of soap over his hands, between his fingers and against his nails.

"My hands aren't dirty," he cried.

She continued to wash his hands and her own, thoroughly. Observing her face in the mirror, she saw that her lipstick had smeared her cheek. She was wearing too much mascara—why hadn't she noticed this before her interview? *No wonder they didn't hire me.* Or maybe the fluorescent light in the room was accentuating everything. Her hair looked fine. Her eyes looked greener. Chris loves me, she thought. The water continued to run. Her unhitched brassiere was barely noticeable underneath her cream blouse.

"My hands are clean, Mom."

She took her hands off his and said, "Wash your face now. We have company. You need to look clean."

He leaned down and splashed water over his face. She felt water dampen her skirt. At the same time, she felt a trickle down her thigh. Was it from Christopher or herself? She wanted to touch underneath her skirt to check. Brian raised his head, forcing a wide smile and squinting. "How do I look?"

"Fine," she said. "Dry up."

Blindly, he reached for the towel on the wall rack. While he dried his face, she wiped the smudge of her lipstick and moved her hands about her hair, to fix it. She took the towel from Brian and dried her hands. "Go say hi to Chris now. His father's here, so behave."

He started out of the bathroom, but she held him, taking his knapsack. He had had it on his back all this time.

"Don't mention you saw us playing, okay?"

***

Bill was already sipping his Coke at the breakfast table when Laney and Brian returned to the kitchen. Chris was standing by the sliding glass doors looking at the back yard. A handful of vegetables was scattered in the middle of the table. Holding Brian in front of her, she searched Bill's eyes for clues that he might know that she and Chris had just fucked. Her hands were clammy and her heart thumping. A part of her wanted Bill to know the truth: *I just slept with your son. Forgive me, but it was right.*

Chris turned from the window. His face looked relaxed, refreshed somehow, his cheeks ruddied, as if he too had washed. There was a calmness about him, a contagious serenity in his eyes that made her wish that she could have lain with him on her bed, stroked her fingers against his cheeks and hair, and clutched her pelvis against his.

"I was just telling my dad how much fun we had in here," Chris said, narrowing his eyes.

Was he being flippant or could he really have told him?

"But my dad said it couldn't compare to picking tomatoes," he continued. "He thinks gardening is better than sex."

Sex: Was he out of his mind? Did he want them to get caught?

"What's gotten into you?" Bill said.

"Into *me*? Maybe it was all the head on that Coke. You should ask Laney."

He *was* pushing her. But he wouldn't actually come out and say that he and Laney had just fucked. He was playing a game. Such a boy—he needed attention.

"Children," she said, giving Chris a frosty stare. She checked for his reaction—he had caught her insult, she was pleased. "Speaking of children," she continued, "Bill, this is my son Brian. Brian, say hello to Mr. Hendrickson."

Brian barely stepped forward—she lightly pushed him— while Bill rose from the table.

Bill walked toward Brian, who still hesitated. When Bill stood in front of him, Brian stuck out his hand for him to shake, but it was as if he were saying, "Don't come any closer."

Bill bent down and took it. "You're such a big boy," he said. "And so handsome, too."

She watched Brian cower: He was always afraid of men. They intimidated him, and everywhere but the Cub Scouts he sought out the protection of women.

"I bet you take after your father," Bill said, continuing to shake his hand.

"Yes, see." Brian ran away from him, to the counter by the phone and pointed to the picture of Jay hiking in the mountains.

Bill walked over to him. Chris followed, intrigued by the picture of Jay, dancing his brows up and down at Laney.

Would he stop!

Brian slinked against the counter, until he was cornered.

"Yes, you do look just like him," Bill said. "One day you're going to be just as big and handsome as him."

Brian looked at Bill circumspectly. "No, bigger."

Chris chuckled.

Brian turned, shoving the picture of Jay into Chris.

Chris crouched down.

Did he do that on purpose?

"Brian, that's not nice," she said.

"I guess everyone wants to get in on the act," Chris said, winking.

Brian started to move away, but Bill grabbed under his arms and said, "Do you know how to fly?"

Brian looked perplexed.

"Put your arms out."

Brian did as he was told, and Bill proceeded to carry him horizontally around the kitchen, dipping him down and racing him along the countertops while making the sound of an airplane. Finally, he set him atop the breakfast table. Brian, excited, swung his legs back and forth.

Laney glanced at Chris. He had already placed the picture back on the counter, and his eyes were sweeping over her, twinkling.

Bill seemed unable to detect anything unusual about the way she and Chris were acting. Perhaps he was thinking what a beautiful home this would make, his future with Laney. But Brian, who watched them silently but closely, seemed to notice the calmness between them. Perhaps he sensed the closeness, the lust, they felt towards each other.

While Brian continued to swing his legs, still pretending to fly, Chris stepped over to the breakfast table and leaned against its corner, tapping a hand on Brian's leg. Brian kicked his leg out, then pulled it back, then kicked it out again.

Bill finished his Coke, watching Brian and Chris. What fine brothers they would make, his face suggested.

The more she looked at Bill, the more he appeared a stranger. His cowboy boots had dirt over their tips, and his body did not compare to Chris's bulgingly lean frame. "Bill," she said, "thanks for all your help today. We'll have to have dinner sometime." She hoped he realized that she was not inviting him over tonight.

"Tomorrow," he said, "right?"

She had forgotten about Erin's soiree. She hadn't yet asked Erin whether she could bring a guest, but she said, almost out of pity, "yes, of course."

Standing from the table, Bill appeared contented. Chris put his fist on Brian's nose and playfully twisted it. Brian squirmed.

"Say Uncle, say Uncle," Chris said.

How easily they were bonding. She could never imagine playing with Brian in this way. There was such intuitive understanding—of each other's limits, of each other's strengths—such camaraderie, such maleness—she was envious.

"Uncle!" Brian finally said, in anguish.

He released his grip, messed up Brian's hair, and said, "That's what you get for knocking my nuts. See you later, handsome."

As Chris stood, Brian kicked him in the buttocks. "Brian!" Laney said.

A smile seemed to be forming on Brian's lips, but he looked away.

"That's okay," Chris said. "I deserved it."

"You sure did," his father added.

Yes, he did, Laney thought, but what did Bill mean? Was he referring to his behavior in the car?

As Chris waded forward in his loose pants, Bill followed, several steps behind, saying goodbye first to Brian then to Laney. "Would you say thank you?" Bill said to Chris.

"Why yes. Thank you, Miss Secord," Chris said, with an enigmatic smile, his eyes squinting. He stepped toward the doorway.

"Would you mind if I have a kiss?" Bill softly asked her.

She half-shrugged. "My son," she whispered. "I don't think it's appropriate."

"Of course." He grazed a finger over her arm and headed toward the doorway.

Chris was watching his father's hand, his gaze imperturbable as stone, looking at it as if it still lay on Laney's.

After they left, she sent Brian, his arms stretched out like the wings of an airplane, upstairs, then returned to the kitchen and finished off Chris's Coke.

15

All through dinner Laney couldn't eradicate the image of Christopher making love to her while Brian stood at the door to the kitchen, watching. They should have heard him, but they had had no regard for anybody else.

Brian ate as he normally did, focusing on his chicken breast and mashed potatoes while saving his vegetable, his favorite, for last. She thought about bringing up what he had seen, but hoped instead that he would forget about the incident.

He was quiet as usual, but had a less worrisome expression than in months past. For her part, Laney was invigorated, but also perplexed. Her body was less constricted. There was an ease and fluidity about her, a nonchalance that permeated her as she held her fork, gracefully ate her dinner. Yet the strong sensations also left her disoriented. Such strange thoughts these were of being satisfied, being loved unconditionally. The experience with Chris was like a dream ending abruptly. She relived the moments in the kitchen with Chris, extending them so that they replayed harder and faster than in real life, with more imagined possibilities. She had touched his small, dark nipples, licked them, and she had taken hold of his penis, and sucked it. But she also began to conspire against herself. How could she have been so foolish to have made love to him after having had sex with his father? As she wrestled with what she had done, the possibilities she had envisioned for herself— the beginning of unbridled promise and beauty and limit-free happiness—revealed themselves as mere fantasies. If she had viewed Chris as a panacea, her depression, mild and numbing, was immune.

In the upstairs bathroom adjacent to Brian's bedroom, after Brian had finished soaking, Laney helped dry him, wiping a long beige towel over his arms and legs. He stood beside the tub, which was filled with bath water. A layer of grime coated the tub above water level. She reached a hand into the tepid water, and the rubber duck swam away from her arm. She pulled the stopper, leaving her hand near the drain. Water warmed her fingers as it made its way downward. She was losing track of where she was. She kept her arm still, enjoying the sensation. With her other hand, she dried Brian's back. The band of gray grime grew wider and murkier against the porcelain tub. As the water level lowered, a circle of suds pooled around her arm, soothing her, caressing her. She pressed her breasts against the side of the tub. She could feel Chris's hands on them. She forced him inside her, again.

She looked at Brian. The towel was spooled around his feet. He stood, naked, waiting. She pulled her hand out of the water, reaching for his underwear and pajamas that were lying atop the closed toilet lid. She slung the pajamas over her wet arm, and watched him lift his foot to step into his underwear. As she saw his naked body, not fully formed, but growing, her mind was catapulted back three years ago, when he was barely a toddler. She had been giving him his bath, and after a minute or two, he suddenly had an erection. At first she was startled, but then she started to encourage it, stimulating him for a couple of minutes. How the expression on his face turned to glee, and with every touch of her hand, every stroke, his pleasure was magnified, and she felt, because no one was watching, because no one had the opportunity to misunderstand, this small secret between mother and son reinforced that she was the best possible mother her son could want.

"Mom," Brian said, disrupting her fond reverie, "did Christopher hurt you this afternoon?"

So he had seen Chris grabbing and holding her. Naturally, he was curious, but he was also too young to know about sex. "No, it was nothing," she said. "Let's go to bed."

"Is that how babies are born?" he asked.

She had to be careful because he might tell a schoolmate or teacher what he had seen. "No, babies are born to a mother and father. And Chris is just a boy."

"But you could have a baby with his father, right?"

Her stomach twisted. Her fear about becoming pregnant by Bill returned. Yet, she had no fear of being pregnant by Chris. "No, two people have to be in love."

"Chris doesn't love you?" he said, calling him 'Chris' too, and not 'Christopher', as if he could read her most intimate thoughts and desires. "He said he did the other night."

She hadn't convinced him he had 'misunderstood' what he had heard. Perhaps she wouldn't be able to be either. "I'm afraid we're just friends."

Brian was not as tired as he should be, and she didn't want to read him a bedtime story for fear it would stir his imagination and keep him awake. So she tucked him in tight and kissed him goodnight.

Her mind was racing. She didn't want the day to end. Telling Brian what had happened in the kitchen was nothing had an unintended effect. The statement was not true, but the words, spoken, showed how easily she could dismiss the event. To a six year old, it didn't seem important. She could possibly convince herself too. She repeated to herself, It was nothing, It was nothing. She didn't get the job at Evergreen. She didn't have to feel guilty about having had sex with Chris. He was old enough to know what he wanted.

She walked about the house desultorily. Random items registered: the wall clock, the time an hour off; a crystal vase, empty; a floorboard that creaked. This was not her house. It was really Jay's, despite the decorations.

She ended up in the living room, fluffing the pillows on the sofa although they looked fine. For so long, she was determined that this spot, where she and Dan had lain, be pristine. She was like a criminal revisiting the scene of her crime, ostensibly searching for anything—loose change, lint from Dan's clothes.

This week's newspapers, the Denver *Post*, were stacked on the coffee table, and she scanned through them, wanting to learn more about the woman teacher who had had an affair with one of her students. The front pages she scanned, the Metro section, column after column, but there were no articles about her. She had been arrested. End of story.

She stared so hard at the newspapers that the page before her became a blur. Could what have happened between them ever be repeated? No, she and Chris would have to conceal their involvement from everybody, and there was no conceivable way that their relationship could survive hiding and pretending. And there would always be the issue of Bill.

She went to the kitchen to toss away the papers, but she couldn't take her eyes off the counter where she and Chris had made love. Placing the papers on the countertop, she traced her finger over the cool granite. She could still feel it against her thighs. She sat on the counter, and her legs rocked back and forth against it, with Chris's body. She looked about the room, and though it was beautiful, it seemed empty. She was not merely lonely but alone. She felt a gaping void. She had tried, through Chris, through Bill, to deny the existence of this void, but now it enveloped her like a gigantic, amorphous blanket that smothered her and from which she could not find issue. She fell against the counter and wrapped her arms about her, her limbs shaking. She had managed to experience sex and at best a fleeting love.

She pulled herself from the counter, stood straight, and said, Stop. Nothing that she had done should have caused this sorrow.

At 8:30 PM, as she lay, fully dressed, in bed, awake and alert as ever, she received a telephone call from Erin. Immediately, her heart started palpitating: Could Dan have told her that they had had an affair? Did Erin want to scream at her and tell her they could not be friends anymore?

"Laney, Dan told me..."

Her heart thumped, and she could not breathe...

"... about the interview. I know you're upset."

"I'm fine."

"I've invited Dan's boss, Eric Reditt, to dinner tomorrow. This way, you can meet him in person and seal the deal."

Laney started to undress, slipping off her socks. "The job doesn't seem right to me."

"There's not a lot happening in Plainview. You have to take what you can get."

"I need to go back into social work."

"Who's going to hire you?"

The innocuous-sounding comment stung like a harsh slap. How friends can sometimes stand in your way, virtually hoping that you don't succeed.

Erin caught herself: "I didn't mean that."

But she knew she did. "That's okay," she said, not feeling she deserved the insult but not wanting, not needing, Erin's approval either. "There was something I wanted to ask you. Do you mind if I bring a friend tomorrow?" As conflicted as she felt about her relationship with Bill, having him beside her would shield her from a potential set up with the CPA Erin was inviting.

Erin hesitated for a moment, and Laney could tell that she had caught her off guard. "You mind if I ask who?"

"Bill Hendrickson."

Erin's voice took on a foreboding tone. "I don't think you should get involved with him."

"Why not?"

Erin spoke haltingly: "He tried to kill his wife."

Laney stopped undressing. Erin had to be confused.

She continued: "He and his wife were going through a messy divorce. They're both drinkers, and they were fighting over money and custody of the boy.

"His wife went after the boy, whether she tried to kill him, I don't know. The father tried to stop her, strangling her, but the son stopped him. Both of the parents were arrested. All the charges were eventually dropped, but they were more or less forced to leave town."

Laney was shocked. Bill hadn't alluded to any of this. Now, he was pressing her to marry him.

"His wife was in the hospital for over four days. The boy

was put in foster care for two months. His father got him back because the boy said his mother was abusing him."

Two months in foster care? Chris had been abused? Sexually? The memory of when she had stimulated Brian—that one time—returned, forcefully. Intense guilt—regret—washed over her. It hadn't been right to touch her son that way, and it hadn't been right to have sex with Chris. What if Chris had been molested—Was that the only reason he was interested in her, as some sort of substitute for his mother? Was she as guilty as his mom? She had inserted herself in the middle of a turgid affair.

"I feel sorry for their son," Erin said. "He's so cute, you know."

"Are you sure about all of this?" Laney asked.

"It comes straight from the Chief of Police in Beckle's Ridge."

Laney needed to hear the story straight from Bill before she could rely on it, before she could be certain whether any— or all—of it was true. Going to Erin's might give her the opportunity to speak with him in a protected environment, to deal with his proposal. "I'd still like to bring him, if that's okay."

"He could hurt you."

She couldn't tell Erin she had already had sex with him and that he wanted to marry her. She would think her absolutely... *different*. "I have to make my own choices."

"Goodnight," Erin said, hanging up.

Laney didn't want to make sense of the situation. She didn't want answers or explanations, but still, she had unrelenting questions: Had Christopher simply made up the story of abuse in order to return to his father? Why had Bill lied about where his ex-wife lived: Denver or "far away"? Couldn't his lies at least be consistent?

She had done this to herself. She had known about some of their family problems. If Bill really had tried to kill his wife, that was not the man she knew.

'Christopher', she said to herself. In hearing the gossip about his past, in distancing herself from the Hendricksons in her mind, she found herself calling him, thinking of him, as 'Christopher' again, some local Eagle Scout, some area student whose name might be mentioned in the *Gazette* for Honor Roll or as an up-and-coming soccer star. It was better, safer, to view him as Christopher, someone with whom she was not overly familiar. There might be repercussions otherwise.

Somehow, she had to restore the status quo between her, Bill, and Christopher. But how to deconstruct a triangle without destroying its shape, its essence? She did not want, and could never, take the place of Christopher's mother. She had manipulated his father to be with him. The triangle needed to be destroyed.

She pulled the sheet up to her chin and stretched it about her neck. She had thought Bill was a caring man, a gentle soul. Yet her eyes remained open. What would he do if he discovered she had seduced his son?

16

On Saturday morning, Laney awoke at 6:30 AM with an urgent awareness that she had so much to do: bring Brian to the Scouts gathering, deal with her car, prepare for dinner at Erin's this evening. The day was going to be a whirlwind. Rarely had she had so much activity planned. She felt a mild sense of dread, especially concerning the dinner and her car, but she was determined to move through her errands.

She headed to the home office, where she wrote, in florid penmanship, a brief thank you note to Julie Crowley. The interview might have been perfunctory and Julie Crowley a bitch, but she was not going to compromise her innate civility. Kill her with kindness, Laney thought. What did it matter that she was not going to get, and did not want, the job?

She called Hank's Garage, and they informed her car would be ready this morning.

She went about the house, doing a light dusting so that Meg, Erin's sister, who would see the house tonight for the first time when she came to babysit, would not think Laney was a lazy housekeeper. She stopped at the sliding glass doors to the deck to look at the garden: *Bill could not have seen anything.* But had Christopher wanted him to, to outmaneuver his dad out of jealousy? Maybe he wasn't as naive as she had thought.

At 7:30 she woke Brian and dressed him in his Scout uniform. As he ate breakfast, she took out the phone book and found the number for Plainview Town Cab. She dialed, but the line rang and rang. She redialed, but there was no answer. Could they not be open now? She looked at the ad in the yellow pages: 24-hour airport service, it said. She hung up the receiver, perplexed.

"What's the matter?" Brian asked.

"Nothing. I'll be ready soon."

Brian had to be at Plainview Elementary by 8:30. He could not miss the meeting because he had to finish his project for tomorrow, Mother's Day. She could call Bill again, and though it was early, he would surely help. But she didn't want to. He would interpret her request as even greater interest in him. She could call Erin, who was most likely up at this hour, but she didn't want to disturb her the day of her dinner party. The last thing she needed was a friend asking for a favor.

Not having a car, she felt stranded, at the mercy of others. Maybe Town Cab would open at eight. That would leave just enough time for a cab to arrive at her house and make the short trip to the school.

At eight o'clock she called again. Still, no answer. She became nervous. Brian was waiting impatiently. "We have to be there at eight thirty," he said.

"We have time."

"Why are you so nervous then?"

"I'm not," she lied.

He seemed aware that she was lying, and, from the wisp of a smile that danced across his lips, pleased.

"You better watch out," he said, his voice becoming so quiet she had to make an effort to hear him—"or I'll step on a crack—" He pushed his foot on the seat of the chair and he landed harshly on the tile floor, "and I'll break your back. In two thousand little pieces." He swished his shoes on the floor, as if crushing bits of glass.

What had gotten into him? "Brian, that's not nice. Is that what they're teaching you at school?"

He nodded, smiling.

"I'll keep you home if you don't apologize."

He turned and stared out the window, to the backyard, at the garden, craning his neck. It was as if he had seen Christopher strain to see his father. "I'm sorry," he said perfunctorily, his voice devoid of emotion.

Who was this boy in front of her? Was he hers? Did he really love her?

She returned to the phone, hit re-dial, and "Town Cab" answered. The dispatcher must have come in late. Laney ordered a cab, asked whether it could come right away, and at 8:25, with scant minutes to spare, the taxi arrived.

The cab driver was a fellow in his early thirties, about Laney's age, but roughened, with a multitude of tattoos covering his arms. It was hard to tell what any of them were because the colors had faded and bled into one another. When she sat in the front passenger seat, the heavy, stale scent of cigarettes assaulted her, almost causing her to gag. The driver asked if he could smoke, and she was going to say, "Are you crazy?" but instead she said, "No. My son's allergic. Asthma." She told him she was in a hurry and the cabbie took a shortcut he knew, though he drove at a leisurely pace, despite Laney's looking repeatedly at her watch. She would have preferred that he had taken her normal route. She hoped the Scouts van wouldn't leave without Brian.

To her relief, they arrived at the school only seven minutes late. Dozens of children and parents were still swarming about the van.

She asked the cab driver to wait in order to give her a ride to the auto repair shop afterwards. As he lit a smoke, she led Brian to the Scouts van with his Mother's Day project, concealed in a large shopping bag. Other parents were milling about the doorway.

As she knelt before him, straightening the scarf around his neck, reminding him to behave, he looked over her shoulder, down the parking lot.

She turned, seeing Chris standing several feet away, on the sidewalk. He looked like a 'Chris' again, in his Eagle Scout uniform with all the patches.

Of course, he would be accompanying the boys on the outing. She should have realized he would be here.

He didn't look himself. His hair was tousled and unstyled, suggesting he had been awake all night or that he was depressed for some reason—Did his glum appearance have anything to do with what had happened in the kitchen? Or perhaps the knowledge of Bill's proposal continued to weigh on him.

He did not move closer when he saw her but remained on the sidewalk. Brian waved hello to him, Laney smiled, but he continued to stand still.

Finally, he gave a small wave back, looking only at Brian and avoiding Laney's eyes.

She finished adjusting Brian's scarf. "Honey, let's get you to the van. It's time to go."

He continued to look past her, at Chris, his body inching toward him slowly but steadily.

"I want to go say hi to Christopher," he said.

"Come on. You'll see him later."

"Why can't I? He's my friend."

"He's busy."

"He's my *only* friend."

He picked a fine time to feel sorry for himself. "We'll talk about this later," she said.

"That's what you always say."

When had she said that before? Did seeing Chris affect him just as strongly as he affected her? Or had seeing him make love to her in the kitchen caused him to view him differently?

She would have to find time later to discuss how he felt. "You have to get going," she said. "I promise we'll talk later." She kissed him on the cheek, nudging him forward.

"Two thousand little pieces," she thought she heard him mumble as he slowly ambled off with his project onto the van. What a bizarre child she was raising.

Chris had his back to her while he was speaking to another mother and a boy. Laney sauntered nearer, aware of everybody around her, conscious of whether they were looking at her or Chris. Here she was, in public view, at a school. She had a dim sense of herself as the female teacher in the newspaper article. But she had to say hello. He would want to also. The crowd might conceal them.

When she reached him, he briefly turned his head, and the quick turn of his eyes confirmed that he was anxious. She watched as the pair said goodbye and the boy walked away toward the van. After the mother departed, Chris did not look at Laney but kept his head down.

She stepped forward. "Hello. How are you?"

His head tilted up and around. His cheeks were sunken. Black circles had formed under his eyes. His cheeks were blotchy, seeming on the verge of breaking out. How—unattractive... he could become.

He stepped back from her, as if she had infringed on his space. Although only a half day had elapsed since they had last seen each other, since they had been intimate, he had turned distant. A part-vacant, part-disparaging gaze overtook his eyes. He was such a strong leader to all the young boys, reassuring and calming before them, yet before her tentative, nervous, on edge.

"My father said he fucked you," he said, his voice quavering. "Did you?"

'Fuck': that word sounded so harsh coming from him, so incongruous with his boyish uniform, his sweet face. How could Bill have mentioned anything to him? He had promised he wouldn't.

"Did you?" he repeated even more harshly.

How could he ask this with all these people around? What if someone overheard him?

"You're not answering!" he shouted.

What could she say? Yes, your father and I 'fucked'. She began to tremble, her throat tensed, choking any words that might come. His eyes were burning, becoming fiercer. He knew.

She stepped back, cowering, as if he had struck a blow. Her mouth became dry, and she breathed in short, irregular spurts. Everybody was watching them. A strong gust of wind rushed over them, tousling her hair, his shirt, nearly tackling her. But he stood impervious. He wanted an answer—the truth—but to give it would be like singeing an open wound. She could barely ask a question: "Did you tell your father what happened between us?"

"I *need* to know." His forehead, his eyes steamed. "Did you fuckin' *fuck* my father?"

How could she explain that she had betrayed him? She couldn't act as if she did. She lowered her voice. "Calm down."

"Did you?"

She stammered— "Uh-hhh..."

"Can't you just answer yes or no? Why are you doing this to me?"

"I didn't..." ... do this to you, she meant, but he interrupted—

"You didn't?"

Was he suggesting that he didn't believe she and Bill had fucked? Was it only what he wanted to believe? The blaze in his eyes was that of a challenge: I challenge you to be truthful. But no matter what she said, he would be able to see the truth.

"Did you?" he demanded, his voice strained. He put his hands on her arms. His grip was tight, becoming even tighter. The vein on the side of his temple convulsed. She pulled back. "When?" he shouted.

"This is all a misunderstanding."

"Letting someone stick his dick in you is a misunderstanding? What are you? The fucking town whore?"

His language made her cringe, decimating her ability to piece together her thoughts. Had she really been so reckless? Would no one have respect for her again? She wanted to hide. Brian was watching them from window of the van. His face pressed against the glass, as if to prompt her: "What now?"

The reflection of the sun on the window made it seem like he was sticking his tongue out at her. Insulted, incensed, hurt, she turned back to Chris—

"Don't speak to me like that," she said, her tone firm, unequivocal.

"Don't you fuck around with me, you bitch!" he said, nearly spitting at her.

His language, his behavior, repulsed her. And his uniform, so neatly pressed, so perfect, so impugnable with its cute badges and small collar—something only a child would wear—she wanted to tear apart. She was not going to allow a *boy* to humiliate her, to dictate how she should feel: "What the hell makes you think such a thing?"

He stammered... "My dad said..."

"What kind of filthy woman do think I am?" she interrupted.

"I don't think you're filthy," he said quietly.

"Then why would you accuse me of going to bed with every man—or *boy*," she said, loudly emphasizing this word, "—around?"

"I'm sorry, I..."

"I'm a mother, and you're just a *Boy* Scout. You should know better."

Sweat trickled down his temples. "At dinner last night, my dad said you went into the garden with him."

"We did. So what?"

"He said he kissed you."

"He did. So?"

"So?" he answered incredulously.

"It was a kiss. Big deal. You have a girlfriend—a girl *your* age. You've kissed her, haven't you? Or haven't you graduated to that level?"

"We're not talking about her. Why wouldn't my father tell me what happened? He would only say, 'A gentleman never tells'. He would only say that if..."

"If what?"

"If you screwed him."

"*Screwed* him. Don't be such a boy. Maybe he doesn't want to talk about these things with you because you're a *boy*."

"I'm not!" he shouted, stomping his foot.

"Then prove it."

"I proved it in the kitchen, didn't I?" he scoffed.

"I don't know what you think you proved." She took a breath, and her stiff frame, her neck, her shoulders, became limber. Her hands, which had been shaking, were still. "Let me make this clear. I won't be spoken to as if I'm just anybody, anymore. Not by you or anyone else." Her eyes bore into his with an icy expression of disgust and revulsion. Her hostile stare had her desired effect: Stupefied, he couldn't speak, and his eyes misted over. All his confident posturing was crushed, routed, and he had nothing to rely on except the distasteful fact that in her eyes he was just a boy.

The Scout headmaster advanced on the sidewalk toward them. He was a lanky gentleman in his forties with a military-style buzzcut, a rigid stride, a neo-Nazi air that made her recoil.

A lump lodged in her throat. Would Chris tell him that they were lovers—out of rebellion, spite, anger?

"Chris," the scoutmaster said, "We're all ready. Is something the matter?"

"No," he said, shrinking down into the sidewalk.

She had won. She had crushed his attack and preserved her self-respect. But she couldn't completely relinquish her doubts about what she had done, about what he might do.

The scoutmaster's gaze was steady and hard. He would not smile. It was as if he detected the tension between her and Chris.

"Thank you for all the help you've given my son, Brian," she said, eager to leave.

"He's a great boy," he answered.

"Good luck on your outing. I'll see you this afternoon."

Chris shook his head, as if he couldn't believe she was walking away. His hand reached forward—she glanced at it quickly, and the scoutmaster's eyes darted from Chris's hand to Laney's, which was slung freely but which also rose toward Chris's.

She lifted her hand, putting it about her hair, as if to primp, as if to itch her temple. She turned and walked toward the cab, not turning back. If she looked back at him, he might put her hand on her shoulder, tell her that he was sorry, that he loved her, that they needed to be together.

When she reached the cab, she turned around. Everybody was watching her. They gazed at her with puzzled, disapproving faces, as if she were that teacher in the newspaper article, but she stood proud, looking back, unmoved.

Chris meandered around the van with the scoutmaster, who was helping a boy inside. He glared at her, pointing to his watch. He raised his index finger.

What did he mean? Was it a warning of some sort? An insult? The other parents mingled, talking to one another, waving to their children on the bus. Ignored, isolated, she felt her brief sense of power slowly creep away, like a ball that a child chases but inadvertently keeps kicking farther from her grasp.

The scoutmaster looked at her, catching her staring at Chris. She turned away.

Chris had pointed to his watch. Did he mean one o'clock? If so, why?

17

The cab driver pulled out of the school parking lot. "I was at your house a few years ago. I used to drive limos for the Plainview Funeral Home. I drove you, your son, and your family from the cemetery back to your house."

She hadn't remembered him, but as she recalled the limousine ride home after Jay's burial, her expression became sorrowful.

"I'm sorry. I shouldn't have brought it up."

"It was my husband's funeral."

"I'm very sorry," he repeated. "How old is your son?"

"Seven." He was obviously trying to make small talk, but she kept thinking about Chris. Did he want to meet her, at one o'clock? Should she make plans to be home at that time? Or should she go to the school instead? But how would he be able to abandon his troop?

"It must be hard leaving him," the cab driver said.

"Oh?" He means Brian, not Chris. "Yes, you would think it would get easier as he becomes older, but it hasn't."

"I don't have any kids of my own yet, so I couldn't help you with that."

Help her, he had said. Could this stranger, who might be an outsider to Plainview, with his tattoos, his earrings, possibly understand her situation? *Someone* had to be sympathetic.

"It must be difficult finding somebody to shoulder the responsibility of a child," he said.

How did he know she was single? What was he hinting at? Was he interested in her? Had he watched her and Chris? She had to deflect suspicion. "Many divorced men have children of their own nowadays."

"I can't see you with someone older."

Why was he saying that—because she had acted familiarly with Chris? Or was he flirting with her? She had to be careful. The details of their conversation might come up later, and he could be integral in painting a portrait of her as some sort of predator. "My husband was older," she said, lying.

"Men are always dating younger women, sometimes as young as sixteen or seventeen," he said, his brow arcing, the piercing rising with it.

Was he guessing at Chris's age? How this might—and would—come back to haunt her. "I'm sure that doesn't happen in Plainview."

"You never know."

Was he setting a trap for her, or was she imagining, succumbing to paranoia?

"Of course. Of course."

We did he mean? Why did he say that twice?

"Of course."

Then a third time! She couldn't appear anxious. "I don't think I'll ever be in that situation."

"You don't think or you know?"

He *was* grilling her. "No, I know."

He smiled at her: such an odd, self-satisfied expression, as if he could read her thoughts, as if he were about to again say, 'Of course.'

He fished out a cigarette from the packet on the dashboard and offered it to her. She declined. She squirmed in her seat. He would have evidence: her address; an eyewitness account of her interaction with Chris; a good estimate of Chris's age. She imagined him at trial. Her conversation with Chris would be presented as flirtation, a seduction. The jury would look at her with disdain while the cabbie described how close she stood to Chris, how she sent her son away, how she and Chris might have kissed without his being able to see.

Her lawyer would be able to discredit him. Look at those tattoos, those earrings. He probably smokes dope. No, he will come dressed nicely in a suit. They will have asked him to cut his hair—It is all part of the show. She will be in an orange jumpsuit, orange because that is used for inmates who are dangers to themselves. Shackled.

The smoke was filling the car. *Do not roll down the window any farther: He will remember me.*

He was quiet, as if his mind was memorizing every detail of her behavior—her twitching, her quick, short breaths—as if he was preparing to trap her again.

They were almost at Hank's Garage. She had read somewhere that generous and parsimonious tippers are most frequently remembered. She would leave him an average-sized tip. She could be just another fare. She shouldn't have him bring her to the dealership. She could trade in her Volvo for the sports utility vehicle that she had wanted for some time.

"Sixteen," he said.

Not Chris's age, the fare.

"Because of the wait," he added.

She paid the fare, handing him a twenty dollar bill. He looked at it, as if he wanted more.

Don't. Make him forget you.

He raised two fingers to his temple.

She looked at him, puzzled.

"That's the Boy Scouts salute, isn't it?" he asked.

"Oh, I must be."

"That's how the troop leader said goodbye to you, right?"

He *had* observed them. He would not forget her. But Chris hadn't saluted her. She had to leave, before every fare in town would hear this tale of the widow with a fondness for boys. "Of course." As she said this, her eyes locked with his, and there seemed an intuitive understanding of how she had spoken to him evasively. His stare was nerve-racking, as if he were a predator eager to pounce on his prey.

"You need change?" he asked.

'*She was a cheap tipper,*' he would testify. "No, thank you," she said, stepping out of the car and walking toward the garage. How despicable she had become: trying to be so clever, so coy. Yet a complete stranger could see her attraction to Chris. Couldn't the scoutmaster? Officer Wilkins? Anybody? She had thought, foolishly, desperately, that the cab driver might be able to help her. On the contrary, he seemed more inclined to torment her.

She paid for the repairs. She shouldn't be concerned whether her Volvo was completely fixed and the dealership sold it to some unsuspecting buyer. She had more important matters to tend to—like her being sent to jail.

She drove to the new dealership by the interstate. Because the dealer would not open until 10 AM, fifteen minutes from now, she waited in her car. Being near the dealership, seeing the glimmering new cars in the showroom, Laney felt ready to start living in the present, not in some remote past or in a dreamed-of tomorrow. Hybrid sports utility vehicles were becoming the quite the rage. Soon she would have her own. Freedom lay just down the street. She could hardly wait for the dealership's doors to open. Although thoughts of Bill and Chris weighed upon her, she knew she could resolve them. One step at a time, she told herself, that is how change is effected. First, she needed the SUV.

She should call home. Home: she had not lived with her parents since college but still considered her parents' house in Boulder home. She had to put an end to the idea of vacationing in Santa Maria. Then she could deal with Bill and Christopher.

She took out her cell phone and dialed her parents' number. The noise of the highway rumbled in the background.

Her mother answered, "Elaine, where are you? You sound like you're at the airport."

Elaine: Her mother called her by her given name because friends only started calling her Laney in junior high school. Her father immediately took a liking to the name, but her mother resisted.

"I'm on my cell phone," Laney said.

"Oh," she said testily.

"Listen, Mom. I'm not going to be able to make it to Santa Maria."

"Do you want to talk to your father?"

"No." Laney hated how her parents would always bounce her from one to the other. "You tell him."

"What's the matter? You don't sound yourself."

"Will you stop asking me what's wrong? Nothing's wrong. I'm going to buy a new car. Everything's fine." Her voice was strained, shaky.

"You sound like you're having a breakdown."

She thinks I'm having a breakdown when I'm finally moving on with my life. No wonder I'm spinning my wheels. "I'm in a rush," she said.

"If you didn't want to talk, you shouldn't have called. What's on your mind?"

There was no harm in letting her mother know she had started other relationships. She was changing. She didn't care whether she approved or not. "I've been seeing someone," she said.

"Good. It's about time."

What an odd reaction. What did she mean: It's about time? Her mother had never encouraged her to date after Jay's death. "It's only been three years."

"Three years! What have you been waiting for? Prince Charming to come up and swoop you off your feet?"

"It's not easy in this town."

"It's not easy anywhere. Whenever everything's going great for you, you always have to mess it up."

"I have no idea what you're talking about."

"I'm talking about that fling you had with Jay's friend."

She knew about Dan? "Who told you about that?" she said, trying to mask her shock.

"Jay did, of course. After you crawled on your hands and knees back to him."

Jay told her? She found it hard to believe that he would share such intimate information with her, especially without telling her about it. But her mother's characterization was not fair: She had been matter of fact when she had confessed to Jay. "I was drunk."

"No need to apologize to me. But as they say, in wine there is truth."

The accusation stung. "What did Jay say?"

"The usual. How could she?"——

Christopher's words, How Could You, echoed through her. She struggled to maintain focus while her mother continued to speak: "He was angry. He knew it was one of those things you couldn't take back, but that you wanted to."

"He forgave me?"

"He was a Scorpio. You can't expect a scorpion to cozy up and cuddle with you after you've just sprayed insect repellent on it. But it's none of my business, that's what I told him."

She was not going to receive the validation she craved from her mother. "Does Dad know?"

"Your father doesn't know anything about this, and he doesn't need to. I'm glad about this new man. Good luck with your car. I'll talk to you soon." Her mother hung up the phone.

Laney held the receiver to her ear until it started to beep.

He was not a man. He was a boy.

The traffic on the interstate became louder, creating a steady, droning din. She felt oddly disengaged. Part of her was relieved. Her betrayal, her stupidity, was lessened. She took comfort that Jay had indeed forgiven her, as best he could. All these years she had continued to berate herself and no amount of self-scolding had managed to purify her. But now, guilt over committing adultery was being lifted by, of all people, her mother. Jay did not take his anger to the grave. He had unloaded it. She needed to do the same.

'In wine, there is truth': Maybe her mother was right. Maybe there *had* been some latent attraction between her and Dan. Why had she been unable to admit it?

The cool wind from the mountains wafted through the

car window. The sky was gloomy and gray, dotted with a few billowing clouds. Here she was, in this unfamiliar part of Plainview, but everything looked doable. Freedom coursed through her. Putting her cell phone in her handbag, she came across the crumpled pizza wrapper with Bill's number on it. Her apprehension over her involvement with Bill and Chris returned. Although the dealership was now open, as she held the pizza wrapper, a series of memories descended upon her. Her going to the Hendricksons' house, looking her best. She was with Bill in the garden. Then she was with Chris at the school, and he was saying, 'Did you fuck my father? How could you do this to me?'

Why hadn't she stopped seeing either of them after screwing Bill? That was wrong enough. No, she had to undo that wrong by committing one even more heinous. If only she had dealt with her feelings for Chris, she would not have put herself into this situation. How long would it be before Bill found that she had had sex with Chris?

She had to expel this guilt before it consumed her. She needed to know whether Bill knew about her and Chris. She would be able to tell from his voice over the phone. He should be home now, and Chris gone. She dialed, and he answered the phone. "Are you on your cell?" he asked.

"Yes, I'm buying a new car."

"You need a hand?"

His voice was calm—he couldn't know. But before she could answer, he continued with an ingratiating tone:

"I can help you negotiate."

"No, I'm fine."

"You sure you don't want me to help? I know exactly where

you are. I can be there in ten minutes."

How did he know where she was? Did her whole world have to revolve around Plainview? Resentment rose within: Everyone was trying to intrude, to *help* her. "No," she said with a bit too much force. She stopped, in a mixture of surprise and shock, as she recognized her anger. "I can do this myself."

"Is something wrong?"

That question again. Everything was right with her—she could deal with anybody or anything—and both her mother and Bill thought something was wrong. "No, not at all." She could not answer his proposal over the phone. He deserved more consideration: a face-to-face talk. "Could I come see you around twelve?" If Chris was having his lunch break at one, he would surely not be home earlier.

"I... can't," he said, his voice cautious.

He couldn't—why not? He had always been available for her. If he could make it here now, why not at his house in a couple of hours?

"You can't?"

"No."

No explanation was forthcoming. She recalled what Erin had told her about him and his ex-wife: How he had almost killed her. She tried to shake loose the feeling. If she couldn't talk to him at noon, she would have to go to dinner with him tonight. "I'll pick you up at seven then," she said. "Can you meet me out front? We'll be rushed." The truth was she didn't want to go inside the house because Chris would probably be there.

"Sure," he said in a resigned voice. "Is there something you want to tell me?"

She could sense the defeat resounding through him. She could apologize for sounding too harsh earlier, but she was not truly sorry. "There is. But we'll have to talk later," she said. From now on, she would speak only the brutal, honest truth. She disconnected the line.

***

She purchased her brand new car! A Lexus RX450—She felt elated. She paid the sticker price, in full, by personal check— She didn't care that she was overpaying.

"Rocky Mountain High" blared on the radio, and she sang along with John Denver.

She drove around town, acclimating herself to the myriad gadgets and knobs. She had skimped on nothing, even splurging on the chrome wheel-wells. She felt so free, so alive, finally entering a new era. She marveled at her perch above the road. How Plainview had changed with the purchase of a car. The town was not claustrophobic or dull, but full of surprises and opportunity. The road had been recently paved. The bright white and yellow lines gleamed. Evergreen trees reflected on the polished hood, and their strong scent mixed with the new-car odor that was so reassuring and refreshing. Brian was going to love this car.

A cab passed—it was not the one from before. She had overreacted earlier to the cabbie. She was being overly sensitive, overly paranoid. He couldn't suspect anything.

She stopped at the supermarket to prepare for the evening at Erin's. She chose a bottle of fine merlot and a box of candles, scented vanilla, as hostess gifts. She bought some extra treats for

224

the babysitter—a pint of Ben & Jerry's Chunky Monkey, potato chips—yes, to fatten her because she was as thin as Erin. She jaunted down the aisles, paid cash—not by her usual check or credit card—and emphatically said, "Thank *you*," to the cashier. She did not even turn down the offer of assistance to her car. Although she had only a couple of bags, she might as well show off her new SUV.

The bag-boy, wheeling the two bags in the shopping cart, followed her out of the store through the parking lot. She had parked at the end of the aisle in an isolated spot because she was afraid the door might get dented.

She turned to the boy, who was several lengths behind, and smiled, in good-neighbor fashion, to him. He did not offer a smile in return. He was a gawky-looking teen—odd eyes and nose and an oblong face, with his hair cut short so that his disproportionately large ears were even more noticeable. He was perhaps a sophomore in high school. No, he could not be as old as Chris.

Although she was not facing him, she could hear the cart rumble behind her, not quite touching her, but closing in. Was he watching her? She became conscious of her gait, trying to control the twisting of her hips, but only making it, at least in her mind, more pronounced.

When they reached her car, the boy said, "You're Mrs. Secord, aren't you?"

She froze, staring into the one of the grocery bags—at the bottle of wine and the chips. How did he know her name? Had he met her before?

She didn't bother to correct him, that she was a 'Miss': "Yes. Why do you ask?"

"I thought it was you!" he said, his voice a nasally whine. He had a cold, in the middle of May.

What did he mean? She fumbled with the keyless entry remote. The salesman at the dealership had showed her how to open the lid of the trunk with the push of a button, but which button was it? One of them was the panic button, which would send the alarm blaring. Another unlocked the doors, another locked them. Her fingers nervously danced over the remote. *It's easy. It's this one. No, maybe this one.*

"You know my friend Chris Hendrickson," the boy said.

Had Chris been bragging of his involvement with an older woman? *Don't admit anything. Don't say anything.* "I do?"

"Don't you?" He giggled, with a schoolboy's gleeful derision, stepping away from the cart and the SUV, descending into a coughing fit.

The red button must be panic—yes, of course. *No, hold it down for a few seconds to sound the alarm. The one with the depiction of an open lock unlocks the doors—but where is the key to unlatch the trunk?* "Chris Hendrickson?" she said, coyly.

"He *told* me," the boy said, stretching out the word 'told.'

Could Chris have told this young, this too-young boy, everything, so soon? Was he that reckless? She should have known. It was her fault.

When the boy's coughing fit ended, he stepped closer. "Did he really almost get arrested at your house?"

She started to move away from the trunk toward the front of the truck. Why would Chris have mentioned that he had nearly been arrested? Did he view it as some sort of accomplishment? What exactly did this boy know?

"Because he went through your yard?"

"Not exactly," she said.

"Then why?"

Why would he have to ask—Didn't he know? "It was a mixup, that's all. The neighbors thought they heard... a prowler. The town murderer." How stupid that sounded. She successfully unlocked the driver's door with the remote and manually released the trunk.

He was looking at her strangely. If Chris had told him that they had fucked, he might be curious about her, in a sexual way. He did not edge closer. He placed the pair of bags in the trunk, exclaiming, "Wow, this car smells so new!"

How wide-eyed and impressionable he was. Christ, he was not thinking of sex. Did every person, every thing she encountered, have to remind her of Chris? Her fears were unfounded: Chris had told him about the escapade merely to impress him.

She handed the boy a couple of dollars as a tip.

"Wow, thanks!" he exclaimed. Her tip was too generous. He will remember me, she thought, as the rich lady with the new car, who pretended not to know Chris, but when pressed, admitted it. The cab driver, too, would be in the courtroom eagerly waiting to testify. Who would be believed—an innocent boy, an impartial, cleaned-up cab driver, or her?

As the boy wheeled the cart back to the store, she observed his slight frame and protruding ears. The supermarket manager, taking the cart from the boy at the entry to the store scrunched his brow in concern. The boy stared at her. She waved at them, feigning enthusiasm, but as she drove through the parking lane, her cell phone rang, startling her, because at first, she thought it was some sound emanating from the car. She jammed on the brakes, and the car jolted. She instantly realized it was her cell phone. As she stepped on the gas—too heavily—the SUV's tires pealed, causing the car to lurch forward.

The manager strode toward her car, but she drove off. She had missed the call.

As she peeled away, she watched in the rearview and side mirrors until the manager and the boy were no longer visible. Her mind would not let up. She was racing through town at fifty miles per hour, but she felt as if she was traveling at half that speed.

She passed the spot where she had pulled over with Chris the other night. She decelerated, looking at it in disbelief. She pictured his face, his body, in the rearview mirror, in the passenger seat, in the reflections on the windshield. She could feel his body against hers and she could feel him inside her, pressing against her. She wanted him. To try to convince herself otherwise was useless. His question of this morning— "How could you have fucked my father?"—grated her. The answer was simple: She had to. Being with Bill, the adult, was the only way she could hold onto that sliver of morality, uncorruptible and sacrosanct, that allowed her to maintain the illusion that she did not hold herself in contempt for being attracted to a sixteen-year-old boy. She had felt better about herself after she had fucked Chris. She felt better about herself when she was with him because his physical presence reassured her of her youth. She never truly cared what he felt, as long as she could make him want to fuck her. Used him, yes, that was what she had done. That night here and that afternoon in the kitchen.

The cell phone chirped: There was a voicemail message waiting for her. She couldn't check it now. She needed to concentrate on driving home. It was probably a wrong number.

It usually was. *Chris* didn't have this number.

She arrived at her house at a few minutes before 2 PM. She turned off the engine, not completely sure whether it was running or not because it was so quiet. At once she felt sheltered inside the compartment yet eager to leave it. Her mother had said she sounded as if she was having a nervous breakdown. Perhaps she was. If Jay were here, would he notice? Or would he think that she was just unusually quiet, absorbed in her thoughts, but not suffering?

She stepped out of the car. This house was her refuge. Seeing it calmed her, made her feel immune to the pressures of the outside world. No, the cab driver and bag boy couldn't have suspected she and Chris were having sex. It was foolish on her part to have thought so. No one knew anything.

Before she reached the front door, she sensed that something was wrong. The lawn beside the driveway sidewalk was flattened by tire tracks, a patch of it uprooted. Why would someone drive over her front lawn? Who? Could Bill have come to the house, enraged? No. Bill was not upset when she had spoken to him earlier this morning. He could not have learned anything new in the meantime—could he have?

Or had Chris come here? At the school, he had pointed to his watch. Had he meant: 'Meet me at one'? He could have been upset that she had failed to meet him.

Or could it have been a complete stranger? Perhaps it was that murderer running loose in Plainview. Her heart pulsated.

As she placed the groceries on the doorstep, a woman walking up the driveway called out: "There you are!" It was Mrs. Flaherty, her next-door neighbor, a widow in her mid-fifties whom Laney scrupulously avoided because she was such a busybody. She was short, menacingly thin, and sported a modified bee-hive. "You just missed the police," she said frenetically. "You had a burglar. He came in a white van and I saw them arrest him."

A white van? She had to be referring to the Scouts van. Chris had been here and been arrested?

Mrs. Flaherty pointed around the garage. "One of the officers just drove away with the van. The burglar found a way in back. Officer Wilkins said he secured it. You know the boy, Christopher Hendrickson, don't you?"

"Yes," Laney answered cautiously. She had to be careful what she admitted to.

"That's what he said. Of course."

Of course: the same unnerving phrase the cab driver had used.

"Here, I'll show you," Mrs. Flaherty continued, ambling past her.

Laney followed her to the backyard, unable to fathom why Chris would have broken in. Why did he have to return after having been caught snooping in her yard the other night?

"I saw the cruiser's lights flashing from my den window. I rushed outside and stood right next to the cruiser while Officer Wilkins handcuffed the boy," Mrs. Flaherty said.

They reached the back of the house, where Mrs. Flaherty pointed to a small window approximately two feet from the rear door. The window was closed, although Laney usually left it open a few inches to air out the kitchen. She thought it too small a gap for someone to slip an arm through, and if there was an intrusion, she had motion detectors enabled throughout the house.

"I heard him tell the officer how he just reached in and

opened the door," Mrs. Flaherty said. "After he arrested the boy, Officer Wilkins informed me he found him upstairs. He didn't take anything. He was in his Boy Scout uniform. Imagine, a Boy Scout burglarizing a lady's home. He was in your bedroom."

She would not act suspicious. Wilkins was already aware that she and Chris knew each other. She moved away from Mrs. Flaherty, to the side of the house. "I should check to make sure everything's okay inside."

"Do you want to come to my house? I could call Harold Greeley and he can watch over your property for you." She was referring to an elderly gentleman who lived down the street.

"That won't be necessary." Laney started for the front of the house.

Mrs. Flaherty troddled behind her. "He might be stalking you. I'm glad I called the police the other night when I saw him snooping. He *was* snooping, wasn't he?"

"Are you referring to Wednesday night?" Laney asked.

"Did he have permission? At that hour? Did his parents know?"

Laney hurried toward the front yard.

Mrs. Flaherty marched behind her. "Surely you didn't give him permission to come *into* the house—through the window?"

"No."

"I knew he was lying to the police! That kid swore up and down you said he could come inside the house."

Laney had tripped herself up. She walked even faster.

Mrs. Flaherty was almost out of breath, but she managed to keep right behind her. "'Why didn't you have a key?' and 'Why didn't Mrs. Secord leave the door unlocked?' I overheard Officer Wilkins ask the boy, but he couldn't—or wouldn't—

explain. His story didn't make sense. I told the officer *that* myself." She eyed the SUV in the driveway rather suspiciously, as if leery of her expensive new car, her tongue clicking. Then she arched her body backwards, as a buzzard might while trying to dismember a carcass. She craned her neck forward, her eyes gleeful. "He is a fine looking boy, too. Wouldn't you say? You just wouldn't think an Eagle Scout would do something like this, unless, unless he was invited—or *thought* he was invited."

What was she insinuating? She had just said she didn't believe he had permission to enter the house.

"Maybe he was, after all, *just* looking for jewelry." Her voice grated. "But I recall, after my husband died, I was very lonely, too."

Why was she talking about how lonely she was? "I appreciate your help, Mrs. Flaherty." She unlocked the front door and started inside, about to close the door behind her.

"Don't worry," Mrs. Flaherty said. "I made sure the officers knew you weren't *that* kind of woman."

"What kind of woman is that?" Laney asked, trying not to appear annoyed.

"You're such a *young*, pretty woman, with so much going for you: a beautiful home, a *young* son. And the Hendrickson boy, some would say, he's *almost* a man."

Laney felt a sharp pain in her chest and she suddenly became short of breath. "What are you getting at?" she said bluntly.

"I didn't mean to imply—no, no."

Laney gathered the grocery bags. "I have to be going, Mrs. Flaherty. Goodbye."

"Be well too, considering."

She wasn't going to ask 'considering what?' She started closing the door.

Mrs. Flaherty put her hand on the door to stop her. "Considering that boy has a crush on you."

Laney pushed the door closed. The entry, the living room— especially that painting of the seascape that Chris had admired the night he had roamed through her backyard—looked so unreal, not her own. She was wrong: The cab driver, the bag boy, *did* suspect that she and Chris were lovers, just as Mrs. Flaherty did. The furnishings, the polished, barely used furniture, which had once provided security for her, now made her feel vulnerable—not because of the break-in but because she was now faced with the possibility that her relationship with Chris would be revealed. He might tell the police she had seduced him, to justify his actions and to elicit their sympathy. Or they might extract a confession from him under questioning.

She went to check the answering machine: There was a message from her alarm company that the alarm was triggered and that the police were dispatched. The same message was left on her cell phone voicemail. She called the monitoring company. They advised her to call the Plainview Police Department for details. A dispatcher told her that Chris Hendrickson, the suspect, was in custody.

No, she couldn't allow her life to be destroyed by some boy's foolish, desperate excuses. She had not encouraged him to pursue her. Yet she was partially   no, because she was the adult, even more so—to blame. She told the dispatcher—without explaining why—that she would come to the station right away.

18

The Plainview police station was situated at the edge of the old town center, beyond the high school. Passing the schoolgrounds, Laney felt the anxiety of the past week assert its control over her. She couldn't look at the campus, the fields, without thinking, without *being*, with Chris. The boy who would had been so insistent on showing off to his friends now seemed equally intent on seeing, claiming, harassing, her. Why had he broken into her house? Why did he have to go into her bedroom? Couldn't he have simply waited for her, or just left? Now, it was only a matter of time before Mrs. Flaherty blabbered her suspicions—what she *thought* she knew, and rightfully so—to the police, all over town.

Laney's hands, trembling, could barely maneuver the steering wheel. Her new SUV now seemed a mistake, something beyond her control. She did not feel safe in it. Why did she have to set the alarm at the house? She hadn't been reacting to news of the local murders—No, she had been religiously setting the system ever since Jay had died. If she had wanted excitement in her life, now she had it. She wanted to hand it back and say, This is not what I bargained for!

What would Chris tell the police? What if he told the truth? That he had come to see her, because they were lovers, and he had learned that she had slept with his father? Would Bill want charges pressed against her? Was there any way she could get out of this situation?

The warning signals had been there from the beginning. She

had asked for disaster. It now descended upon her, unmitigated and unrelenting. Even if Chris did not tell the police that they had been intimate, Officer Wilkins would recall her being at the high school the other day, watching the soccer game, and Chris's coming to her house on Wednesday night. Bill would then learn of his nighttime foray into her backyard.

Hopeful that Chris would lie, she tried to concoct some cover story of her own. Chris was supposed to mow the lawn—but... but during his Scouts outing! She had given him permission to enter. They were supposed to meet—but why, why? Nothing added up unless she revealed the secret ingredient: that they had a sexual relationship.

She reached the station, which looked benign, almost unconcerned. As she nervously drove into the parking lot, the feeling that the entire town was awaiting her arrival rushed through her. *Turn back*, she told herself. *Do not allow them to destroy you.* Is this how the schoolteacher felt when she was first called in? Needing to lie and obfuscate while at the same time confessing to herself, begging for mercy? If Laney returned home, what would she be turning back to? They would certainly take her house, her expensive new car, everything she owned, and Brian. She hated how he came almost as an afterthought. As a mother, she was expected not to feel certain unhealthy desires. What kind of example was she setting for him? She couldn't let them take him away. And wasn't this the truth: She was not caring for him as she was supposed to. She was not meant to be a mother.

Unsteadily she walked toward the station, leaving the doors to the SUV unlocked. Someone could come steal it, she did not care. She felt she had little left, not her self-esteem, nor even hope for tomorrow.

Inside the building, the officer manning the front desk asked for her identification and then proceeded to buzz her through the security door. She was shown to a sterile room devoid of furnishings except for a metal table about three body lengths-long with a dozen matching chairs. The room seemed too large to be an interrogation cell. It looked more suited for conferences or staff meetings. As she sat down, she noticed the corner of the table was scratched with an amateurish doodle, a crisscross of deeply etched lines that she interpreted as a warning, as if it were a protest made by another detainee. *Be wary*, it seemed to say. *Tread carefully. They will get you.* Small video cameras were perched on the corners of the room. Her every move was being watched, recorded. Were there microphones, too?

Her suspicions piqued, she thought about how Officer Wilkins had befriended her. Yes, yes! Now, he would cajole her into confessing about her relationship with Chris and then dutifully arrest her.

The wait was excruciating. She imagined this was what the terminally ill must feel: waiting, for minutes and hours, the only climax was when time would stop. As every minute passed, she was sure that the police had extracted one more incriminating detail from Christopher. He had told them of their encounter in the kitchen, how she had scarcely undressed, how much she had wanted him. What would Bill say now when presented with incontrovertible evidence of her involvement with his son? 'How could you?'—the same words Chris had said to her—and yet, there were reasons, rationalizations, which whirled about her in a maelstrom of confusion and doubt.

When the door to the conference room finally opened, Laney turned to see Officer Wilkins, whose usual good-natured expression had turned to a look of rancor and exasperation. He gave her a strained look and sat next to her, placing a file and a legal pad before him on the table. The legal pad unsettled her. Even if there were no microphones, he was going to record what she said. His notes would form part of a court proceeding against her. The cab driver, too, would be called in. The evidence would be insurmountable.

"Miss Secord, hello," Wilkins said.

"Please, Laney."

"Of course," he replied in a formal tone.

Just what the cab driver and Mrs. Flaherty had said. She had to remain calm.

He took the pen in hand and twirled it above the writing tablet. "I'm sorry to see you under these circumstances."

"Officer, I wanted to come because I think there's been some misunderstanding."

"There has?"

What had Chris told him? His tone revealed little. Was he baiting her, so that she would stumble in a tangle of lies, or was he truly receptive to what she had to say? "Yes, I think so," she said. "I know this boy, and he isn't the type to do something like this. As you know from the other evening, I gave him permission to enter my yard for his Scouts activities. He wasn't trying to burglarize my house, was he?" *Yes, ask questions, dig for information, to guide the planting of the necessary lies.*

"It seems more like a case of breaking and entering," he responded flatly.

"He didn't have any malicious intent, did he?" *Yes, use legal terminology to help obfuscate the issue!*

"It doesn't seem so. But he did lie to us, at first."

What did he mean, 'at first'? Had Chris subsequently come clean—confessing to their affair? "How so?" she asked as matter-of-factly as she could muster.

"He said you told him he could come into the house. When I asked about the alarm being triggered, he said you must have forgotten to turn it off. You didn't, did you?"

Why was he questioning her? What did he suspect? "No," she had to say.

"Later, he changed his story and said you wouldn't have minded that he came in. He said you asked him to meet him at one o'clock, and when you didn't show up, he took it upon himself to go inside and get what he needed."

"He needed something inside the house?" she asked cautiously.

"Apparently your son forgot a picture of your late husband that he and Christopher were going to use in the project they were working on."

That was his pretext for breaking in—a picture? Brian hadn't mentioned anything about taking a picture from the house. "Yes, the Mother's Day project," she said.

"Your son didn't exactly ask him to go get the picture. It was more Christopher's idea."

"You know how kids are," she said. "They both might be telling the truth."

"We didn't find a picture on him when we arrested him. When I asked him why you were going to meet, he said the reason was to get the picture. I asked how you could have known that Brian had forgotten it. He said he was confused. He said you wanted to meet him just to make sure everything was going okay with your son during the outing."

So he had lied for her! She felt triumphant! He would not betray her! She tried to conceal her emotions. She could not let on that she was pleased, that she felt energized by Chris's loyalty. She had to corroborate his story and at the same time embellish it, to make it seem true— "That's not the complete reason," she said.

Wilkins' brows rose.

"Chris has been extremely good to my son, and since Brian lost his father a few years ago, scouting has become his passion and Chris a role model to him. Since Chris has been trying to raise money for a trip to Mount Rushmore, I wanted to give him an extra reward, just make sure he could pay his way. He's not exactly poor, but I know his family could use some help."

"That's very kind. I'm concerned, though, because he's been acting extremely nervous since he's been in custody. His story has changed several times."

"He's probably scared. After all, the alarm went off and he was arrested. He doesn't know what kind of trouble he might get in. I don't mind that he went inside my house. I trust him."

"I don't understand why we found him in your bedroom."

Her throat clenched. "Maybe he didn't find the right room when he went in."

Wilkins looked at the legal pad, which had notes scribbled over it. "That's the same thing Chris said." He wrote something quickly on the pad, tapping the pen against the paper.

She felt tense, as if she had said something incriminating.

"But wouldn't he have opened the door and seen that it was a lady's bedroom?"

"Maybe he was curious," she said.

He ruminated for a moment. "We checked your jewelry

240

box—it didn't look opened, and he had nothing on him. So if that's the case, why won't he admit it?"

"He's probably afraid."

The phone by the door rang. "Excuse me." Wilkins stood to answer it. "He's here?" he said into the phone. "Thank you." He hung up. "Give me a minute. Mr. Hendrickson has arrived." He exited the conference room.

She was glad he left—He was asking so many questions, too many questions. Why was he interested in spending so much time on such a minor incident? Didn't he have better things to do?

What was Bill going to think? She would have preferred to talk privately with him before Wilkins had a chance, but she was not controlling the situation. How long could Chris maintain his story—his stories—their lie—under the pressure of being incarcerated and interrogated, especially when he was unsure what she would say? Although Chris was the one currently in custody, she did not feel blameless. He probably never suspected she had an alarm system at the house. It wasn't in his character to enter her house without permission. And Wilkins was right: How could Chris calmly stay inside the house while the alarm was blaring? Had he realized he had made a mistake and didn't want to appear guilty when caught? Could his reasoning have been that lucid? Or was he merely being stupid—as a boy would, feeling that he was invincible, that he could escape or hide before somebody caught him? That word, 'boy', kept resounding, because he and she were in this predicament precisely because he *was* a boy.

What would Bill tell Wilkins? What will she do if he says that Chris has been behaving strangely all week, since he had met her? What will she do if says, "Chris talks about her all the time"? Should she agree or laugh off the comment? She would have to make sure that Bill said as little as possible, that any seeming contradictions between their stories were not contradictions at all but somehow, somehow, buttressed what she—and God-knows-what Chris—had said.

Officer Wilkins led Bill into the conference room.

"I can't apologize enough for what my son did," Bill said as she stood. He tenderly put a hand on her shoulder, a gesture that Wilkins seemed to pick up on. That Wilkins was watching, perhaps with a hint of suspicion, unnerved her. Her eyes surveyed the video cameras about the room. She felt she was under a microscope, being analyzed, dissected. "It's all right. It's all a misunderstanding."

"It's not all right," Bill said adamantly.

"Mr. Hendrickson, I understand why you're upset. Why don't you have a seat?" Wilkins was now carrying a manila folder as well as a legal pad.

She took a breath, to alleviate her unease. Bill sat beside her while Wilkins took his seat opposite them and opened the file. He smiled at her, his gaze lingering a bit too long over her face and hair—and she wondered—Did Bill notice?

"In running a check on your son," Wilkins said, "we noticed that he had some problems in Beckle's Ridge."

Bill looked surprised. "Yes," he said tentatively.

She could see that his hands were trembling. Could what Erin have told her be true? "I could step into the other room if you'd like some privacy," she offered.

"No, it's all right," Bill answered.

Wilkins' eyes bounced from one to the other, in strange

fascination, but he kept looking back at her. Had he been leering at her earlier, or had he only now started to after Bill had come into the room?

Wilkins' fingers started to jostle the file. "He has a prior arrest for vandalism."

Vandalism, she thought—Chris seemed so sweet, incapable of vandalizing someone's property.

Bill, uncomfortable, repositioned himself in the metal chair. "Yes, three or four years ago. It was an isolated incident, a school kid prank. There haven't been any problems since. My wife and I were separating at the time, and it was hard on Chris."

"At one point, you and your wife were arrested also."

Her body rose slightly from the seat. Erin *had* told her the truth. Bill and his wife had had a terrible fight. But did he really try to strangle her? Could he have done something that despicable?

"We were arrested," he said, "but no charges were filed."

Wilkins' lips pursed smugly, as if to challenge him. "Just because no charges were filed doesn't mean there was no crime."

Bill sat stone-faced, nodding.

What Wilkins was saying was true: There very well may have been a serious crime that was not followed up on, for bureaucratic or personal reasons.

Wilkins continued: "We have a nice quiet community in Plainview. How long have you and your son lived here?"

"A year and a half. This is the first problem Chris or I have had since," he added.

Laney detected a quivering note in Bill's voice. What really happened in Beckle's Ridge? Why wasn't Wilkins pursuing this line of questioning? Yet despite Bill's past, she needed to make sure the present situation was resolved favorably. She couldn't allow him to be blamed for Chris's actions—It wasn't his fault. A father couldn't watch his son all the time. "I can vouch for him, Officer," she said. "They're very responsible people. I don't want the boy to have a record. He has a bright future ahead of him."

Wilkins stirred the file before him.

"Officer, I apologize for what my son did. I assure you nothing like this will happen again. He could lose his designation if the organization learned about this."

"We had to tow the van to the station, so they already know."

She had to get Chris out of police custody as soon as possible, before he said something that might cast suspicion on their relationship. "Officer, didn't Chris say my son told him it was okay to go into the house?"

"He did, but permission from a seven year-old doesn't give him license to open a locked door. There was also the incident the other night."

Bill's head perked up, but Laney tried not to react.

"I didn't want to bother you," she said. "Officer Wilkins saw Chris at my house at about eight o'clock on Wednesday night. I had given him permission to take specimens and things from my yard for his Scouts outing. I didn't tell you about it, but it's my fault, it really is. I should have said something."

Wilkins weighed her admission. "May I ask something personal?" he inquired, his tone softening.

"Sure," Bill said.

"Are you two seeing each other?"

Now he was acting as some sort of psychologist or counselor, rather than a police officer. Was he trying to impress her?

"We might get married, in fact." He took her hand and tenderly grasped it on the conference table. "She hasn't said yes quite yet." Pride registered in his voice, but also a hint of doubt.

Maybe he was coming to accept the possibility—what was surely in his mind, a vague, unlikely, but still viable possibility— that she might say no. She would have to find a way to capitalize, to manipulate, this doubt.

"How does your son feel about this?" Wilkins asked.

"He's fine," Bill said. "He knows I'm going to remarry someday."

So categorical he was, dismissing the notion that Chris was not upset that his father wanted to marry her. Couldn't he put the pieces together, if only on a subconscious level? Didn't he see that the more he pursued her the more rashly Chris was behaving?

Wilkins looked at Bill as if he too did not completely believe the notion. He wiped his brow with the back of his hand, peering at the perspiration and only glancing up when he became aware that she was watching him. "He could be acting out. Kids do that. I'm not an expert in these things, but I would advise taking things slow. He might not be as happy about the situation as you think."

Bill released her hand. A confused, morose expression overtook him, as if Wilkins had destroyed any hope that she might marry him. "It's possible," he said, his voice weak, his tone dejected.

"I'm going to release him to your custody. He'll probably have to appear in court, because he's a juvenile. The JV courts have special procedures they have to follow, though I believe it's up to the District Attorney whether or not to file charges.

But seeing how Miss Secord—Laney,"—he assented, smiling, "—doesn't seem to have an issue with the forced entry, the DA might be persuaded to drop the matter."

"I can assure you, I'm not going to let him off without some punishment," Bill said.

"You need to keep an eye on him. I've seen boys his age get into a little bit of trouble and then something sets them off and all hell breaks loose."

That 'something' might be her.

"I'll make sure this doesn't escalate," Bill said.

"Thank you," Laney said to Wilkins, giving him a sincere look of appreciation to acknowledge the favor he had done.

Wilkins smiled at her as if to say 'You're welcome,' then he turned to Bill: "I'll get your son now." He exhaled as if still on edge while he gathered his file, pad, and pen and departed from the conference room.

"I'm astounded," Bill said. "Suddenly, it seems as if I'm on trial. I'm going to kill Chris."

"He meant well."

"Why are *you* protecting him?" he asked.

The accusation stung her. She had to protect Chris—after all, he would never have pursued her had she not encouraged him. She looked away, back at the table, where the lines of graffiti caught her stare. What was she doing to this family? She had pitted them against each other. Chris should be obeying his father. "He's a boy," she said.

Bill put an arm around her shoulder. "I'm sorry." He leaned toward her, pulling her head against him, but she moved away. Taking consolation from him could only incite his son's wrath.

He looked puzzled. "Do you really think he's rebelling

against us? Maybe he resents how you're taking the place of his mother."

Chris didn't see her as a mother. Didn't he realize that Chris didn't want her to see him because he saw himself in his father's place, beside her, with her, as a girlfriend, lover?

She lifted her head from his chest. "You told him about us?"

"You didn't want me to?"

"About what happened in the garden?" she asked.

"In so many words."

She couldn't believe how thickheaded he was. She should have known he wouldn't be able to keep from bragging, but she didn't think he would tell his own son. Yet she could do little now except try to mitigate Chris's anger. "It doesn't matter," she relented.

Perplexed, he seemed to be on the point of asking why not, when Officer Wilkins opened the door. Chris stood behind him.

She was unprepared for how he looked: his belt had been removed, probably as a precaution. His shirt was unbuttoned randomly and was untucked. His hair was completely disheveled. His eyes, reddened as if from crying, stared stonily forth while his hands kept twitching. Nerves had completely taken hold of him. Red welts had formed around his wrists where the handcuffs had been placed. His uniform hung loosely around his body, as if it were a size too large, and it seemed to be little more than a lump of spruce-colored cotton rather than a symbol of his achievements. She wanted to reach out and touch him, but she was afraid, both of his reaction and of Wilkins.

As Wilkins entered the room, Chris barely stooped forward, his shoulders hunched. The confident posture she had come to expect from him had been stripped, like a horse that had been broken and had lost its will to run. His eyes lacked their usual curiosity, expressing only disinterest.

Bill did not move forward even though there was ample space between him and his son. Anguish quickly overtook his face, and Laney felt as if she were a bystander, witnessing the collapse of a family. She inched closer to Bill, and to Chris, but her movements were tentative, as if she were stepping over the fragile remnants of a fractured glass. Although she wanted to restore the glass to its harmonic whole, as she looked at the pieces, she realized they were too numerous and complex in their misshapen qualities to salvage it. There was nothing to do but walk around them, to avoid stepping on the shards.

She did not make eye contact with any of them, looking at the far end of the room. Finally, Wilkins said, "You're free to go." He spoke to all of them, and at that point, Laney's initial irritation with him turned to dislike. Despite all his questions, his 'counselor' pose, he seemed to have no interest in helping them. He seemed merely dissatisfied that he had been unable to fashion together the elements of a crime—a crime committed by Chris—and by extension, Bill—against her. He was superfluous to the three of them, an extra side to an already complete triangle.

19

After Chris was given his personal belongings—belt, wallet, keys, even a pack of chewing gum the police had seized—they exited the police station. Laney headed straight for the parking lot; she would have time to discuss the matter with him later. She didn't want to risk his telling Bill now about their affair. She couldn't locate her car at first, because she was searching for the Volvo rather than her new SUV, but she soon found it. Yet before she could slip off, Bill's voice roared at Chris, who had managed to slink ahead of them—

"What the hell were you thinking?" he shouted.

"I'm sorry," Chris said.

"You're sorry? All you can say is you're fucking sorry?" He raised his fist. "I should have let you sit in jail for the rest of the night. You don't break into somebody's house."

"I was getting something for Brian."

"So you went around back and pried open the door? Haven't you heard of knocking?"

"I was in a rush. I didn't think it was a big deal."

"A big deal? You don't call being arrested a big deal?"

"*You* were arrested before."

Did he actually try to strangle Chris's mother?—The thought sent shivers through her.

Bill's breathing became huffy. "This has nothing to do with me!" He reached out to grab Chris, but he ducked out of the way.

Laney put a hand on Bill's chest. "Don't. Not here."

Chris, shaking, started to walk off, toward the edge of the parking area, away from where Bill's Galaxy was parked. "Maybe she doesn't like you anymore," he called back. He turned to Laney: "Don't worry, Laney, he won't hit you. Not unless he's drunk."

"Get over here this minute!" Bill yelled.

She was afraid their shouting might attract more attention from the police. "Bill, calm down. You're causing a scene. The police will come out."

"Get in the car right now," Bill ordered Chris.

"Or what?" Chris countered back, his voice nervously defiant.

Bill broke away from Laney and lurched forth, as if ready to tackle him.

"Bill, please. I'm sure Brian wanted something and Chris was just trying to help."

"He's *my* son, Laney. I won't have him fucking things up now that everything is finally starting to go right in my life."

"What?" Chris said incredulously.

"Now that I have Laney."

"*You* have her?"

"How do you think you got out of this mess?"

Chris punched his arm out and round-kicked his leg—at nothing in particular, just at some imaginary target—slicing the air.

"Get in!" Bill demanded.

Chris hesitated.

"I'm your father, now get in before I have your ass thrown back in there!"

"For what?" Chris asked petulantly.

"That's it!" Bill fumed, striding forth, his body tumbling

forward. Chris cowered, backing away and then turning so he wouldn't have to look him in the eye. Bill charged behind him, stopping only when Chris opened the car door. Then, without turning to Laney, he went to the driver's-side door, stepped inside, and hastily started the car. They drove off.

The sun, reflecting against the Galaxy's windshield, obscured Laney's view of them. But when the car reached the road, she noticed that Chris was staring out the passenger window at her. He looked infuriated. He had evidently expected her to defend him.

She found her new car, feeling little solace. This was her future: a shiny piece of metal machinery with enough bells and whistles to numb her. But it couldn't alter the fact that Chris had broken into her house and now he and his father were fighting. She drove away, glancing back at the police station. She felt distrustful of Officer Wilkins; he was going to be watching her house from now on. He had managed to extract not a whit of truth. He was probably jealous of Chris—because he was so good-looking, because he had the world ahead of him. He would not confine himself to a rinky-dink town like Plainview; so Chris threatened him.

When she arrived home, she had just a few minutes before she had to pick up Brian at the elementary school. She wanted to retrace Chris's steps to find out what he was really doing in the house.

Opening the window by the door to freshen the kitchen, she mimicked his hearing the alarm, his stepping outside, his coming back in. He must have gone down the hall and headed upstairs. Then he had to have walked by Brian's room; he could not have missed it because the door was always open.

She traced the steps he would have taken: He went inside the room, saw the picture of Jay by Brian's bed, but left it, closing the door behind him. Then he meandered down the hall to her room. He stopped, looking at her bed, the sliding glass doors to the deck, the fireplace in the corner.

She tried to see the bedroom as he would have: *So this is where she sleeps.*

The jewelry box on the dressing table is untouched, along with the pictures of Brian and a few pieces of crystal. There is a pen next to the crystal dolphin; it is uncapped, as if he had been writing something. The pen has come from the drawer, which is closed. She opens the drawer and sees a small stack of bills, stamps, and address labels. In the back, she finds a compact mirror, replacement checks, an unworn set of earrings, a memo pad from the Santa Maria Country Club. Nothing is out of place except the pen. She again looks at the bed. The pillows are neater than how she left them. The sheets are pulled together, folded more crisply, in hospital corners. This is not how she made the bed. She goes to the bed and picks up the pillows. Nothing is underneath. She unfolds the duvet and sees, three-quarters of the way down the bed, a piece of the memo paper, folded in half.

She took the note and started to read: "No one will ever love you like I can. I would give everything for you. We're soulmates, Laney. If you go out with him tonight, I will tell him about us. Then you won't have to. Don't see him anymore. Please." Then, written in smaller letters near the bottom edge of the paper: "I hope you get this before you go to bed."

Though he had once seemed a challenge, a fantasy that she could control, with the note in hand she detected a veiled threat of blackmail. He would tell his father—so easily—and who else? His schoolboy friends—like the boy at the supermarket,— sure enough. He was manipulating her. He had not told the police, because his game of conquest would then be over. Nor had he said anything to Bill outside the police station, when he had plenty of opportunity. No, he had to continue his pursuit of her, to prolong it.

If she had had any doubts about Chris's lack of maturity, they were dispelled. He had gone through all this trouble to leave her a note, getting himself arrested in the process. He was behaving like an adolescent, willful and spoiled, even desperate. He broke in, the alarm signaling that the police were likely on their way, that what he was doing was wrong.

"We're soulmates. I hope you get this before you go to bed." He was trying to be endearing. He "loved" her. Despite his being with another girl, despite his being arrested today, she felt, with the unmade bed before her, violated and used.

She took the note and placed it in the drawer of her dressing table. She did not want to deal with his attraction to her, her anger. She had to pick up Brian. As she descended the stairs and left the house, keeping the alarm system turned off, she became cross at Chris for making her late. Brian would be waiting for her; she was a bad mother. What should have been a priority—caring for her son—she was giving short shrift to. She stepped into her car, slamming the door.

She backed out of the driveway, and an oncoming car drove by, too fast: "Fuck you!" she cursed. "Fuck you! Fuck everybody!"

Her hands were shaking. She hated this car, those fucking chrome rims that she did not really need, having to go to Erin's dinner party when she wanted to be alone, this claustrophobic town. She stopped the car and held her head against the steering wheel, virtually crouching underneath it. But as the seconds passed, her foot still on the brake, she asked herself what she was doing. No one was going to come help her. She was alone; she had to take responsibility.

She lifted her head, feeling as if she had crawled out of a skin, a body, that was lying beneath her. She was a ghost. A goddamn ghost. She was an actress playing every role imaginable— mother, daughter, friend, lover, seductress, job interviewer, even mythologist—all because she had had enough. All because she had fucked a sixteen-year-old boy.

She sat back against the seat, telling herself that Chris wanted her, Bill wanted her. She looked at her eyes and hair in the visor mirror. All still looked fine. Bill and Chris responded to what was on the outside, and everybody else did, too. No one had to know what she felt.

When she arrived at the elementary school, several minutes late, all the scouts were gone, except for one boy who sat on the sidewalk step next to Brian. Seeing the boy was some consolation to her. She was not the last parent to pick up her son.

Brian looked dejected as he held onto his Mother's Day project, which sat in a bag covered by a white cloth so as not to spoil the surprise.

The scoutmaster, Mr. Diamond, immediately apologized for Chris's going to her house; Laney assured him that there had been some miscommunication. She explained that the police had understood there was a misunderstanding, and the whole matter was dropped. "There won't be any repercussions because he didn't return to the troop, will there?" she asked.

"He did tell me where he was going," Mr. Diamond said, "but I thought you'd be there to show him in."

She carried on about how she had just bought a new car and had gotten delayed at the dealership. She told Brian to go take a look at their new car.

"Chris gave me his word of honor he had permission," Diamond said. "The police said that you told him he could go into your yard for a project he was working on."

"Yes," she said, noticing that Brian still had not moved. "Brian, go see the new car." She pushed him along, and half reluctantly, he walked away with his project, saying goodbye to his friend.

"Chris is not working on any project at the moment," Diamond said.

"I wasn't aware of that," she answered.

Diamond looked troubled, running his hand against the sharp ends of his buzz cut. "He's reached the highest level of achievement in our organization. I'd hate to see him lose it all."

The Eagle Scouts was certainly the least of Christopher's problems! "Could I do anything to help?" she asked.

The boy waiting on the step spoke up: "Dad, can we go home now?"

So the boy was Diamond's son. She felt a twinge of guilt: She was indeed the last parent to arrive.

"Just a minute, Andy." He turned to Laney. "You might not want to encourage him."

"What do you mean?"

"I think he has a crush on you."

Mrs. Flaherty, now Diamond, knew. She laughed. "Chris?

No. I'm seeing his father."

His eyes narrowed, as if he was inspecting something. "I can see the way he looks at you. How he gets nervous and excited around you."

"Don't be silly," she said.

"Aren't *you* the one who's being silly?"

Not base or vile, she thought, but *silly?*

"He has a good future ahead of him. Stay away from him, will you?" He picked up his son and propped him against his chest, holding his arms around him, as if creating a buffer before her. His eyes did not move; they remained on his son.

Shocked, she froze in fear. Was her involvement with Chris that obvious? What did Diamond know? Was he trying to corner her, to make her admit to something—to having a romantic relationship with Chris? She wouldn't. Not to the cab driver, not to Mrs. Flaherty, not to him. She wasn't going to allow him to destroy her, to mock her, so that she would be some kind of joke whom schoolchildren would jeer at, whom the hypocritical townsfolk would publicly hold themselves above but privately sympathize with. No. No one would know. No one *could* know. Not even this man, this father, this sanctimonious civic volunteer—Who did he think he was, accusing *her?* She had a son, too.

She walked off, toward her car.

Brian was standing by the passenger door. "Mom, did Chris get in trouble today?"

She didn't answer; she had heard enough about Chris.

"He was supposed to help me," he continued. "He didn't come back, and I didn't finish my project."

She could see a piece of carved, stained wood jutting from

the bag. She didn't care about the surprise. She didn't feel she deserved any recognition this Mother's Day. But as she looked at Brian, so innocent in his scarf and uniform, she knew he wouldn't understand any of what she was feeling. "I'll help you," she said.

"I don't want your help!" he shouted, pulling away his arm and moving his body toward the door.

She became embarrassed. "Don't be sad." She put a hand on his arm. "I'll help," she repeated.

"No!" he shouted, bursting into tears. "I hate you!"

"You don't mean that."

"I do! First you kill Daddy and now you take Christopher— Chris"—his eyes gleaming at her— "away."

Kill Jay—How, why could he think that? Is that what he truly thought—that she was somehow responsible for Jay's death? She had to ask him; she needed his reassurance. She went to hug him but he flailed his arms and kicked at her. She tried to settle him down by rubbing her hand against his arm, but he was still agitated, breathing heavily. She looked back at Diamond, who was still holding his son, like a shield, like a weapon; they were watching her. She felt worthless. Finally, Brian's fit subsided, though he would not raise his head to look at her.

"Maybe the babysitter can help you tonight," she said.

"I need someone to paint in the words," he sniffled. "Chris said he would. I don't know why he didn't come back. I told him I didn't want that stupid picture!"

"Did you tell Mr. Diamond that?"

"Yes," he said excitedly, nodding his head, pleased with himself.

"What did he say?"

He shook his head. "He asked me how you knew him."

"Did you say I knew his father?"

He shrugged. "I said you gave him a ride home the other night. I said he came to *see* you."

"Did you tell him what you saw in the kitchen?"

He didn't answer.

"Did you?" Her voice was becoming frantic.

When he lifted his head, his eyes were devoid of tears and showed no signs of redness, as if he had not been crying at all. The whites grew larger. He was almost laughing. "You didn't want me to say anything?" he said innocently, an angelic—no, demonic—smile creeping across his lips.

"That's okay," she said, helping him inside the car, realizing she had to get away from Diamond, this school, thinking, *What kind of child was he?*

***

When they returned home, she discovered a message from Bill on the answering machine. He apologized for blowing up outside the police station and said he would be ready at 7 PM for her to pick him up. "Again," he said, "I'm really sorry about what Chris did."

She listened to the message a few times, trying to detect whether his voice was strained because of Chris's arrest or because Chris's subsequently told him that they too were lovers. She had to talk to Chris. She wasn't going to go to jail because of him, because of his foolishness, his stupidity. She had to warn him about Mr. Diamond, who already knew too much. She would tell him that she had found his note, but because the police, Mr. Diamond, and others were focusing on their friendship, they could not continue to see each other. Maybe she can find a way to introduce him to some young girl—Erin might know of one. She could encourage Bill to give him some money so that he and the girl could go on dates. Maybe she could even persuade him to buy Chris a car. It was time for him to have a driver's license. He'd have a whole new world open up to him and she'd no longer be on his mind.

She called the Hendricksons' home, determined that if Bill answered, she would tell him that she would indeed pick him up as planned. If it was Chris, which she hoped it would be, she would try to stop him from behaving so recklessly.

Bill answered; he probably wasn't allowing Chris to take phone calls.

After confirming their date, she asked, "How is Chris doing?" There was a long pause. What *did* Chris tell him? Did he repeat the same stories he told the police?

"He's in the shower," Bill finally answered.

She was relieved. They hadn't discussed her. Chris was in the shower. Instantly, an image of water streaming over his smooth skin, through his hair, down his face and chest, invaded her. She pictured him in that small bathroom with a plastic shower curtain held up by a metal hoop over the tub. She could smell the soap and the shampoo and could feel the steam envelop him. She could see his penis, growing, lathered by his hands, and soon, her hands would join his because she would not be able to resist touching him.

"Are you there?" Bill asked, startling her out of her reverie.

"Yes," she answered.

"He's grounded," he said, "for the rest of the school year.

From now on, it's just school, Scouts, and home. And no Mount Rushmore."

Grounding Chris would help put distance between them. "It's unfortunate," she said.

"One of these days, I'll have him apologize to you," he said.

"That's not necessary."

He drew a breath. "No, he needs to. Especially if you decide to say yes to me."

After all this, he still wanted to get married. Didn't he have a clue? "Don't you think now isn't the best time to consider that?"

"If we're serious, we have to start acting as a family. Provided that's what you want."

Don't attempt it over the phone, she told herself. "We'll talk tonight, okay? See you at seven." She hung up.

From the counter she took the picture of Jay hiking up the trail. He forgave her. Why couldn't she believe it? Her mother was right. She had not forgiven herself. She had become involved with a father and son; but why? Did guilt over betraying Jay have that powerful a hold on her? Was she trying to destroy any chance of having a healthy relationship? In college, she had studied about self-destructive people. Could she be one herself? Was she ruining her life? She stared at the photo of Jay, hoping for some answer. But none came. She put the frame back on the counter and readied herself for the dinner, putting on makeup, steaming her dress free of wrinkles. She had a party to go to. Nothing held any importance for her. Her resolve turned to routine.

The blankets and sheets of the bed were rumpled from uncovering Chris's note earlier this afternoon. With time to spare, she curled on the bed, slipped under the sheet, brushed her legs where Chris had placed the note, buried her head against the pillow. She imagined she was holding him and resting against him. She could see him emerge from her bathroom, fresh from a shower. She knelt before him, kissing his feet, his shins, his knees, and she felt thrilled, alive. Then she said stop. She was torturing herself. She didn't want Chris to love her. She had to stay active. Fantasizing only sent her into a private hell. She had to get a job, find something busy, something life-consuming, so that she would have no time to dwell. Yes, tomorrow. No, tonight. What should she do? The house was all set. Brian was racing to finish his gift for her. He did love her; no one could accuse her of being an inattentive mother. She had to stop judging herself.

She radiated in her sleeveless burgundy organza dress. She put on little jewelry because she wanted to project a professional image. Dan's manager would be at Erin's house tonight; she could at least make him regret not coming to her interview.

Erin's sister, Meg, arrived at 6:30 PM with Erin's kids, Samantha and Luke. Meg was a younger version of her sister, shorter, but just as skinny. She had the same frilly hair, curls upon curls that looked like the strands of a mop. A natural with children, she was studying for her master's degree in education to become an elementary school teacher. Though she had never had a boyfriend that she knew of, Laney envied her natural charm and optimism.

As she watched Meg round up the three kids, who chased after a remote control electric car that Luke had brought, she offered Popsicles, which she thought they'd love because of the heat, but the children continued to dance around Meg, following the car. They viewed Meg as an equal, a friend, rather than as a mother. "I just got engaged," Meg said, raising her left hand to show the gold band around her ring finger. Her face beamed. "Erin introduced me to him. We're getting married in October. I hope you can come."

She thought Meg would never get married. Even though Erin had failed to tell her she had fixed her sister up, she said, "I'm so happy for you. I can't wait to meet him. Would you mind doing me a favor? Brian is working on a surprise for Mother's Day. He's desperately trying to finish it for tomorrow. Could you help him with it?"

"I'd love to." Meg's face flushed with eagerness and pride.

Laney felt a twinge of jealousy: Meg was embarking on the journey that she had set out on six years ago, only to find herself stranded.

As she drove to Bill's, she compared herself to Erin and Meg. Where had she gone wrong? If a stranger were to meet the three of them, he would think she would have the greatest chance of happiness. But she clearly had the least. She had not set goals for herself nor set out to achieve them; she had meandered in both her personal and professional lives. Meg's work with children should inspire her. She definitely needed to reconnect with her own field of social work or she would never have the stability she craved.

When she arrived at Bill's and approached the front door, the spot on the sidewalk where Chris's initials were etched caught her eye. Underneath, something else had been carved in the cement. Could they be some girl's initials? She knelt, jealousy spiraling through her. They were initials. "SB." And there was a plus sign between them: "CH + SB. 4EVA."

Shocked, she stared at the cement. She had fantasized that maybe Erin could set him up with a teenaged girl, but the fact that he was actually seeing someone *now*, while acting as if *she* were the only one, sent her into a whirl. Was she reading the letters correctly? Was that a squiggle or—No, there was no doubt that was a plus sign. Why hadn't she noticed this—this declaration, this pronouncement, this notice to the world— earlier? Maybe the carving wasn't fresh at all—maybe he had carved the initials years ago, after he had experienced some first love. Maybe it had been a joke. She blew at the cement block, to rid it of dust. But the letters looked as if they'd been recently etched, so clean, smooth, and undisturbed were their lines.

How silly, yes incredibly fucking *silly*, she was to think he didn't have some girl his own age. She had seen him with her the other day at the ice cream parlor on his lunch break. He was flirting with this "SB," touching *her*.

The "4EVA" gleamed at Laney—What about the supposed "soulmates" he said they were? All lies—manipulation. She stood, adrenaline racing, her limbs steady, wanting to seize something, grip it, wrench it—yes, wrangle Chris's hand, force him to wield a chisel so that these initials, this "4EVA," would be scratched out, obliterated.

Bill opened the door, apparently having heard her car. She smiled, pretending that she had just nonchalantly strolled up the sidewalk, noticed, thought, felt nothing. He looked handsome in a white dress shirt and a brown tweed sports coat over pressed khaki slacks. His hair was freshly styled.

"You look very nice," she said.

"Thank you," he said. "Chris has been sulking since he got home. I think you should go see him."

Her fingers twitched. Why was he asking her this—Why was he grinning at her strangely, so smugly? "I should?"

"Maybe you could mother him a bit."

Mother him? She couldn't stop a glare, a scowl, from overtaking her face.

"If you don't want to—"

"No. That's all right." The thought that this was some sort of trap—with the police waiting inside—rushed through her, but she pushed her way beside him through the door.

No; no police lurked inside ready to pounce on her. She barreled through the living room, a stale smell assaulting her. Chris's room was just down the hall on the other side of the living room.

His bedroom door had a Boy Scouts emblem tacked to it. Still, *forever*, a *boy*. How could she have let him actually fuck her? A touch of scorn—or was it anger?—blazed in her eyes. She knocked, barely waiting for an answer. Chris looked up. He lay sprawled on his bed wearing a tight-fitting T-shirt and shorts, a mathematics textbook and notebook wedged under his arm.

She looked back at the door, to check whether Bill was in the hall, but she didn't see him. She closed the door, though not fully, an inch or so shy, to ensure that if Bill sauntered by, she would hear him.

"You found my note?" he asked, his eyes expectant.

"Mr. Diamond knows something's going on between us," she said. "We can't see each other anymore."

He looked down, taking his pencil and brushing it over the textbook, as if he were trying to shade the page.

Her eyes roamed over, between, his shorts. Ashamed, she caught herself and glanced off. "Did you say anything to your father?"

"What difference does it make?"

"I *need* to know."

"Why don't you just go? I'm sure you'll have a lot of fun tonight," he shot back sarcastically.

"I *am* going to go out with him tonight."

"I meant what I said in the note. We're soulmates."

"What do you mean 'soulmates'?"

"We were meant to be together. Forever."

'Forever:' that silly fucking word again. "That's kid stuff. I don't believe in soulmates."

He hopped up. "I'm not a kid. I can move out of here and get my own apartment. No one can say anything then. We won't have to worry about my father or the police or anybody."

"What about that girl you're seeing?"

"What girl?"

"Don't lie. SB," she said.

Surprise overtook his face, and she couldn't help feel satisfied. "You saw her initials?" he stumbled. "We're just friends."

"I've seen you with her. She's your girlfriend, isn't she?"

"What are you—stalking me?"

"*Me* stalking you?"

"It was a joke." He let out a nervous laugh. "She likes me. I've known her forever, before I met you. We're like brother and sister."

"Brothers and sisters don't usually put their initials in the sidewalk with a plus sign between them."

"A joke," he said.

"Are you sleeping with her?"

"We're pals. It's harmless." But he was smiling smugly, his lips pursed in a mischievous grin.

"Listen. I made a mistake. This was all wrong of me. We've got to put an end to this before you fuck up your—*my*—life. I've got a son. I wish you the best." She turned to the door.

"Don't go." He jumped off the bed and ran to her, putting his arms around her waist. He nuzzled the nape of her neck and kissed her. His pelvis pressed against her hip—He was so much taller than she was.

"We can do it again," he whispered. "I love you more than any SB." Leaning against hers, his body pushed the door closed. "Don't be jealous," he cooed.

"I'm not jealous!" She squirmed from him. A floorboard creaked in the hall. Was it Bill? Her heart pounded as she managed to open the door. No one was in the hall, but the sound of footsteps rattled in the den. She straightened her dress, Chris trying to close the door. "Tell him you love *me*," he said, his voice bellowing.

"Do you want your father to hear you?" she said like a mother castigating her child.

"Yes!" he snapped back.

"Well I don't!" She listened for footsteps, signs that Bill was near.

She had no choice; she could not encourage him. "I *don't* love you," she said, her voice emphatic. Yet she could not control her eyes as they traveled across his body.

His chest thrust against his T-shirt, stretching the fabric. "You used to."

"No. I didn't ever love you. No stop your whining."

His face became graver. "Then you *used* me." His voice grew cold, echoing between them as if they were in a vacant chamber.

We all use one another, she wanted to say, but saying so would only inflame him. He would learn the lesson himself, someday.

"I don't like being used," he said, his voice strained.

Whether he was seeing this 'SB' or not, she could guilt him. "Neither do I."

"You have no idea what I'll do."

She shuddered. He *might* try to send her to jail. He was more manipulative than she had thought. "I'll take my chances," she scoffed with a bit too much bravado.

"You'll regret this."

"No, I won't." She *would* have to take her chances. What was he planning? Was he merely spewing wild, angry, empty threats? He didn't actually say, 'I'll go to the police.' And if he told Bill that she had had sex with him, Bill would be so embarrassed that she had cheated on him with his own son that he wouldn't, couldn't go to the police.

She reached the end of the hall, sensing that Chris was still watching her by the door. Did he move forward, or did he stay in his room? She could not look back.

She expected to see Bill in the den, but the front door was wide open. She walked outside, where he paced the driveway, admiring her new car. "This is a real beauty," he said, sounding completely untouched by the turmoil his son was going through.

"Maybe you shouldn't leave him alone tonight," she said, trying to subdue her nervousness.

"I've forbidden him to leave his room. He has to learn his lesson."

Hearing Bill share the same sentiment about Chris having to learn on his own, she couldn't help a self-satisfied smile from creeping over her lips. Chris was confined to his room. He wasn't going to venture after her. She shouldn't worry. She only had to deal with Bill.

***

"You wanted to talk, right?" Bill asked.

"After dinner," she said. "Let's enjoy our evening."

They arrived at the Malloys' house, where the other dinner guests—Dan's boss, Eric Redditt; Alex, the single but overly thin, owl-eyed CPA whom Erin was so excited about; and Rachel and Neal, whom Erin privately said to Laney "made a nice Jewish couple"—were already settled in. Alex was not drinking alcohol, Erin explained, because he was a Mormon. "Isn't it funny how both the Jews and the Mormons call us non-believers Gentiles?" she noted.

"You think of the strangest things," Laney said.

"I think of *everything*," she replied, arching her brows.

Her retort made her instantly think that Erin knew she and Dan had had an affair.

The evening would have proceeded smoothly except that Erin kept trying to fix Laney up with Alex. She praised the purity of the Mormon religion and went on about the beautiful house he had just bought in Chesterville, a dozen miles from Plainview, even farther out in the boondocks. "A four-bedroom Colonial, and he's never been married." She acted as if she wanted to get rid of her.

Dan talked business with his boss, attempting to pull Laney into the conversation, but she had already made up her mind not to pursue the job. She gravitated toward Rachel, who she learned worked for the Department of Social Services in Denver and offered to get her on the inside track of job listings. Laney set a lunch with her for next week to discuss prospects.

Alex, though self-spoken, managed to charm the group with tales of his missionary work with the Australian aborigines. Chris seemed a world away, until Erin sarcastically said to Alex, "I bet you were a Boy Scout!"

"An Eagle Scout, in fact," Alex replied.

"See, you too do have something in common," she said to Laney.

What did she mean? Could she have heard some gossip about her and Chris? Alex, Dan, Erin, Rachel, Neal—especially Bill—seemed to be looking at her.

"Darling, you look like you've seen a ghost," Erin said. She turned to Alex: "Her son's a Cub Scout."

"How old is he?" Alex inquired.

"Seven," Bill answered, taking Laney's hand and earning a contemptuous glance from Erin. She felt as if Chris were before them all, confessing, confirming, that he loved her. She could feel her temples tense, and Bill's hand—his fingers rubbing against her skin—made her uncomfortable, but she didn't move. She didn't want Erin to push Alex on her any harder.

"My son's an Eagle Scout too," Bill said proudly. "He's only sixteen."

Only sixteen, she thought. He made him seem like an infant.

"That's awfully young to reach that designation. I didn't become one until I was twenty-one," Alex said.

"When you became legal," Dan joked. "I guess kids do everything younger nowadays." His eyes darted to Laney and he winked.

The wink jolted her: Was he implying that he knew she had slept with Chris? How?

Dan continued to gaze at Laney and winked again, this time

more privately. Erin noticed the gesture and abruptly stood: "It's time for dessert," she announced curtly, turning from Dan to Laney with an icy glare.

As she strolled toward the kitchen, Erin shot another piercing sneer at Laney and she shook her head. Laney feared Dan might have, against her advice and at the urging of his marriage counselor, told Erin about their affair. "I'll help," she said, freeing herself from Bill's grasp.

When they were alone in the kitchen, Erin turned to her: "I'm sick and tired of this," she growled fiercely. "It's bad enough that you flirt with my husband before me, but do you have to do it in front of all my friends?"

"I wasn't flirting."

"Don't give me that. I saw the way you kept looking at him, encouraging him. There are some things you can hide—but looks, especially after three years of marriage, you can't disguise."

"You're completely misinterpreting this," Laney protested.

Erin stepped back, toward the counter, and stood motionless before the chocolate soufflé; then she turned back— "I know what happened between you and Dan, when Jay was visiting his parents in February, three years ago, and you two went out to dinner together, alone."

"What are you talking about?"

"You know." Erin looked at her harshly.

"No, I don't."

"Don't lie to me. It's time we stop playing the charade or else I can't be your friend anymore."

Erin was threatening her, and a stab of anger rose in her chest. "What did Dan say to you?" Laney asked, trying to remain calm.

"Nothing. I wouldn't give him the satisfaction. When he

didn't want me to go to dinner with you two, when he came the fuck home at 3 AM, I knew. After three years of therapy, I finally reached a breakthrough yesterday. I realized Dan and I could never go back to being head-over-heels in love like we were when we first met. I had always fantasized we could. But I know now that what's stood in our way is my friendship with you. I never confronted you about your affair with him, and all the anger I harbored against both of you I should have released. It's been consuming our marriage."

So now *she* was suddenly to blame for Erin's bad marriage. Sure, it's always someone else's fault. But she would have to let Erin have her say: "I'm sorry."

"You're sorry! You're sorry?" Her voice rocketed to a panicky spiral. She was practically laughing, but Laney dismissed the dueling emotions of forgiveness and anger that Erin was exhibiting.

"I wanted to tell you myself."

"Tell me! What kind of fucking whore,"—She was screaming— "fucking whore," she repeated, whispering, "are you? No, no," she continued, her brows raising, her voice scalding, "It's not your fault."

Laney reached for her arm, stuck on that word 'whore.'

Erin recoiled: "Don't touch me! You think you can just come prancing"—She was screaming again— "prancing," she whispered, "over here time after time as if nothing ever happened? How do you think that made me feel?"

"I'm sorry." Her voice grew more distant, as if her response was preprogrammed, automatic.

"Like a fool," she answered her own question. "A goddamn fucking fool," she whispered. "Everyone in town knows."

"I never said a word to anybody."

"You *are* blind. Of course you didn't, you—prick-tease! Every guy who comes your way, you have to see if you can get a rise out of him. I'm surprised you haven't moved in on Rachel's husband already!"

Is that what she had done to Chris and Bill? Merely reaffirmed her attractiveness to herself by sleeping with them? No, her feelings were genuine, felt deeply. "You're my best friend, I shouldn't have," she said, hoping this second apology would end the confrontation.

"You should have! I'm glad you did! I realized what kind of person you really are."

"What is that?"

"A selfish bitch. You only think of yourself."

Laney could see that she hadn't lost any of her self-righteousness. "You don't mince words."

"What's the use? I wouldn't get through to you otherwise. No wonder you won't go out with Alex, he's too good for you."

"You have every right to be upset." Any more insults from Erin would stop all sympathy.

"Of course I fucking do! Don't patronize me!" Her fingers were twitching, as if they were nervously grasping, wringing, a wet towel, edging closer and closer to Laney.

"I didn't put you in therapy," she snapped back. "You did this to yourself."

"So it's my fault?"

"I take responsibility for my actions. You have to do the same."

She was on the verge of crying, yet held steady. "I was your friend. How could you do this to me?"

Laney watched her for a moment and at last grew sickened by the self-pity. She too had wasted three long years blaming herself. There was nothing to gain by succumbing to—or inflicting—guilt. The only way to exonerate herself was to admit the mistake. "I *was* selfish," she answered stonily, being careful not to evince any compassion. Doing so would only protract Erin's tirade. "Thank God I was, because now I know I need to be selfish more often, all the time. I'm tired of playing the selfless victim. I'll live my life the way I want to." She walked out of the room. She could not be responsible for how others felt—Chris, Erin, or Bill. She had to focus on her own life.

20

Laney was eager to wrest herself free from the party. Throughout the remainder of the evening Erin had made direct—deadly—eye contact with her. She said nothing, just listened, stared at her, analyzing the way she ate her dessert, how she sipped her coffee, thinking God-knows-what. She'd glance over at Dan and study his reactions to Laney, not commenting or reacting. Laney had never felt so unwelcome in their home.

She reaffirmed her desire to meet Rachel for lunch. The dinner had at least served as a positive step in resuming her career in social services.

Bill needed no cajoling to leave. "I'm nervous," he admitted. "I called home earlier, but Chris didn't answer."

She hoped Chris was all right, but her intuition gave her doubts. Her anxiety was compounded because Bill would, during the car ride home, expect an answer to his proposal.

"Erin and Dan make a nice couple," Bill said in the car.

He had no idea their marriage was not as idyllic as it appeared. How flawed his perceptions were. Or was he trying, indirectly, to bring up his proposal?

The SUV twisted through the dark streets. Conifers and firs towered overhead, forming an impenetrable barrier impervious to the wind. She hadn't yet driven this car at night, and she was still adjusting to its height, the brakes, the steering.

Bill seemed jittery, over-eager. "Have you given any thought to what we spoke about?"

"I'm too nervous to talk and drive. Let's wait until we get to your house, okay?" She was tempted to put a hand on his leg to reassure him, but she resisted the impulse, feeling he might misinterpret the gesture. Instantly, she berated herself for not allowing herself to touch him. She should have heeded her desire. But apprehension—over Chris, over the proposal—had caused her to distrust, to discount, this impulse. Couldn't she at least touch him? After all, she had had sex with him. But he was now flicking his thumb against his middle finger, scraping the nail against the skin, his expression becoming harder.

When they reached his house, the lights inside were on, but the Galaxy wasn't in the driveway.

"Where the hell is my car?" Bill's hand dashed into his pocket, searching for his keys as he rushed out. He darted back a few moments later. "Chris is gone."

"I thought he was grounded."

"If he went out with that girl, I'm going to kill him."

So Chris did have a girlfriend. He had lied to her. Bill spoke seriously, as if he actually could kill somebody. Had he tried to kill his wife? "He's probably just out with friends."

She had an uncomfortable feeling Chris might have gone again to her house. He might be waiting for her to return from the party. She hoped this wasn't the case.

"He should have left a note."

Her cell phone rang. When she went to answer it, she noticed a message waiting in her voice mailbox.

"I hadn't heard back from you, so I wanted to let you know everything is okay," Meg said.

"I didn't check my messages," Laney said.

"I called to make sure it was okay to let Chris Hendrickson come over to help Brian with his surprise for you. Brian pleaded with me to call him. It's not a problem, is it?"

"Did I hear her say Chris is there?" Bill interrupted.

Laney put her hand up to stop him from talking. "Meg, thanks for all your help."

"He's putting the tools away."

"Why would Chris be there?" Bill asked. "Tools? Did she say 'tools'?"

"This is a bad connection," Laney barked into the phone. "I'll be home soon." She hung up. Fuck—Chris was at her house and Bill had overheard Meg. How would she explain his being there? She would have to tell Bill the truth. "Brian desperately wanted Chris's help on his Mother's Day gift, so he had the sitter call him. It's my fault. I should have told Meg he was grounded."

"We better go."

"Yes," Laney said.

"What's gotten into him?"

She could hear equal parts concern and anger in his voice. "He's not a boy anymore," she said. "He's a young man."

"Don't defend him."

"Come on, Bill. I'm not defending him. Don't you remember when you were young what it felt like to do things you were told not to?"

She drove slowly, taking the long route home, hoping that Chris would have left her house by the time they arrived.

"Shouldn't we take the back road?"

"There are no lights on the streets there. I'm not used to this car yet."

She caught a quick glimpse of Bill. He looked slack-jawed—his lips parted as if he wanted to say something but couldn't.

"I'm not young anymore," he said.

"I'm sorry," she said, not really hearing him, not really caring. "I can't marry you."

"You need more time," he said, but his statement was half-question, half-declaration.

"We're not right for each other."

"You probably want someone with the fancy house and the six-figure job, like that guy at dinner."

"I'd rather be alone."

"You've been alone for three years. Let me in."

She had let him in, as well as his son. How could she explain what she felt? Only disaster would result. She could barely see where she was driving. She tasted salt on her lips and felt as if her makeup was rising in swirls on her face. She could not tell him how she was feeling, the extent of her angst, her anger at herself for becoming involved with both of them! She had no choice but to let her feelings boil inside of her, bubble, burn, devour her—yes, leave nothing but her moribund hopes and fears, sorrow, and the knowledge that she had forever driven a wedge between Chris and his father. She had poisoned, contaminated, their relationship, and Bill could never know why or how.

She steadied herself, biting her lip, looking into the sideview mirror at the blackness, the blankness of the road behind her, so that she would not succumb to the temptation of giving him a clue, a sole, arbitrary clue, as to how she had betrayed him. The car seemed to be driving itself. The foot on the gas did nothing. Steering was so effortless it was useless. She didn't need to be here. She didn't need to see him ever again—She couldn't! How could she continue to lie to him, smiling at him, pretending, in feigned compassion, all the while ensuring not a misstep, not a stumble, but a fall that would take him to the deepest, loneliest depths of being deceived and used?

So she drove as slowly as she could, stonily, will-lessly, the guile in her heart pumping forth through her veins like acid. But as much as she tried to avoid reaching her house, the SUV seemed to whirl them there. Bill's Galaxy was parked in front of her garage, its taillights on. As Laney pulled into the driveway, Chris stepped out of the car. *That is why*, she wanted to tell him. *Your son. Do I need to tell you everything? Is that what you want?*

As Bill charged from the SUV, Meg enthusiastically waved to Laney from the front door.

"I grounded you!" Bill yelled, pointing at Chris. "Give me the keys and get in that car right now!"

Chris watched as she strode forward. His eyes roamed over her shoulders and bare arms and uncovered legs. He appeared taken in by the sight of her in her sleek black dress. As he looked at her, she knew she was beautiful. She tried not to stare at him, but couldn't help notice his lost, almost helpless expression. She had courted him, loved him, but then had withheld her desire for him. He was being destroyed. His hands trembled, his shoulders slumped forward. He was no longer the proud, eager boy who had come to her door. He had no uniform to hide under, merely jeans and a polo shirt that was a size too small, the collar overlay shrunken and downturned. She was staring at him. She could not stop herself. When she realized Bill was watching her, she imagined a look of horror on her face, a face that must have told all as she scrambled to conceal her feelings, for Chris.

"Tell him," Chris said to her.

She shrugged. "Tell him what?"

"Are you okay?" Meg asked.

"We're fine," she answered. "Make sure the children are okay."

Meg he stared at her, but she gazed back with a punishing look. Meg retreated to the foyer.

"I love her," Chris said to Bill.

Laney froze. How could he be so stupid?

"What?" Bill asked.

"I love her."

"She's a grown woman for chrissakes!"

"I told you!"

"Give me the keys," he demanded angrily.

"She loves me, too. Tell him, Laney."

She responded with a steely silence.

"Tell him," he pleaded.

Bill recognized hurt in his son's voice, but ignored it. "Son, get in the car."

"I want you to know, Dad." He took a step away from his father toward Laney.

"I have no idea what you're talking about." Her indignation was now unmistakable, virtually palpable.

Bill looked as if he believed her, but as he continued to glance at her face, her bare neck, her shoulders, he seemed to want to believe *Chris*.

"What happened in the kitchen was nothing? Fucking me was—"

A large crow swooshed over their heads behind the garage.

"Liar!" she screamed. "Nothing like that happened and you know it!"

"You bitch!"

"Don't talk to her like that," Bill shouted. "Are you trying to destroy our relationship?"

"*Your* relationship?"

"How can you," Laney said, addressing Bill first, then turning to Chris. "How can you—even insinuate that we had sex. I should have the police come over and arrest you again!" She noticed she was twisting her gold wristwatch—Bill's eyes were watching the back of her hand, the dial, the sparkling band. She stopped, feeling that her nerves were giving her away, that she was losing Bill.

"Goddammit!" Bill yelled forcefully, his arms, his hands, his face shaking—in disbelief. No, it wasn't disbelief! He glanced at Laney with a distrustful air, quickly looking away as if he couldn't bear the sight of her. What did he mean by 'Goddammit!' Was it an indictment—of her?

Chris's foot kicked at the ground. "We fucked in the kitchen." His tone was accusatory and spiteful.

Upstairs, Brian's bedroom light flicked on, shining over the driveway. Laney glanced up at the window and saw him standing before it, confused.

"I don't know what the hell you're talking about!" she screamed.

"Get in the car!" Bill shouted. "You've embarrassed all of us enough."

"Just say you love me, you bitch!" Chris raised his hand to strike her—She quickly turned away. His hand struck her across the cheek, against her eye.

The pain did not register. She became more resolute. She deserved the slap.

Bill lunged at Chris, tackling him onto the driveway. Chris freed himself from his father's grip and punched him square in the face.

Laney heard a loud pop. "Stop it!" she yelled, but the fighting drowned her out.

Chris's fists flailed against him—against his arms, his face, his stomach, his back.

"You want a piece of your old man?" Bill heaved Chris off him. "Come and get me." He beckoned him closer.

He lurched forward, but Chris clocked him on the side of the head—once, twice, then in a frenzy, pummeling him, forcing him into a crouching position on the ground. Chris reached for his throat to strangle him— "How do you like being choked?" he spat, eyes ablaze. "You think Mom liked it when you tried to strangle her?"

The crow zoomed overhead, cawing. It perched on the eave over the front door.

Gasping, Bill let go of Chris's legs. He slumped to the ground. He closed his eyes, squeezing them tightly shut. "I had to protect you. You're my son."

"Not anymore, I'm not." Chris was about to kick him in the face but she reached in to grab him. He pushed her aside, pausing to observe his father's bloody face, a whitish pale blue.

"Don't," Bill groaned.

He smacked his father across the face with the back of his hand, as if brutally punishing a child, sending him backwards toward her.

He ran to the Galaxy and opened the driver's door.

Blood was streaming from Bill's nose. "Get back here!"

"Fuck you! Fuck both of you! I'll spill it all out!"

"Chris!" she shouted, running towards the car. "Don't!"

"He can have you!" he said, disgust in his voice like phlegm. "I'm going to tell everyone we both fucked her! They'll drive both of you out of this motherfucking dumb-fuck town!" He slammed his arm against the driver's door. "I'm going to crash this piece of shit car and you'll both have to live with it the rest of your sorry-ass lives!"

He started the car, the engine harshly turning over and rumbling as he sped onto the lawn then back into the driveway.

Meg rushed beside her, her mouth agape as she reached a hand toward Laney's face. "Are you okay?"

"Make sure Brian's in bed."

"I'm going to kill that son of a bitch!" Bill shouted, his eyes blazing with fury. "And I'm going to kill *you* too!" He looked at her with a look of vile contempt. "Give me your keys." Blood spurted from his mouth.

"No," she said.

"Don't give me that, you fucking liar!"

"I'll call the police," Meg said.

"No," Laney said. "Go back inside."

Meg stood frozen, unable to move.

Laney turned to Bill: "Did you try to kill your wife?"

Blood continued to trickle from his nose. "Fuck you."

"What happened?"

"Give me the keys!"

"No," she said firmly. "If you want to save your son, tell me."

"The divorce was finalized this afternoon and she gave up all custody rights. I didn't hit her," he added, his tone hesitant. His lips quivered when he finished speaking. His eyes drew up in surprise—seemingly at himself, because of what he had said. His hand brushed over his mouth, as if to wipe away the lie.

She had lied to him by concealing her involvement with Chris. It was only fitting that he would lie to her now about his past. She had to hurry before Chris reached the police station. "Get in. I'll drive."

She rushed to the driver's door and he ambled after her.

She backed down the drive, faster than she should have, eyes darting from the driveway to the road. The Galaxy was already out of sight. She sped down Heather Lane toward town.

"I want to know one thing," he said, stanching the flow of blood from his nose and lips. "Did you fuck him *before* or after me?"

"If you want me to say I'm sorry, I won't," she said. "I cared for him."

"You had to fuck him?"

"I couldn't help it." Her voice broke. She wanted to say more, but knew she shouldn't.

"You're a fucking whore. You deserve each other."

"I don't regret it."

"Fine, it's over."

She raced to Lake Street—the quickest way to the police station.

"You got what you wanted. You're a cunt," he said.

She deserved it. "I don't expect you to forgive me. I care for you. I'm not that cold. What I did was wrong in the eyes of everybody but my own. I'm not going to sacrifice myself to satisfy anybody else, anymore. What I think and feel is the only thing that's important. I've suffered more than anyone. Fuck you all. Call me selfish. Call me a bitch. Call me a whore. I am what I am. And I'm finally proud."

He looked at her blankly, as if she were not near him but a ghostly apparition that he refused to acknowledge.

Chris's car was heading south on Lake Street toward the center of town. Was he heading to the police station? How could he be so vindictive? She raced after him. Bursts of wind hurled against the sides of the truck. The Galaxy bolted forward, the chassis careening as Chris maneuvered around a tight curve. The Lexus quickly caught up, handling the curve without difficulty. She flashed the headlights.

Chris reached a fork in the road and bolted down the desolate stretch. He was taking a shortcut to the Plainview Police Department! She chased behind him, but how much faster could she, should she, go? An oncoming car passed by, honking at Chris while she floored the truck, pushing through the rising whirls of wind, whipping into the oncoming lane. She was side by side with the Galaxy. She motioned for him to pull over, but he sneered, shaking his head—Fuck You! The car veered toward the side of the road.

He hurtled back onto the hardtop, even faster, ambushing her. She quickly glanced at Bill, who was scraping at the dried blood on his hands. She decreased her speed to let Chris pass ahead of her. Trees whirred by her sides, a blur of blackened gray masses, like the final images of a movie reel.

They reached the town center. The police station was just a few blocks away, a right turn off Franklin Street. Chris started to turn, then he swerved away. Was he really going to see Officer Wilkins, or was he taunting her? He steered onto another side street—an even shorter route to the police station! The moon glowed brightly overhead. Several teenagers were milling about the sidewalk, near storefronts. She would not let him go to the police. She would cut him off. She increased her speed, even though the speed limit was 25 miles per hour. She looked at the speedometer. She was going 75. They were driving wildly. She wouldn't, she couldn't, slow down. His car barrelled around the corner. He had to have been going 85 or 90. She heard screeching brakes, then a loud, piercing crash that was like an earsplitting scream.

She slammed on the brakes. The braking system expertly brought the truck to a cruising speed. Her hands floated above the steering wheel. She saw only a melange of color: the green and yellow lights on her instrument panel, a faint blue glow which surrounded the lighter and the knobs of the radio like halos. The clock flashed "12:02 AM."

She turned the corner. The sight of Chris's car, upside down, smashed against the brick wall of Hank's Garage, brought her back to consciousness. The police station's lights gleamed around the corner. Had he been going there or somewhere else? Perhaps home? A siren from the station sliced the air. Two teenaged girls, both high school aged, cowered against each other on the sidewalk in front of the garage, covering their mouths. Laney parked the SUV in the middle of the roadway, not bothering to pull over.

"My God," Bill said.

"Stay inside," she ordered him. In a complete state of shock, he obeyed.

She stepped out. One of the girls trembled. She watched each step Laney made, as if she were taking a step closer and closer to the edge of a cliff but the girl was too afraid to tell her to stop. Her friend shook her and pulled her aside.

Laney ambled toward the Galaxy, her footsteps unsteady. A police car arrived, its lights swirling, the siren growling to a halt. A black alley cat, its tail nervously straight up, shot across the road into the agitated darkness.

The roof of the Galaxy had caved in, flattened to the chrome lines of the trim on the frame of the door. Shards littered the street. The engine continued to whine. Laney walked to the driver's side. Blood pooled on the pavement next to the door. Chris's head and hands were twisted in the broken glass of the window, covered with blood, as if at the last moment he had desperately tried to jump from the car. His eyes, though open, were lifeless globes of white and black that seemed to have no bearing to his body. His teeth shone white under his bleeding lips.

What gripped her more than anything—more than the pooling blood, the whine of the engine, the hurling wind, the morbidly growing crowd, the sobbing, screaming girls, the approaching policeman—was the eerie, almost desperate embrace of shadows circling near.

ACKNOWLEDGMENTS

I would like to thank all those who read early drafts of the novel. Their insightful commentary and feedback have helped make *Monday, Sunday* what it is today. I am forever grateful.

Fenton Grace

ABOUT THE AUTHOR

Fenton Grace was born and raised in New England and currently resides in Southern California. For more information please visit www.FentonGrace.com.